D1527899

PAUL HEATLEY
SLEEPER
CELL

AETHON THRILLS

aethonbooks.com

SLEEPER CELL
©2023 PAUL HEATLEY

1

The town of Minnow is twenty-two miles northwest of Anchorage, Alaska. It's four thousand two hundred and eighty-eight miles away from Washington, DC.

Georgia Caruso lives on the outskirts of Minnow. It's a small house, cabin-style, and she's lived here for the last four years. She wakes early, as she does every day, and wraps up warm before she leaves the house to jog. She lives alone. She has no partner and no pets. She runs through the woods near her home, her boots crunching through the snow and her legs rising high to avoid falling. The terrain here is rough. The snowfall has been thick and heavy. There are fallen trees that must be either jumped or climbed. It doesn't take long before her heart is hammering and her breath is heaving.

She runs down to the stream a mile and a half from the back of her house. She pauses by it, hands on hips, her breath misting in front of her face. Her muscles ache. They burn. She can hear her blood pounding in her ears. That's good. She doesn't want it to be easy. Doesn't want to get soft and complacent.

She's only just getting started. The run is her warmup.

The stream is running gently, cracked ice clinging to the edges of its banks, shards of it being carried away. A sign that spring is coming. Usually, through the darkest depths of winter, the stream is frozen over. She crouches down beside it and scoops some up in a cupped hand. Drinks it. It's cold, so cold it hurts her teeth and burns her throat on the way down. It tastes good, though. Clean. She stands and begins the run back.

The house is eerily silent as she re-enters. She'd be alarmed if it wasn't. She goes down into the basement. It's been converted into a gym. There is rubber matting spread across the concrete floor. There are racks of dumbbells against one wall and a cable machine against the one opposite. Already sweating, she takes off the heaviest of the clothes she's been running in, remaining in only her running leggings and sports bra. She kicks off her snow boots and slips into sneakers. Stretches out a little. She's already limber from the run. She does some push-ups, and then she moves on to the weights.

She works out for a further hour. By the time she's done, she can barely move. She lies on the rubber matting to catch her breath. Sweat trickles down the side of her face. If she glances down, she can see where her heart is pounding against her chest.

She's able to drag herself back upstairs. Her house is two floors. The bathroom is upstairs. She tells herself, gritting her teeth as her thighs scream at her in protest, that it's all just an extension of the workout. That this burning is good. That this extra journey up these steps is a good thing.

It's a quick shower. She cleans herself under warm water, soaping herself up and rinsing it off. Then she braces herself and turns it to cold. Her body stiffens, and her breathing turns to panting. She steels herself against the cold. She closes her eyes and breathes through it. Holds herself under for a minute, then gets out and towels off. Her record is seven minutes under the cold water. She keeps track. Counts it off in her head. She catches a glimpse of herself in the mirror while she brushes her teeth, but she doesn't linger over her reflection. Does not stop to admire the muscles she has built, nor the way they ripple with her movements. She does not work on herself for aesthetics.

In the bedroom, she dries her hair. Puts it up into a bun that sits neatly atop her head. She makes her bed. Makes it tight, like she was in the army. She dresses. Black trousers, freshly pressed the night before. A plain white blouse, likewise pressed. A beige cardigan.

Breakfast is light. A slice of brown toast with a poached egg sprinkled with chili flakes. She washes and dries the plates when she's done. Puts them away. Leaves the house and gets into her Ford pickup truck.

Much like the stream, the road into Minnow is not as bad as it was just a few weeks ago. There isn't much else in the area where Georgia lives. Just a few other houses, all spread far away from each other. There aren't any businesses or places of interest, and for this reason, the road can sometimes be forgotten by the plows. She knows some of her 'neighbors' have complained to the local council about this many times. They've come to her door to ask her to raise her voice in their protests. Georgia has nodded politely and signed anything they've asked her to sign, but it hasn't made much difference. Sometimes the plows come, and sometimes they don't. It probably depends on the driver.

Today, however, there is no need for one. The road is mostly clear. It's been almost a week since the last heavy snowfall. Now it lies piled up at the sides of the road, slowly melting. Spring is coming.

Georgia's truck is old, but it's hardy. When the road has not been cleared, it battles through. It just takes her a little longer to get into Minnow, is all. On clear days like this, it doesn't take long at all. She drives in silence, the radio off. It's rare that she ever has it on. The only sound is the engine.

In town, she goes to the store before she heads to work. Gets a sandwich for lunch. The store is quiet, and there is a strange hush. Usually, at this time, the store is busy. The residents of Minnow call in to get provisions for the day before they head off to their jobs. Georgia counts three other customers. There should be dozens. This is strange, and she doesn't like it. She wonders if there's something happening that she's missed or forgotten about, but she doubts it. She keeps on top of local happenings. She doesn't like to be caught off-guard.

The other shoppers are moving slowly. Their brows are furrowed. They look confused and unhappy. Georgia almost wants to ask what's wrong, but she doesn't. She takes her sandwich up to the cashier and pays for it. The cashier is young, and she almost looks like she's about to cry. Again, Georgia almost asks her what's wrong. Still doesn't. Bites her tongue. She doesn't get involved. She keeps herself to herself.

She gets to the library and opens up. Switches on the lights. She looks to the desk where she'll spend most of her day, looking out over the two desks directly in front of her and the rows of shelves filled with books. It is deathly quiet in here, too, but this one is expected. This one is appreciated. She puts her sandwich in the fridge in the staff kitchen and then gets to work putting out yesterday's returns.

She's barely started when someone enters. Georgia looks up, smiling, ready to exchange a wordless friendly nod when she sees that it's Camilla. Camilla is sixty-six years old and has worked at the library since the day it first opened. She's not supposed to be in today. Georgia's smile turns into a frown, which deepens when she sees that Camilla is wearing the same downcast expression as the people she saw in the store.

"Georgia," she says, shaking her head and taking a seat at one of the desks. "Have you heard the news?"

Georgia goes to her, setting down the armful of paperbacks she'd been carrying around. "No, what news?"

Camilla shakes her head again, but this doesn't answer Georgia's question. She wonders if someone has died. Someone prominent in town, perhaps. This would certainly explain the funereal pall she experienced in the store.

Georgia remains standing, looking down at Camilla, waiting for her to share. Camilla takes a moment to gather herself. She pulls off the scarf she's wearing and rubs at her forehead.

"There's been a terrorist attack," she says. "You haven't heard? How couldn't you have heard? It's all over the news, all over the radio."

"I haven't switched either on yet today," Georgia says. "What kind of attack? Where?"

She checks in with the news often, usually in the evening. Keeps up to date. There's been a spate of domestic terrorist attacks lately. Three in the last two weeks. Texas, then Virginia, and most recently at Fort Jackson in South Carolina. All three attacks were on military bases. Bombs planted. There were casualties and heavy injuries. No one has been caught yet, but responsibility has been claimed by a group calling themselves the ARO —the Anti-Right Outreach. She wonders if this latest attack, which seems to have shaken everyone up more than the previous three, is anything to do with them.

"They killed him," Camilla says. "He's dead. The car rolled right over the top of him. They showed it on the news—I couldn't believe it."

"Who?" Georgia says.

"Jake O'Connelly," Camilla says. "The vice-president."

"He's dead?"

"That's what I've been saying!"

Georgia thinks. The vice-president is dead. A fourth domestic terrorist attack in just a fortnight. It's brazen.

"Who did it?" Georgia says.

"Those *bastards*," Camilla says, almost spitting the words, "the ARO."

Georgia expected as much. Every attack they've made has been brazen. Planting bombs on military bases, and now this—killing the second most powerful man in the country—but this seems like a colossal leap.

She scratches the corner of her mouth. "Where'd it happen?"

"In DC," Camilla says. "He was on his way to open a new children's hospital. It was supposed to be the *president*." She covers her mouth with one hand like she can't bear the thought. "If it had been *him*—if they'd gotten *him*—oh, Lord, Georgia, can you *imagine*?"

Georgia has stopped listening. She's thinking, hard. She thinks she knows what this might mean. She feels her blood running cold at the prospect. She hopes she's wrong. But if she's not…

"Georgia? *Georgia*?"

Georgia snaps back to attention. Looks down on Camilla.

"Are you all right?" Camilla says. "You looked like you were somewhere else there."

"I'm—I'm fine," Georgia says.

She sees how Camilla looks at her. She looks concerned, but she also looks surprised. Maybe even suspicious. Georgia wonders if perhaps her reaction to this news Camilla has brought her has been too cold.

She softens herself. "I'm just—I'm just stunned, is all. This is a lot to take in…" She shakes her head in imitation of Camilla and takes a seat opposite her on the desk. "I think it's just taken me a moment to process… This is awful, Camilla. So truly awful."

Camilla nods and reaches across the table to take her hand, patting it comfortingly. "I'm worried for this country, Georgia," she says. "I'm not going to lie, and I'm not going to sugarcoat it. They almost got the *president*. They got the vice-president, and that's bad enough! They could throw this country into chaos— heck, they already are!"

Heck is the strongest language Georgia has ever heard Camilla use, along with her earlier use of *bastards*. It's an emotional day for her. "It's terrible," Georgia says.

"I dread to think where this is all going to go next. I just… I don't suppose you're old enough to really remember 9/11, are you?"

"I was seven." Georgia doesn't remember much from back then. Or for years after. What she *does* remember…

"Take it from me," Camilla says, getting back to her feet and winding her scarf back around her neck and lower face. "They were dark days. Everything changed then, Georgia. I don't think anything's ever really been the same since. I can see that happening again with this. They need to put an end to it as soon as they can."

"Who does?"

"The government! They need to find this ARO, lock them up, and throw away the key. Hell, they might even need to *execute* them."

Georgia has never heard Camilla espouse any support for capital punishment before, either.

"We shouldn't be made to feel like this," Camilla says, though she's wrapping up, almost done, and heading for the door. "Good, honest, hard-working American citizens like us, and like everyone else here in Minnow and all across the country, we shouldn't be made to feel like this. We shouldn't have to be afraid." She's back to shaking her head. "I mean, if they can get the *vice-president*, they can get anybody, can't they?"

Georgia nods along. She stands from the table and accompanies Camilla to the door.

"I don't suppose there'll be many people in here today,"

Camilla says, half in and half out of the building. "People will be too upset."

"Do you want me to close up?"

Camilla considers this, then says, "No. We should probably stay open, just in case. If people need to find solace in books, then we need to make sure that we're here to provide them that comfort."

She reaches out before she leaves and pats Georgia's arm. "Try to be strong," she says. "Don't let it drag you down. And if you feel like you need to have a little cry, well, you just hide away in the bathroom and let it all come out. There's no shame in that. You'll feel better for it."

Georgia nods and pats the back of Camilla's hand in turn, but she has no intention of crying. She doesn't feel anywhere close to tears.

Camilla leaves, and Georgia stands by the door for a moment, watching her trudge away through the snow.

A car passes slowly by the library, blocking Camilla momentarily from view. Georgia feels eyes upon her. She looks into the car. The driver is looking her way. He promptly averts his gaze, and then he's gone.

It was only a fleeting glimpse of the man, and Georgia didn't get a great look at him within the confines of his vehicle, but she didn't recognize him. Minnow is a small town with fewer than four thousand people. Georgia doesn't know everyone who lives here, but she at least recognizes most of them. That's why she came to Minnow. That's why she chose to live in such a small and remote location. Far easier to keep track of new faces.

She could be making too much of the man looking at her, she knows. It could have been nothing more than an idle glance in her direction, and their eyes just happened to meet at that exact moment. Or maybe he *was* watching her, but not for the reasons she could be worried about. Georgia has been told she's an attractive woman. She doesn't look in the mirror often, but when she does, she can see that this is objectively true. It could be that the man liked what he saw. That he was admiring her.

Or it could be that she *should* be paranoid.

Georgia watches the road a moment longer. It's empty. The car does not come back by. She can't see any sign of it. She lets the door fall closed and steps back deeper into the warmth of the library. She doesn't forget about the car, though, or what she was able to see of the driver. There's nothing wrong with a little paranoia.

Or, as in her case, a lot of it.

2

Keith Wright's ears are still ringing. His heart is hammering. There is dried blood on his left temple.

He's in a police station in downtown DC. He's being interrogated. It's not a cop talking to him. An agent of some kind. Two of them. They introduced themselves when they first came in, but Keith doesn't remember what they said. NSA, he thinks. Keith can barely hear. It's more than just the ringing. It's the pounding of his heart. The blood rushing in his ears. His ragged breath. He's trying hard not to have a panic attack. He's taking deep breaths. In through his nose, out through his mouth. He fills his lungs and his diaphragm, then empties them back out. Back when he was a Navy Seal, they would box breathe before they went into a potentially dangerous situation. Four seconds in, then hold for four, then four seconds out, then hold for another four, and repeat. Sometimes box breathing still works for him, but a situation like this requires deeper breaths. The deepest he can manage.

The NSA agents are watching him, watching him breathe. They exchange glances. Only one of them has spoken so far. The other sits silent, his arms folded. Up until the glance, his eyes have never left Keith. Keith has felt them burning into him. Into his face. Into his skull.

"Something wrong, Mr. Wright?" asks the agent who's done all the talking so far.

Keith doesn't answer. He can't. What's important right now is calming himself down and stopping his vision from swimming. There's nothing he can do about the ringing in his ears, but he can do his best to stop the panic attack.

He's not sure what he's doing here. There was an explosion. Keith was near it, but he didn't see it happen. Heard it, though. Felt its effects. He'd been in a meeting. That was this morning. It's evening now. They've held him at the station all day. It feels like it's been longer. The station is full. He was in a holding cell earlier. There were three cells. They were all full. Overflowing. Keith imagines a lot of the people in them aren't sure what they're doing here, either.

The meeting had ended, but Keith hung around. He packed up. He wasn't in a rush to get anywhere else. His shift at the diner didn't start for another hour. He put away the chairs. Folded them. Stacked them. He was heading out when it happened. He was at the door. His hand was upon the door handle.

There was an explosion. The pressure blew the door inward off its hinges. Keith was able to get his arms up on reflex alone, preventing it from breaking his face. He's surprised it didn't break either of his arms. In a way, the door kept him alive. It shielded him. If he'd stepped outside a moment sooner, he'd be dead.

He thinks he was knocked out, but he's not for how long. When he pushed the door and the rubble off, his ears were ringing. He could feel the blood running down his face. Could taste it. Everything hurt from being thrown across the room. His mind began to race, wondering what had happened, what the explosion was, and where it had occurred. Wondering if it was some kind of accident or an attack.

He'd heard, like everyone else, about the attacks recently. The bombings on the military bases. The news of these bombings, and the death and destruction they entailed, had stirred things in him. Memories. Memories he'd rather forget. On more than one occasion, he'd had to turn the news reports off, feeling the early stirring of a panic attack. Keith was a Navy Seal before he couldn't do it anymore. Before his PTSD almost overwhelmed him.

But this was nowhere near a military base. If it was an attack, it didn't fit in with the pattern of the others.

He went outside with caution, not sure what he was going to find.

It *was* a bomb.

It was chaos.

People were screaming and crying. He could hear them through the ringing in his ears, though muted. He saw overturned vehicles. He waded out through the rubble, feeling dazed like he was in a dream. Blinking hard and hoping he'd wake up. He didn't. And the closer he got to things, the worst they looked. He almost stepped on a severed arm, no sign of the rest of the body. He saw a woman, young and dark-haired, on her knees, screaming. There was a deep gash in the center of her scalp, and her right eye was missing. Blood ran down her face and matted her hair. Paramedics reached her before Keith could.

There were paramedics and police everywhere. Agents in suits. It was easy to tell who had just arrived on the scene and who was present when the bomb went off. The former were rushing around, trying to help, trying to tend to the hurt. The latter was dazed, trying to make sense of what had happened. Most of them were bloodied, too. Hurt.

Amongst it all, Keith saw a girl. A teen, about seventeen. She stumbled, dazed, confused. She looked like she'd banged her head, but she wasn't bleeding. He got closer to her, and so far as he could see, she wasn't hurt. No one was tending to her. No one seemed to notice her. She was left to wander alone.

"Are you all right?" he said.

She looked back at him with empty eyes. She blinked. "I can't find my mom," she said.

"Okay, okay, well, I'll help you find her," Keith said, though he wasn't hopeful. If they'd been separated, that probably wasn't a good sign. "What's she look like?"

The girl was called Kayla. While they were searching for her mother, they came across another guy. He looked unharmed. Like maybe he hadn't been caught up in the blast but had come over to help. They described Kayla's mother to him, but he hadn't seen anyone by that description. He had an accent. British, Keith thought, but not a dialect he could place.

The three were standing together when the police pulled up on them. They bundled Keith and the Brit into separate cruisers. He didn't see what they did with Kayla.

Keith didn't understand. He still doesn't understand. They were treated like they'd done something wrong. He was just trying to help. He knows the cops are busy, knows they're suddenly finding themselves overwhelmed with everything going on, but no one would talk to him. No one would explain what was going on, why he'd been hauled in.

He hasn't had a chance to ask yet. The second they brought him to the interrogation room, sat him in the chair, and started in with their questions, he felt his anxiety begin to rise. The ringing in his ears grew louder.

The agents exchange another glance, and Keith realizes he hasn't answered them. That he's been silent for a long time now. "Why am I here?" he asks. It takes a lot of effort to speak. He clears his throat. He swallows.

Both agents look at him for a moment. They study him. Keith doesn't feel comfortable under their unblinking scrutiny. The one who speaks lowers his eyes a moment. The other never looks away. Never blinks. The speaker looks back up. "You were a Navy Seal, Mr. Wright, is that correct?"

Keith nods. "That's right. Long time ago, now."

The speaker grins. "Don't sell yourself short. It's an impressive feat. But you left the Seals?"

"Honorable discharge."

"And why was that?"

Keith shifts in his seat. He looks to the door behind the men. Looks to the camera up in the corner, its constant red light staring back at him like an eye. "Why is that relevant? You haven't answered why I'm here."

"How long ago did you leave the Seals?"

"I was thirty-four," Keith says. "Four years ago."

"Why did you leave?"

"I was discharged."

"Why were you discharged?"

"You're not telling me why I'm here."

"Why were you discharged, Mr. Wright?"

Keith blows air out his nose. He grits his teeth. "Panic attacks," he says finally. "Why am I here?"

"Shortly after you left the Navy Seals, you joined a message board. Do you remember that?"

Keith blinks. That was a long time ago. He barely remembers it.

"*Do* you remember it?"

"Barely," Keith says.

"It was called—" The speaker refers to something under the table. His phone, perhaps, or a notebook. He recites a name back to Keith. "*Who Will Survive In America?* That right?"

"I remember what it was called."

"That's a song, isn't it?" the speaker says, cocking his head.

"Probably not the one you're thinking of," Keith says.

"Come again?"

"You're thinking of Kanye West, right? Fine, but that's not where it got its name from. It was a different song. *Comment #1*, by Gil Scott-Heron. That's where it took its name from."

The speaker blinks. "Well. Regardless." He sucks air through his teeth. "Bit of a dark place, ain't it? The message board, I mean."

"I didn't stay on it very long."

"Six months."

"Like I said, not very long. Some people had been on it for years. Some had been on it from day one, and they were still active, and it started five years before I joined. What's that got to do with anything?"

"Like I said," the speaker says, "dark place."

Keith shrugs.

"A lot of anti-American activity on that message board." He looks into Keith's eyes. Holds his gaze. "Seems like something of a hotbed, particularly for ex-military personnel such as yourself."

"There's a lot to be disgruntled about among the ex-military," Keith says, thinking he has an idea now why he might be here. "Especially among Black ex-military. That's why I joined originally. I wasn't exactly feeling well cared for after all I'd done for Uncle Sam. I figured it might be a good place for me to get some of those things off my chest."

"And did you?"

"I never made a single post. I'm not much of a sharer. I just liked to read. It let me know that I wasn't the only person going through everything I was suffering."

"You said you were on the board for six months."

"Yeah, I was, and I left when I started to read some things I couldn't get behind."

"Such as?"

Keith bites his tongue. He probably shouldn't say too much.

He'd seen men talk about doing something that would *make* America care. Taking all that training they'd been given and turning it against their country. Make them regret throwing them away so casually, like they were nothing.

The speaker stares at him. "Did you see threats being made, Mr. Wright?" he asks. "Did you see men talk about making bombs? Is that why you left?"

Keith says nothing.

"Did you think, maybe, that you should have reported what you were reading?"

"They were all talk," Keith says. "And I didn't think—I didn't —" His chest feels tight. He's short of breath. He can't get his words out. He breathes in through his nose and tries to calm down. His breath hitches. It takes a few attempts for him to fill his lungs.

The agents don't say anything while he calms himself. They just watch. Keith grips the edge of the table with both hands. He's able to speak again. "Shouldn't I have a lawyer in here?"

"Do you *need* a lawyer?" the speaker says, raising an eyebrow.

Keith grits his teeth. He runs his tongue around the inside of his mouth. "What about a phone call?"

The agents look at each other. They begin to stand. "All right," the speaker says. "You can have your phone call on the way back to your holding cell. Wait here. We'll send someone in for you." The two agents leave.

Keith is alone. He takes deeper breaths. One hand pressed to his chest. He feels how his heart hammers. He takes deep, long, meditative breaths. Feels it slow. Become steady.

One of the guards comes to get him. Outside the interrogation room, the station is loud. Keith realizes the ringing in his ears is finally diminishing. He doesn't notice it so much anymore. Instead, he hears the shouting and protestations of people being booked in and of the ones being held in the cells. The guard leads Keith to a phone. He stands nearby.

Keith takes a moment. Thinks whom he should call. He calls Dominic Freeman. Keith's closest friend. He works at the diner, too. Another short order cook. The only person Keith trusts to get him out of here. He'll know what to do. Keith dials his number from memory. It doesn't ring. He waits a moment. Can feel the eyes of the guard nearby boring into the back of his skull.

Keith is about to tell the guard that the line is faulty when there's a quiet burst of static on the line. Keith goes to hang up, thinking there's a fault, when he hears a voice. "Can you hear me?"

It's faint. Keith isn't sure he's heard right. "Hello?" he says.

The voice doesn't respond, not directly. It speaks to him, though. The voice comes through clearer now, though still surrounded by static. "Keep the girl safe."

"What?" Keith says. "What girl? Hello?"

The line goes dead.

Keith looks back at the guard, who's pushing himself off the wall he's been leaning against. "Let's go," he says.

Keith tries to protest. "There's something wrong with the phone. I haven't made my call."

The guard isn't interested. He doesn't want to hear it. "You made your call," he says. "Your *one* call. Now let's go."

Keith can see that complaining isn't going to get him very far. The guard doesn't want to hear it. He's not interested. Keith walks away from the phone, shaking his head. The words, however, resound in his head.

Keep the girl safe.

They get near the holding cells. The shouting and protesting get louder. Keith can barely hear it, now. The ringing in his ears is gone. In its place is the confused mantra.

Keep the girl safe.

3

Charlie Carter was eating breakfast when it happened.

He was inside the diner, having pancakes. His back was to the wall, he could see out the window and the crowd gathering, lining the streets. The children's hospital, with its ribbon across the entrance, waiting to be cut. He could see the convoy. He knew what was happening. He'd seen it on the news the night before. The president was coming to open St Nicholas. Charlie thought it was a little on the nose to name a children's hospital after Santa Claus, but whatever.

He'd been in America for three full days. The day before that, he spent the entirety of it traveling. From Newcastle Airport to Amsterdam, with a two-hour layover. Then, from Amsterdam to Washington Dulles International Airport. He didn't sleep on either flight and when he finally touched down in America, he was jet-lagged. He made his way through customs blinking hard and stifling yawns, searching out the driver holding up a placard with his name on it. Charlie felt the heat engulfing him. His shirt clung to his back, and a trickle of sweat ran down the back of his neck and under his collar. He'd been abroad many times, but he never got used to the high temperatures of countries warmer than his own. It had been grey and raining when he left Newcastle.

By the time he woke up the next morning, the jetlag had faded. He always recovered from it fast, and he dreaded the day he didn't. That would maybe be the day he put an end to all those long-haul flights.

The explosion blew in the windows of the diner. Having seen the explosion, Charlie had already dropped to the ground and thrown up his table as a shield. He'd grabbed the person nearest to him, a young woman at the table to his left, and sheltered her beside him as the glass shards filled the diner. Luckily, it wasn't very busy. Unfortunately, the people who *were* inside, other than Charlie and the lady he'd managed to grab, were cut up and bleeding. Some of them were screaming. Others were moaning in pain. The waiting staff and the cooks were all right—they'd all been in the kitchen when it happened. They came through, looking confused, investigating the loud noises, and being shocked at what they found. One of them got on the phone and started calling emergency services.

Charlie tended to the first person he came across. An older man with a gash across the top of his scalp. Charlie got a waitress to bring him the first aid kit. The first thing he noticed was that there weren't enough bandages in it for all the people that were hurting. He sent her to get some clean dish towels, too. To the man with the wounded scalp, Charlie administered the Turban technique. He moved on to the next person. A woman with a gash in her upper left arm. The waitress, who was first aid trained, assisted him.

When he'd seen to the wounded people in the diner, Charlie went outside. People were screaming out there, too. Car alarms were screeching. There was a lot of noise. A lot of things to take in. The emergency services had just arrived on the scene. Charlie hurried over to help where he could.

Then, at some point, he came across a Black guy and a teenage girl. He didn't catch either of their names, but the next thing he knew, he was being bundled into the back of a cop cruiser like he'd done something wrong.

Then he was brought here, to the station. Sat down in this room. With all this in mind, after all his efforts to try and help, Charlie has to wonder what he's doing in an interrogation room with a couple of NSA agents.

"Mr. Carter—" one of the agents begins.

"Just call me Charlie," Charlie says.

"Mr. Carter will do us fine," the other agent says.

"Suit yourself," Charlie says.

He sees how both of their eyes narrow. He hasn't said much, but they're probably struggling with his accent. He gets it every time he comes to the states. Or anywhere else in the world, for that matter. Sometimes even in his own country, especially if he's down in the south.

"Mr. Carter," the first agent says, "what is the purpose of your visit to Washington, DC?"

"Work," Charlie says.

"Care to elaborate?" agent two says.

"I get paid to train some lads up to work security. Private firms, mostly."

Agent one blinks.

"You're ex-British Army, is that right?" agent two says.

"That's right," Charlie says.

"What's so special about an ex-British soldier that they'd fly him all the way over here to provide some training?"

Charlie shrugs. "Plenty do. And not just in America. I go all over. Like I said, it's work. It's my work. I make a canny living from it."

Agent one frowns. "*Canny*?"

Charlie shrugs again. "Decent."

"That still doesn't explain what makes you so special," agent two says. "Why not an ex-American soldier? It would save them a lot of money on flights and taxis."

"They do," Charlie says. "But they also like to mix it up a bit. Get a few different techniques in."

"Uh-huh," agent one says. "When did you arrive in Washington?"

"Four days ago."

"And other than your training seminars, what have you done while you've been here?"

"Not much," Charlie says. "I go to the seminars, and I go back to the hotel. Might wander out and find something to eat. This isn't a holiday for me. I'm not here to sight-see."

The two agents watch him intently. Charlie reclines in his seat and watches them right back. He doesn't have anything to be worried about. He's not going to look like he does just for their benefit.

"Lads," he says, "can we get to the point? What am I even doing here? I was trying to help. You're wasting time talking to me."

"We have records of you in South America," agent one says.

"Been a few times," Charlie says. "Nice for a visit. Wouldn't like to stay there too long, though."

"Save your sarcasm," agent two says.

"Nothing sarcastic about it, mate," Charlie says, though it's not entirely true. He knows there's a tone to his words. It comes from his annoyance. He's frustrated that they're not being clear with him. They're talking in circles rather than just coming out and saying what they want or why he's here.

"You did some mercenary work," agent one says.

"Ah," Charlie says. They have his attention now. "*That's* the trip you're talking about."

"It wasn't too long ago, Mr. Carter," agent one says. "Just last year, in fact. From what we understand, you left the British Army when you were twenty-nine. Five years before you turned up in Honduras. Of course, Honduras might just be the only record we have of you in South America. Or, indeed, the only record we have of you doing mercenary work. Could be that you were doing it for the whole five years between leaving the Army and showing up there. Maybe you were working all around the world. But if not, that's quite a wait in between. Civilian life not cut it, the daily routine started to get to you, and you felt like you needed to get back in the action?"

Charlie doesn't answer.

Agent two takes over, leaning forward and clasping his hands atop the table. "What we can't find," he says, "is any record as to why you left the Army. And when we've reached out to the government, they're curiously tight-lipped about it." Agent two cocks his head, inviting Charlie to provide an explanation.

"Decided it wasn't for me," Charlie says, folding his arms.

Agent one grunts. "Sure it wasn't something more than that? Special forces, perhaps, Mr. Carter?"

"Don't know what you're talking about."

"MI5, maybe?"

Charlie snorts. "Think you've got Geordie James Bond on your hands, that it?"

Agent two's eyes narrow. "I don't know what a *Geordie* is, Mr. Carter, but what we've got on our hands is a terrorist attack, and what we have with you is a man with the potential know-how to perpetrate just such an attack. You handle many bombs in the SAS, Mr. Carter?"

Charlie stares at him.

"That's right, isn't it?" agent two says. "SAS."

"This is ridiculous," Charlie says. "And I'm not saying another word without a representative from the British embassy in here with me."

The two agents attempt to question him further, but Charlie doesn't budge. He keeps his arms folded, his lips sealed, and his eyes fixed on the wall behind and just above their heads. Eventually, they exchange glances and give up. They don't make any mention of getting him someone from the British embassy as they stand to leave, but they do ask the guard waiting outside to transport him back to the holding cells.

Charlie doesn't know the ins and outs of American law, but he has a feeling that the current treatment of himself and the other people being held prisoner could be considered unconstitutional. What little he does know, mostly gleaned from TV shows and movies, is that unless they're all charged, they need to be released after twenty-four hours, which means they're about halfway there now. Of course, that could be completely different when the authorities are dealing with a terrorist attack. Charlie begins to wonder if they might be planning on holding him indefinitely. Transporting him to a more secure facility, perhaps. Whatever their intent, Charlie already knows his stance going forward—silence. He won't say another word without a representative from the British embassy present.

The holding cells are loud. There are a couple of guards banging their batons against the bars and telling everyone to shut up. The people held are cramped in these cages, and there are stirrings like there are angry stirrings and shouts like there's a riot building.

Charlie is shoved into a cell. He pushes a few people out his way as they lunge past him for the open cell door, calling to the guard. Charlie gets past them and looks back to see the guard pushing them back in. He points to someone else and barks a name, then takes this person out of the cell. No doubt along to the interrogation room Charlie has just vacated.

Charlie sees a familiar face. The Black guy from back at the explosion, who he was with when the cops took them away. He's sitting on a bench with his back against the wall. His hands are clasped, and he's frowning, staring down at them. There's space beside him on the bench. Charlie takes a seat.

"They spoke to you yet?" he says.

The Black guy looks up like he didn't hear him approach. "Hey," he says, nodding once. "Yeah, they spoke to me."

"Did you do it?" Charlie says, grinning.

The Black guy's frown deepens. "What?"

Charlie chuckles and then holds up his hands. "Just a joke," he says. "If they dragged you in on something as flimsy as what they were asking me... Well, I reckon they probably wanna put their energy somewhere more productive. I'm Charlie, by the way." He holds out his hand.

"Keith." They shake.

Charlie feels eyes. Like he's being watched. He looks around the cell. A wannabe tough guy looking to assert his dominance? He thought this kind of behavior was saved for the prison yard.

He finds the eyes. Two pairs of them in the adjoining cell. A couple of skinheads standing in the corner, leaning up against the wall and the bars. Charlie can see tattoos on their necks and arms. One of them has something on the side of his skull. It looks like a splash of ink at first, but then it starts to make sense. An iron cross. Charlie recognizes the symbology. He sees it on their arms, too. Knows what their tattoos represent. 88's and swastikas. They're Nazis.

Charlie realizes the eyes he felt weren't upon him. They weren't watching him. They just passed over him. They're watching Keith. Staring at him. Charlie nudges him. "Friends of yours?"

Keith looks up and sees the Nazis staring. They grin at him, showing their teeth. Keith shakes his head and looks back down at his hands.

Charlie looks around the two cells. "Plenty of other Black people present," he says. "And Arabs. What makes you special?"

"I'm sure everyone else has had their turn," Keith says without looking up. "I was brought back here just before you got here. It's probably just my turn. It'll be the kind of intimidation bullshit guys like that like to play. I ain't interested."

Charlie looks back at the Nazis. They look at him now. One of them, the one with the iron cross on the side of his skull, winks at him.

4

Kayla Morrow was brought to the station hours ago. She's lost track of time. She's been left alone in a room at the top of the building. The door's locked. An agent brought her here. He said he was with the NSA. Said they had to keep her here until they were able to get in touch with her parents. He's been back once since to bring her a bottle of water and a packet of chips. She tried to speak to him, to ask him questions, but he was in a rush and didn't hang around. Didn't provide her with any kind of update regarding her parents. He locked the door again after he left. Kayla isn't sure why she's been locked in. She'd like to ask, but there's no one to direct her question to.

The room itself is plain. There's a chair and a desk, and she thinks it might be an office, but perhaps an office not currently in use. There's nothing on the walls, no filing cabinets, nothing on the desk. No sign that someone makes this their regular workspace.

It's hard for Kayla to sit here, not knowing where her mother is or how she is. If she's even still alive.

Kayla feels her eyes burning, but she doesn't cry. She can't. She's all cried out. The tears came freely when she was first locked in here, worrying about her mother. There's nothing in the room for her to see her reflection in, but she's sure her face is puffy and that her eyes are bloodshot. She sits at the table with the hood of her jumper pulled up over her head. Her right knee bounces. Her sleeves are pulled over her hands. Her jumper smells like smoke from the explosion. The smell puts her right back there, in amongst all the carnage.

She just wants someone to come and talk to her. She wants to go home. She wants the door to open and her father to walk through to collect her, and she wants her mother to be right behind him.

The longer it takes, the less likely she knows it is that her mother is going to come. The less likely it is that she's all right.

She wonders, though, why her father hasn't come yet. The police, and the NSA agent, claim they've been trying to get in touch with him. How hard can it be? She's given her home number. She's given the number for his cell. Even if they can't get hold of him, surely he's seen the news? He knew where Kayla and his wife were going. Why isn't he looking for her?

It's getting late. She pushes herself up from the table and goes to the door. There's no window in it. She tries the handle on the off chance, but it remains locked. She knocks on the door, hoping to get someone's attention. No one comes. She sighs. Shakes her head. Presses her forehead against the door. The cops and the agents haven't been any help to her. It doesn't even feel like they're trying to help.

So far, the only person that has tried to help Kayla, really help her, was Keith. They took him away, and she doesn't know where he is now. Maybe here, in this building. Maybe they took him somewhere else.

Kayla isn't sure how she came to be near where the bomb went off. She doesn't know how she lost track of her mom. Kayla thinks the blast may have knocked her memory. The last thing she remembers is being in a store. Kayla had been in a changing room, trying on a new dress. She remembers seeing herself in the mirror. She liked the dress. She doesn't know what became of it. The next thing she knew, everything was chaos. People were hurt. People were dead. She'd never seen anything like it, not outside of television.

And then she realized she didn't know where her mother was. She called out for her. She felt herself growing frantic. She couldn't breathe. Her chest was getting tight.

That was when Keith found her. He sat her down and helped her ease her breathing. Talked her through it. He calmed her down. Told her he'd help her find her mother.

They didn't get far in their search. Another guy came along. Kayla didn't know who he was, but he had a strange accent. Shortly after he arrived, the cops pulled up on them. They took Keith and the other guy away. The NSA agent picked Kayla up right after, but he didn't bundle her in the back of his vehicle. He didn't place her under arrest. He asked her where her parents were. Kayla is seventeen. She can imagine at that moment, lost and worried and afraid, she probably looked much younger than she is. When she told him she didn't know where her mother was and she was concerned for her, that was when he took her away with him, reassuring her on the journey to the station that they'd find her mother and get in touch with her father.

Kayla returns to her seat on the other side of the desk, facing the door. Before she can sit, she hears it unlock. She halts, watching. The NSA agent from earlier, the one who brought her here, the one who brought her water and chips, the one who has largely abandoned her for the day, pokes his head in. "How you holding up, Kayla?"

"Not great," Kayla says, straightening up, pushing the seat back under the desk, and hoping that she's finally leaving this room. She can't remember his name, so says, "Agent…?"

He takes the hint. He smiles and says, "Nivens. Lloyd Nivens. I shouldn't expect you to remember—you've been in here a long time. It's been a long day. I'm sorry I haven't been able to check in on you more often. As I'm sure you can imagine, things have been…busy. Very busy." He steps fully into the room.

Agent Lloyd Nivens reminds Kayla a little of her father. They look about the same age. She'd estimate he's in his forties. He has dark hair, which is greying at the sides.

"I'm afraid I don't think I'm bringing news to make you feel better," he says.

Kayla feels her stomach sinking. "What is it?"

"We haven't been able to get in touch with your father," he says, his face solemn. "And we haven't found your mother, either. The good news is, we haven't seen her name on any of the lists of the dead we've managed to compile so far."

Kayla swallows. She feels a dry click in her throat. "Have you found *all* the bodies?"

Lloyd's face lets her know he'd hoped she wouldn't realize this. "Not yet, no. Trust me, Kayla, we're working very hard to try to find your mother and your father. Both of them. But until we can, I'm afraid we can't let you leave."

"I just want to go home," Kayla says.

"I know that. I'm sorry. We just want to make sure you get there safely. I can't let you leave here without a guardian." Agent Nivens looks apologetic. "It's getting late now, and I'm sure you'd like to rest. I'll send a couple of guards along, and they'll take you somewhere you can sleep."

Kayla doesn't respond. She doesn't have anything to say. She just wants to leave. She doesn't want to sleep. She wants to get on a bus or call a taxi. She wants to go home.

"They won't be long," Nivens says, stepping back toward the door.

"Why do you keep locking it?" Kayla says before he can leave.

"For your security," Nivens says. "The station is very busy right now. We don't want anyone getting in here who shouldn't."

He slips out before Kayla can ask anything else, and once again, she's left alone. She pulls the chair out from under the desk, scraping it along the ground in frustration. She drops herself into it and pushes her hands into her eyes. Nivens said he would send someone to get her soon, but from what she's seen today, his idea of *soon* is very different from hers.

5

James Trevor wasn't anywhere near the presidential motorcade when it happened. If he had been, he'd be dead, too. He was close enough to see what happened, though.

He was down the block a little way on crowd control. There were a lot of people. James felt boxed in. His police uniform felt tight. The gathering wasn't particularly rowdy, though. They just wanted to see the vice-president. He remembers wondering how many of them turned up thinking it was still going to be the president. He wondered, too, if they'd heard about the bombing at Fort Jackson. Whether they had or not, they were in high spirits. They waved their flags and shook their banners, and there were plenty of smiling faces.

James had worked crowd control plenty of times before. He knew what to look out for. Suspicious types with suspicious packages or anything that could have looked like a weapon. He wasn't seeing anything like that. Just people present for the opening of a new children's hospital. And plus, there were plenty of Secret Service agents around, too. There were snipers on the roofs of the nearby buildings. They were watching the crowds, too. Everyone was in touch with each other. No one could see anything out of place.

Then the explosion happened, and it all went to hell.

James remembers seeing something right before it happened. Something had caught his eye. A distant figure emerging from the multi-story parking lot. They were just an outline—or is that just how he remembers them? Some debris struck him in the temple, and he wonders if this affected his memory in any way. He presses a tentative finger to that temple now. It's bandaged, and a spot of blood has soaked through. It stings, and it makes him wince, but it isn't too bad. His arm is worse.

But for now, he doesn't think about his injuries. He remembers the vague outline. Walking up the road. No one else seemed to realize they were there. The multi-story had already been swept. It was being guarded. No one expected anyone to emerge from there. James was getting on his radio, advising those on the rooftop to get eyes on this new figure, when the bomb went off. He never got a chance to call it in.

The debris clipped him in the side of the head and knocked him down. He didn't realize what was happening. All the air had been sucked out of the world. He couldn't hear anything, and then he was struck. He was on the ground. There was blood in his eyes. He couldn't feel anything.

But then someone fell on him, and he felt again. They landed on his left arm. They broke it. James felt pain, the kind of pain he hadn't felt since he was a child, and he'd broken his collarbone. He screamed but couldn't hear it. The person who had landed on him wasn't getting off. They were heavy, and James couldn't wriggle free. He had to twist his body and use his feet to kick them off. They rolled onto their back. It was a woman. At least, he thought so. He saw why she wasn't moving. The center of her face had been caved in. The chunk of concrete was still embedded there. He couldn't make out any of her features.

James grits his teeth, remembering. He'd never seen anything like it before.

A children's hospital, for Christ's sake. Who could ever expect anything like this at a children's hospital?

People take shots at political figures all the time, sure, but you keep kids out of it. This is supposed to be America. This kind of thing isn't supposed to happen here.

Lying in his hospital bed, waiting to be discharged, James thinks on how it will be a long time before Saint Nicholas's is going to be able to open, if ever. The explosion, while far away from the building itself, was able to cause enough damage. Most people know the hospital was a passion project of Louise Stewart, the first lady, an ex-pediatrician. She and the president, Frank Stewart, have no children of their own. This wasn't always the case, though. Their daughter, Mary, died when she was just ten weeks old. Sudden Infant Death Syndrome. This was decades before Frank Stewart ever became president. One of the wings of the new hospital was to be named after Mary. They'd never had another child. They'd never revealed whether this was by choice or biology.

President Stewart and the first lady were supposed to be there to open the hospital themselves. After the attack on Fort Jackson, they'd had to cancel. The president had more pressing matters to deal with. The vice-president went to open Saint Nicholas's in his place. The ARO has claimed both attacks—the one on Fort Jackson and the killing of the vice-president. James wonders, what are their goals? Just chaos, or do they have something more insidious in mind?

James had been informed of the change at this morning's briefing. President Frank Stewart had to stay at the White House. Robert Fielding, his Chief of Staff, had advised a press conference, promising to hunt out the Anti-Right Outreach. Warning them that there was nowhere they could hide. These acts of domestic terrorism would not go unpunished, and the president would not stop until they'd all been hunted down and brought to justice. Robert said it was a show of strength for the American people. Something to reassure them.

Instead, this has happened, and no doubt the American people aren't feeling very reassured.

James doesn't even know if the press conference happened. He was too busy, and he hasn't had a chance to check since.

By the time he was able to stand, his left arm uselessly clutched his ribs, and sound was returning to the world. He felt like he was in a warzone. People were screaming. There were bodies everywhere, though it was impossible to tell who was dead and who was living. It was impossible to tell anyone apart. Everyone was doused in dust and grime. Eyes and mouths in blank faces.

James stumbled through the chaos, not sure what to do. Not sure how he could help. He was dizzy from the shot to the head. Blood was still running into his eyes. When he tried to wipe it away, he just replaced it with dirt which stung and blinded him further.

Someone grabbed him at some point. Another cop, though he couldn't make out who they were. They dragged him along, not realizing his arm was broken. They helped him into the back of an ambulance.

And then, the next thing he knew, he was here. In this hospital, in this doctor's examination room. They've checked him for a concussion, but he was clear. They've put his arm in a cast, and the cast is in a sling. James sits on the edge of the examination table and feels numb. He stares at the wall opposite, at the posters warning of the dangers of smoking or alcoholism. The nurses washed the dirt from his left hand and arm before they put him in the cast, but the rest of him remains filthy. He wants to take a shower. He wants to go home. He's not sure what he's waiting for. He thinks they've forgotten him.

He doesn't blame them. They sound busy out there, and all things considered, his wounds are minor. James listens to the sounds in the corridors outside his room. The doctors and nurses running around, barking orders. The wheeling of gurneys and wheelchairs. The moaning of people in pain. The occasional scream. He's heard people crying, too.

He needs to contact Shira. No doubt the attack has been on the news—it was probably live. There were camera crews there when it happened. How much did they show? Was Shira watching—how much did she see? He needs to get in touch with her to tell her he's all right. That he's still alive. She must be worrying.

There's a knock at the door. James turns to it, briefly hoping that it might be Shira. Matt Bunker pokes his head around the door.

"There you are," he says.

He looks relieved to see James. Matt Bunker is not a cop. He's Secret Service. "Still hiding out in here. Leaving all the work to the rest of us, huh?" He steps fully into the room and crosses to the examination table. He checks the bandage wrapped around James's head, then whistles low as he looks at the cast. "You want me to sign that?" He's grinning.

"You're in a surprisingly good mood," James says, his voice hoarse, and he realizes these are the first words he's spoken since the explosion. "All things considered."

"Just glad to see you're alive," Matt says, his expression solemn now. "Plenty aren't."

"How bad is it?" James says.

"Pretty damn bad," Matt says, crossing the room to a window. He looks down. The lights of ambulance sirens reflect on his face. "Have you looked down?"

"No, I…" James doesn't finish what he's thinking. He's been

dizzy. Stunned. He hasn't been able to focus. His thoughts keep drifting back to the explosion.

"Can you hear that? The ambulances haven't stopped running. They're still rolling up now."

"I assume that's why they've forgotten about me."

"It's a mad house out there, buddy," Matt says, jerking his thumb back toward the door. "It's chaos. Truth be told, the doc probably *has* forgotten all about you in here. He's got about a dozen more pressing things he needs to take care of."

"Shit," James says. "How bad is it?"

"O'Connelly's dead," Matt says, "but you probably know that already."

James nods. "Saw it happen."

Matt grimaces. "The ARO claimed responsibility. They've gotten awful bold with this attack."

"Jesus Christ, you don't say," James says. "They've killed the vice-president." He shakes his head. "I mean, setting off bombs on military bases wasn't exactly small fry, but this is a whole other level."

Matt nods. "President Stewart's held a press conference."

"What'd he say?"

Matt waves his hand in the air. "What you'd expect. We, the American people, won't stand for this. We'll hunt them down, bring them to justice, etcetera, etcetera. He and Jake were close. He hides it well, but he's all cut up inside."

Matt stares out the window, and James watches his back. "How did you know I was here?" James says.

"I didn't," Matt says, turning. "I've come to check in on our wounded, and I recognized your name, and I wasn't going to ignore the fact an old friend could be lying here wounded."

"Were you at the hospital? The bombing, I mean. I didn't see you there."

Matt shakes his head. "I was called in to help with the clean-up. Everyone's been called in. All leave has been canceled—*I was on leave. I was out at the lake when I got the call.*"

"I appreciate you calling by," James says. "I need to get in touch with Shira. I need to let her know I'm all right."

"Then let's get out of here," Matt says. "I'll take you home."

"I think I need the doctor to sign me off."

Matt waves his hand in the air. "I'll deal with that," he says. "I'll call your department and let them know what's happened."

"I appreciate that," James says, sliding off the table and straightening with a grimace.

James follows Matt's lead. It's chaos out in the halls. There aren't enough beds for everyone. James wonders how many people were injured in the blast. He wonders how many were killed. The corridors are filled with people on gurneys and others who sit on the ground, cradling themselves and each other. They all look as dirty as James still is and shell-shocked. They stare off into the distance. James can see blood on a lot of them, as well as broken bones. A gurney is pushed by, and the screaming woman atop it is missing the bottom of her right leg.

The hospital is overwhelmed. They're struggling to deal with this sudden influx of patients, coupled with the ones they already have as well as other non-related emergencies. The explosion will have further reaching implications than the immediate vicinity outside Saint Nicholas's. James sees the doctor who was checking his skull earlier rush by, clutching at his stethoscope. He doesn't notice James. It's clear he has more pressing matters on his mind.

"How were your friends?" James says, catching up to Matt.

Matt's expression is grim. It's clear it hasn't been good news for a lot of his co-workers. "They're hurt," Matt says. "The ones who survived…"

They aren't able to take the elevator down. It's too crammed. They take the stairs. Even here, it's busy. They finally manage to make their way outside. It's getting dark. The air is cold, and

James breathes it in deeply. He closes his eyes and feels the grime around his eyes crack.

"Can I use your phone?" he says, opening his eyes.

Matt hands it to him as they reach his car. Matt dials Shira's number from memory. She answers almost instantly. "Hello?" she says, sounding confused, not recognizing the number, but also frantic, almost terrified, knowing that a call from an unknown number is likely not good news.

"Shira," James says. "It's me."

6

Minnow has remained quiet. Georgia imagines it's probably the same across the country.

Three people came into the library all day. None of them were interested in checking out books. They all just wanted someone to talk to. They all said the same thing. How they'd never seen anything like it. How they couldn't believe this had happened.

Knowing she'd likely be distracted by the news all evening, Georgia ate at one of the town's bars after she locked up the library. She didn't go to the diner. Too many windows. Too well lit. She wanted the darkness of a bar.

She took a booth in the corner at the back from where she could see the rest of the room and, particularly, the door. The bar was quiet, though. She'd eaten there a few times before, and it was always lively. Minnow is a small town, and there aren't many places for people to go. The proprietor even lets teens in, so long as they behave themselves, and he won't serve them anything alcoholic. Lets them play pool at the table in the corner of the room opposite where Georgia sat. There was no one playing pool. Barely anyone drinking or eating. Everyone had stayed home, most likely. Watching the news. Waiting for updates that likely won't come tonight.

The bartender had the television on, and he stood glued to it, as did the few other patrons present. They sat at the bar, staring up. They barely said a word, only occasionally muttering to themselves or asking each other if they could believe this.

Georgia finishes her panini with salad and fries, and then she leaves. Her truck is parked down the side of the bar. She goes to it, but she doesn't get straight in. She parked under a streetlight on purpose. Standing in the cold, she checks the snow around her truck. The prints she sees are her own and the ones that were already there when she first got out. She noted them. Memorized them. Satisfied there are no new pairs, she still doesn't get into the truck. She circles it. She looks under it. She checks the front and the back. She doesn't see anything out of place. Nothing there that shouldn't be, like a little black box with or without a blinking light. No kind of tracker. Nothing out of place.

Now she gets in her truck. She pulls away from the bar and heads out of town. Heads home. On her way, she watches her mirrors. Shortly after she leaves Minnow, she spots lights behind her. They keep her distance, but they follow. Other than herself and this other vehicle, the roads are quiet. Georgia keeps one eye on the lights. She's almost halfway home now.

The lights disappear. They might have turned off, but there's nowhere around here for them to go. They could have turned around, realizing they were lost. Or they could have just killed the lights, and they're still coming after her.

Georgia sucks her teeth, thinking. It's so dark behind her that she can't make out the outline of the vehicle that was there. Can only see the trees that line either side of the road. She looks up ahead. She knows this road well. She drives it every day. She kills her own lights, then pulls to the side of the road for a moment. Gives her eyes a chance to adjust to the dark. She keeps checking the mirrors. The vehicle she spotted earlier doesn't approach. Nothing passes. When the darkness has cleared, she starts the engine up again, leaving her lights off. Nothing approaches from behind.

She gets home without incident, but she can't shake the feeling that she was being followed. She doesn't get straight out of the truck. Watches her home for a while and the road that leads to it. She winds her window down a little. Listens. The night is still.

She grabs the torch she stores in her glove compartment and gets out of the truck. Like back at the bar, she circles her home. She pauses by the front door, casting her torch over the ground. There are footprints. One pair. They don't belong to her. The print is a few sizes bigger than her own, and the pattern from the bottom of the boot is different. They're angled toward the door, like someone has been knocking or trying the handle. She tests it for herself. It remains locked. The footprints move off to the right. She follows them. They go all the way around her house. She finds where they've paused at each of the windows. Looking in, no doubt. There's no sign of an attempted break-in, though. Eventually, the footprints walk away from her house and toward the road. The only tire tracks are her own. The footprints head off down the road, sticking to the side. She follows them for a little while. Realizes that there is a pair heading back toward her house, too. The same pair she's following away from it now. However they got here, they left their vehicle further back. Maybe at the same place, the vehicle she thought was following her stopped.

She stands by the side of the road and turns off her torch. She listens, and she watches, staring off down the road. She hears some noises, but they're small. Small movements from small animals. She turns and heads back home in darkness.

Despite there being no signs of a break-in, it's hard to get comfortable. Georgia knows she won't relax tonight. She walks around her home and checks every room. Checks the basement. Checks the lock on every door and window. Makes sure her security lights are turned on.

She changes out of her clothes, but she doesn't get into something more comfortable. She puts on her workout gear. Stuff she can run in, move in. Fight in. She goes down to the living room, leaving all the lights off. She draws the curtains. She takes a seat on the sofa, and waits. It's unlikely she'll sleep tonight.

7

About an hour ago, the two skinheads were taken away together.

Charlie nudges Keith. "They've been gone a while now," Charlie says. "Think they've freed them?"

It's getting late now, and the cells have quietened, their occupants calmer now than they were earlier. Their indignation had been worn away. Keith hasn't been particularly chatty. For the most part, he's sat and stared at his hands. He looks up at Charlie, then to where the skinheads have been leaning against the wall in the neighboring cell.

"Probably just being questioned," he says. "Everyone's had a turn."

Charlie grunts. It was two guards, and one of the agents came to collect them. He looks around both cells. Some people are trying to get comfortable on the floor, trying to grab some sleep. Charlie has noticed that, apart from himself and the Nazis, there aren't any other white people being held. The men here are all either Black or Arabic.

Charlie leans back and rests his head against the wall. He

closes his eyes and thinks of Niamh, back in Newcastle. His wife. Thinking of her makes him smile. Nothing else in here will.

"You married, Keith?" he asks, opening his eyes. "Or have a girlfriend, maybe? A boyfriend? I don't judge."

"None of the above," Keith says. "You like to talk, don't you?"

"I've given you at *least* half an hour of peace."

"It's been about four since they put you in here."

"Speaking of," Charlie says. "They gonna let us out, or what? They have to do something eventually, right?"

"Different rules when it's a terrorist attack," Keith says. "Best thing we can do for now is just to try and get comfortable."

"That's not a very comforting thought, though, is it, Keith?"

Keith shrugs. "It is what it is, man."

A door opens at the end of the corridor, and the two skinheads are escorted back to the cell by the same two guards that earlier took them away. There's no sign of the agent this time. The skinheads promptly push their way through the crowded cell and take up their spot in the corner again, leaning against the wall and the bars. They notice Charlie looking. They grin at him. They look very pleased with themselves. They've been smirking since they returned.

"They look happy enough," Charlie says.

"Fuck 'em," Keith says.

Keith has his eyes closed. Charlie would like to try and grab a nap, but he doesn't feel comfortable in a place like this, with all these men he doesn't know. Potentially dangerous. Soon, they'll probably turn the lights off for the night. They'll be in darkness. The last thing that will be on his mind is sleep.

Charlie looks outside the cell to the door the skinheads were just brought through and where earlier he was brought through, too. There's a camera above this door. There's one above the door directly opposite it, too. They're both pointing into the cells.

There's a little red light on the top of them to show they're active. Charlie finds himself staring into this red light, into the camera.

Keith distracts him, suddenly sitting forward and opening his eyes. "Did you get a call?"

Charlie turns to him. "A call? No, I didn't. They didn't offer one."

"Didn't offer me, either—I had to demand it." Keith strokes his chin. "I was gonna call my buddy, Dom. He would've known what to do. Would've got me a lawyer, or whatever else I needed. Thing is, must've been some crossed wires or something. I never even got to dial out."

"Okay," Charlie says, not understanding the point of the story.

"Yeah," Keith says, staring into the distance and frowning. "There was this voice, instead." Keith shakes his head. "It was…strange."

"What'd it say?" Charlie says, intrigued. "You can't leave off there, mate. You need to deliver the payoff."

The door opens. The two guards come back through. They have someone with them. They're short. They have long hair. Charlie realizes he's seen them before. It's the girl from the site of the explosion. The girl that was with Keith.

Keith has seen her, too. He's already getting to his feet. "It said to keep the girl safe," he says absently, his eyes fixed on the guards and the girl.

Charlie stands, too. Something catches his eye. Above the door. The camera. The red light is off. It's not recording anymore.

8

The guards don't talk to Kayla. They lead her through the station. She doesn't know where they're taking her. She's not in cuffs, but she almost feels like she should be. One is in front, and one is behind. The one behind is holding her by the right arm. His grip is tight. Tighter than it needs to be.

The station is calm. There isn't any shouting or rushing around like there was earlier when Kayla first arrived. Everything is more subdued.

The guards lead Kayla through a quiet part of the station. The back of it, perhaps. It's not the way they led her when she got here. They only pass one other person. A cop reading notes on a clipboard barely glances up as they pass. He nods his head at the guards with Kayla without raising his eyes.

"Where are we going?" Kayla says.

The guards don't answer. The one in front doesn't turn his head. Kayla tries to look back at the one behind her, but he's looking straight ahead. Won't meet her eye.

They stop outside a door. The guard in front pulls out some keys. There are a few keys on the keyring. He uses one of them to unlock the door. Opens it. Kayla can see inside. Can see where they're going. The cells. Two cells. They're full of people. Full of men.

Kayla frowns. She doesn't understand. They must just be passing through this way. But then the guard in front, and he's flipped to another key on the keyring. He opens the lefthand cell. The one closest to them. The guard behind pushes Kayla inside.

"What?" Kayla says, feeling like a deer caught in headlights as the men inside, some of whom looked like they were trying to get to sleep, look up at her.

They look very awake now. All eyes are on her. She turns back to the bars.

"No—this isn't right," she says, but the guards are already turning away. "This is a mistake—I'm not under arrest! Let me out!"

Kayla hears a familiar voice from the next cell. "Hey," it says, though it's not speaking to her. It's talking to the guards. "Hey, what're you doing, man? You can't put her in there. What the fuck's going on here?"

It's Keith. Kayla looks at him, and when she turns back to the guards, they're already gone. Back through the door. They've locked it. She hears the key turning, its teeth scraping through the tumblers.

The British guy with the strange accent is standing next to Keith. He's frowning. He looks just as confused as Keith does and as Kayla feels. He looks to his right. Kayla follows his gaze. Two men are in the corner of the cell. They have shaved heads and tattoos. They're both staring at her, and they're smiling. They look like they're going to eat her up.

"Kayla," Keith says, motioning to her through the bars, beckoning her closer. "Come here. Stay close to us."

Kayla goes to him, grateful at least to see a familiar face. She takes one of his hands in both of her own, and Keith squeezes.

"You stay right here," Keith says. "Don't move from this spot.

You got that? Stay right next to us. Me and Charlie." He turns and looks to the British guy for confirmation, who nods. "We'll take care of you. You got that? Just stay next to us."

Kayla nods, pressing herself up against the bars as if she could force her way through them and into the cell, closer to Keith and Charlie.

Keith turns to the two skinheads. He jabs a finger at them. "And the two of you stay the *fuck* away from her."

The skinheads are smirking. The one with the tattoo on the side of his head is watching Kayla. He licks his lips.

9

The roads are busy with emergency vehicles but little in the way of civilians. James notices blockades, too. The city is on lockdown. He's not surprised.

"Have they been caught?" he says.

Matt shakes his head. "No, still out there somewhere."

"I saw someone," James says, remembering something. "Right before the explosion."

Matt glances at him as he drives, waiting for him to continue.

"I couldn't make them out, though—or at least I can't remember." He points to his bandaged temple. "If I got a good look at them, the head injury must've knocked it right on out. But I saw them coming from the parking lot. The multi-story."

"There were people on patrol in that building," Matt says.

"I know there were," James says, remembering how it looked before he was ushered into the back of an ambulance with a couple of other people. "I don't imagine any of them survived."

"Teams are still sifting through the rubble," Matt says. "But no, I don't imagine they did. You remember anything else about this person you saw?"

"Not really."

PAUL HEATLEY

"That's not much to go on."

"I know. It might come back to me, though. I remember. I'll call you."

Matt drops James off at the entrance of his building. He declines James's offer to come up. "I'm sure Shira's missed you," he says, "and I'm certain she's been worried sick. She doesn't want to see me."

James thanks him again, then gets out of the car and waves him off. During the journey home from the hospital, his body seized up. His muscles ache. His limbs are stiff. His headache feels worse than it did earlier. He goes inside and makes his way up to his apartment.

Shira is waiting for him as he opens the door. She gives a start, probably not recognizing him at first through all the layers of dirt still coating him, but then she throws her arms around him. James wraps his left arm around her waist and moves his right to the side to avoid it being crushed.

Shira Mizrahi is from Tel Aviv, Israel. She's as tall as James is —five-eleven—with long black hair that she currently wears in a single plait running down the middle of her back. Before she moved to America, Shira was in Mossad. She retired a year before she came to the States. At only thirty-five, the same age as James, she's had a busy life. She doesn't talk much about her past, though, nor why she left Mossad, and James never pushes her.

She retains the athletic build she cultivated while a field agent and James feels that strength now while she holds him. She notices how he holds his arm out and looks down at them. "I didn't hurt you, did I?"

"No," James says, smiling. "You didn't hurt me at all."

She takes a step back and cups his face with both hands. "I'd

50

kiss you," she says, her eyes gleaming with tears, "but you're filthy."

"I'm gonna kiss you anyway," James says and grabs her with his good arm, pulls her close, and kisses her.

She could stop him if she wanted. Even if James had the use of both arms, she could probably still kick his ass. She lets him, though, laughing, and then the dirt from his face is smeared onto hers and onto the front of her green sweater.

"Now I need to shower, too," she says.

"That's not the worst thing," James says, holding up his right arm, "you can help me keep my cast dry."

Later, after they've showered and changed into fresh clothes, Shira asks if he's hungry. "Do you want me to make you anything? There're eggs in the fridge. There's not much else. I was going to go shopping, but with everything that's happened…"

"I'm not hungry," James says, "but thanks. I just want to put the TV on. I want to get caught up on what's been happening today."

Shira nods then heads into the kitchen anyway to make something for herself. James goes back to the bathroom and takes a couple of painkillers from the medicine cabinet, then goes into the living room and turns on the television. He lowers himself onto the sofa with a groan.

Soon after, Shira returns. She'd managed to find enough ingredients to throw together a shakshuka. She's put some on a plate for James, too, which is accepts gratefully. As soon as he smelled it, he regretted saying that he wasn't hungry.

They sit and eat together in silence and watch the news. It shows highlights from the president's press conference. It shows the scene of the explosion and then talking heads who were there or nearby. They finish eating and put their plates to one side.

Shira slips her hand into his. "I thought you were dead," she says.

"I'm sorry," James says. "I'm sorry it took so long for me to get in touch with you."

She rests her head on his shoulder. She takes a deep breath through her nose. "It was live on the local news. I was watching. I was sitting right here, drinking coffee, and watching. They cut away as soon as the explosion happened, but I saw enough. I spent the next few hours wondering how close to the explosion you were." She shakes her head a little, keeping it on his shoulder. "The car the vice-president was in, they showed enough to see what happened to that. It took the worst of the blast. I knew no one could have survived that."

James puts his arm around her. He runs the tips of his fingers up and down her arm. "I wasn't anywhere near the motorcade," he says. "I was off to the side."

Shira nods.

James places a hand over his eyes and rubs at his brow. "I don't even know who died."

Shira strokes his back. "I'm sorry, James. I'm so sorry."

Footage on the screen gets James's attention. It's footage of the explosion.

Shira notices. "They've been playing it all day. They cut away before the blast reaches Cadillac One."

James sees it for himself. Sees the vice-president waving to the crowd outside the hospital as the frame freezes. On the left of the screen, he can see the explosion coming from the multi-story. "It should have been checked," James says. "It *would* have been checked. How could it have been missed?"

He stares at the screen. The reporters are talking solemnly over the top of the frozen image, but he doesn't take in anything they're saying. He stares at the roiling fire emanating from the multi-story, at the spreading smoke, at the death that almost claimed him. He can see the cars that were claimed in the explosion and the ones that rolled so close to him. If they'd stopped just five seconds later, ten, would he be dead, too? What became of the men in the other cars? He can see that they were already stopped, that they were getting out. They would have been caught up in the explosion. They're probably dead, too. Or else, if they're not, they're crippled for life. Was that the best James could have hoped for?

He turns to Shira. He might never have seen her again. She sees him looking. "Are you all right?" she says. "What's wrong?"

James realizes he's shaking. He wraps his arms around her and pulls her close. He kisses her cheek, her ear, and the top of her head.

"I'm still here," he says, holding her tight. "I'm still alive."

10

Kayla sits on the floor of the cell, her back against the bars. Keith remains near her on the other side, holding her hand. She barely speaks, but she hasn't cried. She seems almost shell-shocked. Keith stays on one knee, ready to react if he has to, watching the Nazis, who haven't once looked away since Kayla arrived.

Charlie is nearby. He stands with his back against the bars, his arms folded, watching the inside of their own cell.

"It's gonna be lights out soon," Keith says, looking up to Charlie.

Charlie grunts. "I figured as much."

Keith glances back over his shoulder into their cell. It's calm. It's calm in the other cell, too. The only people who still seem lively are the Nazis. They'd make Keith uncomfortable at the best of times, but with them locked up with Kayla, he's surprised he hasn't felt a panic attack coming on. He keeps his breathing steady. Stays calm. He has to keep it together.

Charlie looks around.

"What's up?" Keith says.

"How long has Kayla been in here now? Maybe ten minutes?"

"Something like that."

"Before they brought her in, the cameras stopped recording. The little red lights went off. Did you notice?"

"I wasn't looking," Keith says.

"Yeah, well, they still haven't come on."

Keith twists his body a little and tries to see for himself, but before he can, the lights go out. The cells are plunged into darkness.

"*Shit*," Keith says. He feels Kayla's grip tighten in his. He gets to his feet, and she does the same.

Charlie has straightened, his arms unfolded. "I thought they would've given some warning," he says.

Keith is blinking, blinking hard, willing his eyes to adjust to the sudden dark. There is movement all around them. People mumbling, groaning. Some people getting to their feet. Keith can see outlines. They're coming into focus. He can see Charlie's features.

Then Kayla is screaming.

"*Keith*!"

He spins. He sees the two dark shadows approaching, striding confidently. The skinheads. One of them reaches behind himself. Bring something forward. Keith recognizes the shape of it. It's a knife.

"He's armed!" Keith says.

"What the fuck?" Charlie says, spinning.

They keep Kayla between them as the Nazis approach.

"Stay by us," Keith says to her, his voice low, speaking into her ear. "We can't protect you if you run away."

"Stay calm," Charlie says on her other side. "Let them get close. Try not to panic."

Kayla isn't moving, but she seems close to panic. Her fight-or-flight response has kicked in, and it's screaming at her to fly.

Her shoulders are heaving. Her knees have bent, ready to spring into action. Her whole body is tense, ready to run.

The Nazis get close. Keith can see their faces now, too. They're grinning. They're both armed. They're not prison-made shivs, either. They're combat knives. They should never have made it through security. He can't imagine how they did.

The skinhead on the right, Keith's right, makes a grab for Kayla. Keith grabs him by the wrist and pulls him toward the bars. The skinhead thrusts through with his knife. Keith lets go of him and jumps back, narrowly avoiding being punctured. Before the skinhead can pull his arm back through, Charlie has intercepted. He's grabbed him by the wrist, and he pulls back on it, snapping the skinhead's right arm against the bars. The skinhead screams. He drops the knife.

Keith scoops up the knife and gets back to Kayla. The skinhead in the bars has slumped to the ground, cradling his arm as it dangles uselessly. He's still screaming. The one remaining makes a lunge for Kayla, jabbing. She ducks under, but the skinhead spins back, arcing the knife through the air. It almost catches her in the back of the neck, but she's still moving. The other occupants of the cell are backing up, keeping out of the way. Kayla tries to push through them to get clear. The skinhead gives chase, slicing the air desperately. Kayla is rounding the cell, getting back to the bars. She's crying Keith's name.

Keith's vision is blurring. His heart is hammering. His chest is getting tight, and breathing is getting difficult. This isn't the time. He can't afford this, not right now. Kayla can't afford this.

Out of the corner of his eye, he sees Charlie reach through the bars with both arms and grab the fallen skinhead by the back of the head, then drags him forward into the bars. The skinhead's skull connects with a dull thud that sets the bars to ringing. The skinhead slumps, unconscious, or close to it.

Kayla gets back to Keith. The skinhead doesn't charge in.

Keith has his left arm protectively across Kayla's chest, and with his right, he holds out the knife. He's trying not to make it obvious that he's struggling. He's blinking, though. Blinking more than is natural. It feels like his legs are about to buckle.

Through the dark, the skinhead sees. He charges in, trying to catch Keith unprepared. Keith almost stumbles at his attack. Almost falls. Charlie has seen, though. Has seen that he's not quite right. He pulls Keith back and takes the knife from him. The skinhead jabs the blade through the bars. He doesn't thrust his whole arm through as his friend did. He's not going to make the same mistake.

He's made one mistake, though. His concentration is focused on Keith and Charlie. He hasn't forgotten Kayla, but he's not expecting her to pose any kind of threat.

Keith is on one knee. He's catching his breath. Calming his blurring, swimming vision. He's watching, though. He sees Charlie's defensive stance. He's not being lured in by the skinhead. He's patient. Waiting for his opportunity. It comes soon. It comes courtesy of Kayla.

She creeps up on the skinhead. Gets behind him. Gets close. Keith sees how she's hesitant. She's gritting her teeth. Her eyes are narrowed. She's never done anything like this before. With all the strength she has, she pushes the skinhead toward the bars.

The skinhead is caught off guard. He lurches forward, losing his balance. He drops the knife on his way. The front of his body hits the bars. Charlie is lightning fast. He grabs the skinhead by the back of the neck with his left hand and with his right and drives the point of the knife under his ribs and then up into his heart.

Charlie leaves the knife in. He pushes the dead body away from the bars. It lands flat in the center of the cell.

All hell is breaking loose. The other people in the cells are going wild, jumping up and down. One of them pulls the knife out of the dead skinhead. Another grabs the knife he dropped. They're holding them high in the air, waving them around.

Charlie helps Keith to his feet. They stand near the bars with Kayla. "Did you have to kill him?" Keith says.

"Him or us," Charlie says, though he's not looking at Keith. He's watching the doors leading into the cells. He grunts suddenly. "The cameras have just come back on."

11

The lights come back on, the doors fly open, and guards come charging in. They're shouting red-faced for the occupants to get back, to get away from the bars.

Charlie gets closer to the front. He sees the two guards that brought Kayla here. They're looking into the cells. The left-hand cell. One of them notices the dead skinhead in the center of the floor. His eyes widen a little. He nudges the other guard. They search the cell with their eyes. They see Kayla standing with Keith. They turn, and they leave, pushing their way back out.

Charlie sees it all. He looks back at Keith. Keith saw, too. They exchange concerned glances.

More guards are coming now. They're wearing riot gear. They have shields, and they're banging their batons against them.

In Kayla's cell, one of the men that took a knife starts stabbing someone else. Things are getting wild. The cell door is opened. The guards clad in riot gear charge in. They start busting heads.

The two guards return. They're not alone. They have someone with them. He's wearing a suit. He looks like one of the agents

Charlie has seen going around the station. NSA, most likely, just like the one who was questioning him. This one looks a little older. His dark hair is greying around the sides. He looks into the cell. Sees the evidence of what has transpired. He sees Kayla. He steps into the cell, the two guards following. They avoid the beatings the riot guards are handing out.

"Agent Nivens!" Kayla says, seeing his approach. "They put me in here," she points at the guards on either side of him. "Why did they put me in here?"

Agent Nivens doesn't speak. His face is firm. He reaches for Kayla and grabs her arm.

"What the hell's going on here?" Keith says, grabbing Kayla's other arm and holding her in place.

Charlie fights his way back over to them. "Why were the cameras switched off?"

The agent frowns at this. He looks back at the guards, then back at Keith. "Let go of her arm, sir," he says. His voice is like steel. "Sir, you're obstructing my duties. This won't reflect well on you."

Keith doesn't respond, and he doesn't let go of Kayla, either.

Agent Nivens flicks his head at the two guards, and they step forward to wrench Kayla free from Keith's grip. Keith struggles with them. Charlie steps closer, but he doesn't intercept. He sees a different kind of opportunity.

The guards pry Keith's fingers loose and then restrain Kayla. They drag her from the cell, following the agent's lead. They leave out the right door.

Keith wheels on Charlie. "I really could've used your help there, man," he says.

"I *did* help," Charlie says.

Keith raises an eyebrow.

"I don't trust them," Charlie says, nodding his head in the

direction the two guards and the agent have disappeared. "They locked her in that cell with a couple of Nazis—*armed* Nazis. And suddenly, before they're miraculously armed, they were taken away by those same two guards."

"I hear what you're saying," Keith says.

"Uh-huh. And now they've got Kayla, and I don't feel easy with that, and I'm sure you don't, either."

"No, I don't, but what the fuck can we do about it now? They're gone, man!"

Charlie looks around, then reveals what he's been concealing in his left hand. "I swiped one of their keys."

Keith stares at them.

"Now, are we in on this together? Because the second we open that door and go out after them…"

"I know what it means," Keith says. He chews his lip. He nods once. "Open the door."

Charlie does, pushing his way through the crowd gathered by the door. He tries not to make it obvious as he slips the key in the lock and turns it. He moves fast, though. Keith stays close. Charlie pulls the door open.

It doesn't take long for everyone else to notice. They start pouring out. Charlie feels Keith's hand on his shoulder, holding him back. "Give them a minute," he says.

The guards outside the cell, watching those with the riot gear, turn at the sudden rush of inmates. A melee breaks out as the inmates rush the guards and attempt to escape.

"Now," Keith says. "Let's go."

The guards are all occupied. Charlie and Keith slip by, stepping over and past entangled, battling bodies. They get to the door, the same one Kayla, Nivens, and the two guards left, and they slip out.

"Where now?" Charlie says.

Keith takes a step forward and sucks his teeth. He looks around. He turns to an open door on their left. Charlie follows his gaze. There's a glow coming from inside. A wall of monitors shows footage from every room and corridor in the station.

"There," Keith says, pointing.

12

Kayla tries to resist. She tries to pull her arms free from the grips of the guards and digs her heels into the ground, but she barely slows them. They haul her bodily along the corridor, through the station, following Agent Nivens.

They take a quiet route, similar to when they took her down to the cell. Kayla's throat is dry. Her heart pounds. She thinks about the Nazis in the cell, trying to kill her. The cell that these three men put her in. And she wonders, are they trying to kill her? They won't speak. Won't explain themselves. They drag her along without a word.

Suddenly, the corridor isn't so quiet anymore. A cop appears, running, presumably back toward the brawl in the holding cells. He hesitates when he sees Kayla frowning. He stops.

"Sir," he says, addressing Agent Nivens. "Can I be of assistance?"

Nivens waves him off. "That won't be necessary. They need you more in the cells."

Kayla seizes an opportunity. "Please!" she says. "I think they're trying to kill me!"

The cop blinks. One of the guards slaps his hand over Kayla's mouth, silencing her.

"Who's this?" the cop says. He motions to Kayla.

"We're moving her to somewhere more secure," Nivens says.

"What was she talking about? Who's trying to kill her?"

Kayla struggles against the hand. It slips. She bites into it. The guard yelps and pulls his hand away. "*Him!*" she says, frantically nodding at Nivens.

Nivens pulls out his gun and shoots the cop in the face. Blood sprays out the back of his head, and he crumples to the ground.

Kayla screams.

"Shut her up!" Nivens screams, wheeling on the two guards. He looks down at the dead cop, his blood spreading across the floor. "*Fuck.* When I'm gone, clean this up and wipe the security tapes."

The guards say that they will, but Nivens is already moving, and they're rushing to keep up. They don't go far. Through the door at the end of the corridor and down the steps into the parking garage. Agent Nivens' head is on a swivel as they pass by the parked vehicles, heading toward an SUV parked in the far corner that Kayla assumes is his. The garage is empty of people. Even if there were anyone around, Kayla couldn't call them, couldn't scream for her. His mouth is still covered, and the guard is clamping her tight. Her jaw aches.

Nivens reaches the SUV and pulls open the rear door. "Cuff her," he says, "then get her inside." He pulls out his keys and steps toward the driver's door.

One of the guards reaches for her arms, attempts to hold them behind her back. Before he can get them in place, someone appears behind him, wrapping an arm around his throat and pulling him back. The other guard is grabbed, too. She sees who takes him. It's Keith. He spins him around, one hand on the back of his neck, and slams his forehead into the side of the car.

Nivens is reaching for his gun. The other man, choking out the guard, is Charlie. He shoves the guard at Nivens, and they both fall. Nivens has dropped his car keys. Charlie grabs them. "Get inside," he says to Kayla and Keith. They do. Kayla notices that Keith looks like he's struggling to breathe. He has one hand on his chest.

On the ground, Nivens pulls his gun. Charlie kicks him in the face. A shot goes off, but it's high and wide. The bullet hits the ceiling. Nivens goes down, his nose bloodied. Charlie reaches for him, but one of the guards lunges and wraps his arms around Charlie's waist. Charlie brings up his knee and buries it under his jaw.

Nivens has gotten up, and he's running. He dropped his gun when Charlie kicked him. Charlie gets into the SUV now, behind the steering wheel. Kayla and Keith are both in the back. Keith has let go of his chest now.

"All right," Charlie says, starting up the engine. "Let's get out of here. Hold on."

Charlie reverses, and as they pull away, they hear a gunshot. One of the guards is firing upon them. Charlie slams his foot on the accelerator, and they pull out of the underground garage and onto the main road.

13

J ames is at the site of the explosion.

He didn't sleep well. There was a pain in his arm, but it wasn't that. His mind was racing. How could he be expected to sleep? His country had been torn apart—his whole world.

And all the while, he saw the outline of the person coming from the multi-story just moments before the explosion. No face. Just a shape that becomes bigger and bigger in his mind, an amorphous shadow threatening to overwhelm him.

Come the morning, he woke Shira and told her he needed to go to where the bomb went off.

Shira is by his side. She drove him here. James made sure to bring his badge, though he knew the men securing the area. They let him through. They don't question Shira accompanying him. Most of them know her, too. They tell James they're pleased to see he's all right. They joke about his broken arm and say that he's always gone to extremes just to try and get some time off from the job.

James and Shira walk out into the center of the area, looking around. "What is it you're looking for?" Shira says.

James doesn't answer, not straight away. Things are calm here now. Not like the last time he was here, just yesterday. For a moment, he hears the roaring in his ears again. He hears the screaming.

"I don't know," he says, his voice trailing off as he turns and looks around.

There are still firefighters in the area, picking through the rubble. James looks the area over. He takes his first real look at the damage the explosion caused. The multi-story where it originated is almost completely gone, just the back half of it remaining. The parts of it that weren't evaporated in the blast are piled at the bottom. Blackened scorch marks cover what is standing.

Debris remains scattered across the road and the ground. No one has attempted to clean it up yet. Crime scene investigations are still ongoing. Forensic teams scour every inch of the land, leaving numbered markings and snapping photographs.

The bodies are gone, but their blood remains. Splashes of it on the roads and the sidewalks. James finds himself staring at a dried patch close to where he stands. The early morning sun is beating down on the back of his neck. The blood has come from a head wound. He can tell because the person bleeding had fallen, and it's in the shape of their skull. He wonders if they survived.

Shira touches his arm. She's wrapped up in a thick coat, and her braid hangs down the middle of her back. The color is drained from her face. She looks uncomfortable here. She sees all the same signs of death as he does.

"Are you all right?" she says, looking concerned. "Being back here?"

"I'm fine," James says, turning away from the darkened blood.

His eyes fall on the remains of the convoy. Cadillac One is still there, on its roof. All of the vehicles from the convoy are still here. James swallows. There's blood around these, too. Especially the ones closest to the front. Especially Cadillac One.

"The timing would've had to be precise," James says, looking toward the multi-story.

"How do you mean?" Shira says.

"Barely any damage to the car," James says, pointing. "It was all about the force of the blast."

"If they'd still been inside the vehicle," Shira says, understanding, "they'd still be alive. It was the rolling of it that killed them."

"Exactly," James says.

Shira stares at the car, looking at how it has landed, at the blood stains coming from under it. Her face is twisted, imagining how these men were killed. "What are we doing here?" she says, turning away, not able to look at it any longer.

James strokes his cast, feeling a twinge under his cast. "To help out."

"With what?" Shira says. "It looks like the fire department and forensics have this covered."

"With trying to find out how this happened. Who did it." James scans the nearby buildings. "I saw someone," he says. "The shape I told you about."

"Whoever it was, they're long gone now."

"Uh-huh. Matt told me there was a blackout around here right before the explosion. All the security cameras went out, so they don't have any footage."

"I'm assuming it wasn't a coincidence."

"Would be a pretty big coincidence. Seems like they were hacked."

"The ARO are more versatile than people give them credit for, it would seem," Shira says.

James grunts. He starts walking, moving away from the sight of the explosion. He stares up at the buildings, checking their security cameras. The ones closest to the site, he assumes, were part of the blackout. They're all pointing in the direction he needs them to. He walks on further, past the outskirts of the explosion's damage.

Shira follows. She's looking up, too. "This area looks like it's been abandoned," she says. "These buildings are all empty." There are shops and cafes, their window displays vibrant, but the lights are off, the doors locked.

"I don't imagine they'd get much business," James says. "Not until things down the road have been cleaned up a little."

They leave the barricaded area opposite where they entered, nodding at the cop standing guard as they pass and keep going. Past the blast scorched buildings and the scattered debris. Past the bloodstains. They go down the block to where there is no damage. To where life is continuing, where there is no evidence of the explosion at all. Where people are out and where the roads are full. There's a numbness, though. It's clear in the faces of the people James and Shira can see. There's a heaviness that hangs in the air. A cloying oppression that lingers following yesterday's events. A lack of safety, of security. The knowledge that anything can happen at any time.

James wonders if this was the ARO's intention. If this oppression, this fear, was one of their goals. They haven't been clear on what they're trying to accomplish. Thus far, it's been nothing but chaos and confusion. Of course, until yesterday, James wasn't paying all that much attention to what they were doing. Their attacks were far away. They weren't anywhere near him. They didn't affect him or the people around him.

He feels a twinge in his broken arm, a seeming reminder that just because something is far away doesn't mean it can't creep up on you.

He turns and looks back toward the explosion site. Shira looks back, too. "What are you trying to see?" she asks.

"I'm getting an idea of what's in view," he says. He points. "I saw them *there*. We can still make it out from here, *just*. Maybe, further down the block here, the security cameras weren't affected. Maybe one of them was able to capture what I saw. Maybe they got a clearer look."

Shira nods and then looks around, checking the nearby buildings for cameras. "There," she says, nodding. "That one looks like it might have what you want."

The camera is on the front of a supermarket. It's pointing at the doorway, but its angle is high. Maybe high enough for what James needs. They go closer to the building, turn and look back. James sucks his teeth, unsure. "I don't know," he says. "It's barely got any view from here. I mean, *maybe*."

"Only one way to find out for sure," Shira says.

They head inside the supermarket. It's quiet. There aren't any customers inside, standing amidst the rows and studying the shelves. The only other person in the store is an older man behind the counter, sitting back and reading a newspaper. He looks up over the top of his glasses as they enter. He must pick up a vibe from them. Perhaps, since yesterday, he's grown accustomed to seeing people like them. Investigators, special agents, cops. He doesn't peg them for shoppers; that much is clear from the curious expression on his face. It's doubtful he eyes up every potential customer this way. His eyes narrow when he spots James's sling, though.

James and Shira go to him. James is already pulling out his badge. "Hello, sir," he says when they reach the counter. He shows his badge. The old guy grunts at it, like this is what he was expecting. It's no kind of surprise to him. "My name's James Trevor. Are you the proprietor here?"

The old man grunts and nods. "I am," he says. "Help you with something?"

"I sure hope so," James says, putting his badge away. "The security camera outside, on the side of the building—that functional?"

The corner of the old man's mouth twitches. "Any reason why it shouldn't be?"

"We'd like to access the footage if that's all right with you."

The old man grunts. "Figured someone would be around sooner, asking. Was starting to think maybe we were too far away for our footage to be any good." He nods his head toward James's broken arm. "You get caught up in it?"

James nods.

"I heard a story that most of the security cameras nearby were turned off before it happened. Wondered if that had happened to mine."

James leans closer. "Had it?"

The old man shakes his head. "No. Checked this morning— they were working. Got a pretty good shot of the blast, too. I'm sure the news would be willing to pay me a pretty penny for it—if I were so inclined." He looks at Shira. "Who are you? I didn't see your badge."

"Don't have one," Shira says.

"She's with me," James says. He holds out his broken arm. "She was good enough to offer to be my driver."

"Uh-huh." The old man looks like he's having doubts. "This footage," he says. "I'm not so sure… Aren't you supposed to have a warrant when you want something like that?"

"We can *get* a warrant," James says. "But if you show it to me with your permission, then we don't need it."

The old man still looks like he has concerns, eyeing Shira. No doubt he picked up on her accent.

"Like I said," James says, "I was at the explosion. You saw my badge. You can see my cast. I was working crowd control when it happened. A lot of people died. I saw them. I consider myself very lucky that I'm still alive today. There's a lot of people, and a lot of friends and family and others who cared for those people, that can't say that. Because someone killed them. And I think I might have seen them."

The old man cocks his head.

"Not fully," James says. "There was distance, and then the explosion happened right after. There's a reason that whoever did this killed the security cameras nearby. There was a chance that whoever planted the bomb would've been caught on the cameras. I believe I saw them. And I believe there's a chance your camera may have picked up on them. But I can't be sure—and if they don't turn up on your camera, then I need to keep going down the block and hope I find one where they do."

"You're not on duty, are you?" the old man says. "Not with that arm."

"No, sir. I've been put on leave."

"And you're still out looking into things." It's not posed as a question. "Trying to find who's responsible." He looks James up and down.

He glances at Shira again, but he doesn't look as suspicious as he did before. Something about his demeanor has changed. When he looks at James and Shira now, it's with respect.

Using the counter, he pushes himself to his feet. "All right," he says. "Help me out and go set the sign on the door to closed, then follow me into the back."

James goes to the door and turns the sign around, then he and Shira follow the old man into the back of the store. It doesn't look like anyone else works here, and James wonders if it's always been this way. Just this one man, day in and day out, open every day, never taking any vacation time, just struggling to keep his business alive.

The storeroom is small and cramped, filled with boxes of chips and candy and crates of soda and beer. They pass through it and go into a small office at the back. There's a flickering television screen on a desk in the corner, flicking through the various security cameras inside and outside the store. There's a computer next to it, sitting idle. The television moves through its cycle, and James catches a real-time glimpse of what he's hoping to see— past the corner of a building is the multi-story parking lot.

"You know how to use this?" the old man says.

"Yeah," James says, lowering himself into the chair. He brings the computer back to life and gives it a moment to warm up.

"Good," the old man says. "Always takes me an age to work the damn thing out. Y'know, I must've been robbed about a dozen times—hell, I've lost count by now—and every single time the cops come, and they check this footage, and you know what happened next? Nothing. There's never been a single arrest made off the back of it. You ever been one of those cops?"

"Can't say that I have," James says, watching the computer screen, running through the footage from yesterday, and checking the timestamps. "I'm not usually in this area. I walk a different beat. But when you get called to crowd control, you go where you're needed."

"Sounds like you weren't too happy with the police response," Shira says to the old man.

The old man shrugs. "They blamed it on the footage. Said it was too grainy. They couldn't completely identify the men they saw. How's it looking to you?"

It *does* look grainy, James thinks, but it's clear enough for him to see what he needs. If the person he's looking for turns up on the screen, he can pass the footage on to Matt and see if he can get it cleared up.

"It'll do for what we need," James says, distracted, scrubbing through the footage to get to what he needs. He can see the crowds gathering in fast-forward, filling the area with no idea of what is about to happen.

"Looks like you're almost there," Shira says, leaning in, watching over his shoulder.

He reaches the explosion. "Too far," he says.

He rewinds, slowing it down, watching closely, praying that this isn't a dead end. Praying that someone shows up.

He hits pause. "*There.*" He jabs a finger at the screen, at the grainy figure emerging from the corner. He sees now that they were able to survive the blast—that they were so close to the corner of the building blocking the multi-story from view that they threw themselves into cover behind it.

Shira leans in closer, squinting. "That's who you saw?"

"That's the outline. Exactly as I remember them."

"They don't look any clearer here."

"No, but it's something." James can see a face, but the features are blurred.

"Smaller than I expected," Shira says.

"They're in motion. It's hard to tell their dimensions." James turns to the old man. "Can we take this footage? I have a friend. He works for the government; he might be able to get this cleaned up."

"Sure," the old man says. "Anything that might help."

James pulls out his phone and starts calling Matt. He turns to Shira while it dials. "Even if they can't do anything with this, it shows them—it shows them come into view. Matt can get the manpower to scour the rest of this area, maybe find some footage a little clearer."

Matt answers. "James," he says. "I'm a little busy right now. Is this important?"

"It's important," James says. "I've got something for you. Some footage."

"Footage of what?"

"A person of interest," James says. "The person I saw coming from the multi-story, right before it went boom."

14

Georgia is in the library, but she hasn't done much work. Instead, she paces the floors, checking the windows. Looking outside, watching the road.

No one attempted to break into her house last night. This morning, when she checked the snow outside before she set off on her run, there were no fresh prints. Part of her had half-expected something to happen on her run to the stream, an ambush, perhaps, but nothing did. She had the area to herself, as usual. On her return, she checked the snow again. Still nothing.

She wasn't followed on her way into Harrow. Her eyes darted regularly to her mirrors. In town, she found herself studying the faces of everyone she saw. Checking them for familiarity or lack thereof. Checking to see if anyone was looking back at her, watching.

More people have used the library today, though the number of them is lower than usual. She puts out returns, back on the shelves they came from. It doesn't take her long. She takes her seat behind the counter. It's peaceful in the library. She takes a deep breath. The smell of old books fills her nostrils. She looks at the people in the building. An old lady sitting at one of the tables reading a romance, and a guy, not much older than a teenager, sitting at the table opposite reading a horror. In the corner, the kid's area, a mother reads quietly to her toddler.

People come and go as the day rolls on. A couple of hours before closing time, a man walks in. Georgia feels the hairs on the back of her neck begin to stand. The man is familiar. She recognizes him, though only vaguely. When she was watching Camilla walk away, he was the guy who drove past, his head turning to her as he went.

He's looking at her now. There's only one other person in the building besides the two of them. The teen from earlier, still reading his horror novel, nearing the end. The stranger smiles at Georgia. He makes his way toward her.

Georgia doesn't move, but her muscles are tense. She's like a spring, ready to uncoil if necessary. She keeps her face blank, giving no indication that she recognizes him. She keeps reminding herself, over and over, that when he was looking the other day, it could have been nothing. He might have even been checking her out.

But when she couples his stare and his current approach with the footsteps around her house, and the tire tracks near to it, she tells herself there are no coincidences. He has an officious air about him, too. He's balding on top, but the hair he does have there, and at the sides of his head, is slicked back. He's wearing jeans, and his checkered shirt is tucked into them, but he doesn't look suited to this outfit. It fits him like a too-small glove. Georgia imagines he would be more comfortable in a suit. He looks like a bank manager or a stockbroker.

Or a government official.

As he gets closer, and it's more and more apparent that he's walking directly toward her, Georgia forces herself to smile. The same smile she wears whenever someone is coming to her for advice or guidance or to check if a recent title has come in yet. It doesn't come to her as naturally for this man as it does for her regulars or even strangers who have gotten lost and are hoping for directions. This man isn't a stranger. She knows he isn't. He's been in Minnow for at least a couple of days.

He stops when he reaches the counter. "Hello," he says, resting his hands on top of its varnished wood.

Georgia can see he's let stubble grow through, but even this looks out of place. He's accustomed to being clean-shaven. It's obvious from the way he scratches at his neck and under his jaw, and she can see from the red fingernail marks already there that the short hair is getting longer than he's accustomed to, and it's itching.

Georgia forces herself to nod. "Hello," she says. "What can I help you with?"

"Well," he says, spreading his fingers and leaning closer. "I was wondering if you have a local history section."

Georgia frowns. "Of Alaska?"

"No, no—of right here, in Minnow. I'm new in town, y'see. I'm hoping to get to know the area a little better."

The man has not lowered his voice, despite being in a library. The horror-reading teen has heard every word he's said and snorts.

The man looks back at the sound, then returns his gaze to Georgia.

"There isn't much local history for *right* here," Georgia says. "Minnow started off as a logging settlement, and slowly over time, people began to settle here. That's about as much history as there is for here."

The teen chuckles at her response.

"I see," the stranger says, ignoring the teen. "So, nothing much has ever happened here at all, then?"

"No, not really," Georgia says.

"And probably never will," the teen contributes.

The stranger ignores him again. He grins. "Sounds like the perfect kind of place a person could just disappear into, huh?"

Georgia's spine stiffens. She forces her face to stay the same. "Is that what you're doing?"

"I'm just ready to retire somewhere quiet," the man says, though he can only be in his late forties. Too early to retire unless he really is something like a stockbroker and he's made millions. Georgia doesn't believe this, though. There's something about his air, his presence. The way he looks so out of place and uncomfortable in his clothes. He scratches his jaw again, grimacing a little as he does so.

"You don't sound like you're from Alaska," Georgia says, though she can't place his accent. It's blurred, generic. The kind of accent they use in Hollywood. The same kind of accent Georgia usually has, but not now. Right now, she's using an Alaskan twang to avoid him asking any questions. She's practiced it over the years. She knows it's good.

"Wouldn't retire here if I was," the man says. Georgia notices he avoids saying where he's actually from.

"We have a section on Alaska," she says, pointing. "The top three shelves over there. It might not sound like much, but it's always full."

The man nods and then steps back from the counter. "I'll go take a look," he says. "Maybe one of them will have something about Minnow, huh? Even if it's just a footnote."

"Maybe," Georgia says as he walks away.

The teen at his table catches her eye. He smirks. Georgia forces herself to roll her eyes like they're in on some private joke together, but she doesn't think this is a joking matter. She's uncomfortable. The presence of this man has set her on edge.

He's not in the Alaskan section long before he re-emerges with a general history book full of pictures. He smiles at her and holds it up as he passes, then takes a seat at the table opposite the teen. His body is pointing toward Georgia, to her counter. He opens the book at random and spreads it out on the table.

Georgia busies herself, but every so often, she can feel his eyes on her. When she looks up, he's engrossed in the book. Georgia doesn't think she's imagining things. She trusts her instincts. She moves away from the counter, out of his view. She disappears into the shelves, pretending to straighten them out. She keeps an eye on the stranger. He doesn't turn, doesn't try to find her.

She stays in the shelves until it gets close to closing time. She returns to the front. She notices how the stranger glances back, looking at the teen. She wonders, is his presence a problem? The teen doesn't see him looking.

It's five minutes until closing. Georgia decides that now is good enough. She announces she's about to lock up. The teen looks to be nearly finished with the novel. He starts racing to the end, flicking the pages fast.

The stranger looks at him. Georgia notices how his lips purse. He closes the book about Alaska. "Just leave it there," Georgia says to him, smiling. "I'll put it back."

"Oh, that's okay, I'll—"

"I don't mind," Georgia says, keeping her smile plastered on. "That's what I'm paid for."

The stranger hesitates, then straightens and nods. "Okay," he says.

He comes closer to the counter. "It's a fascinating book. I don't see anything about Minnow yet, though. Maybe tomorrow."

Georgia understands the implication. "Maybe," she says, giving no other reaction to what he's said. "If you bring proof of your new address—a utility bill, something like that—I can always give you a library card, and then you're free to take the title away with you."

"I'll do that," the stranger says, not missing a beat. "But I'll have to wait until I get my first bill. Shouldn't be too long now." He smiles broadly.

"I'm sure it won't be. These things never are."

The stranger nods and then starts heading out.

"Oh, sir," Georgia calls after him.

He stops as he reaches the door, looking briefly confused as he turns back.

"Since you're new to the area," she says, "one thing you should know, when it gets dark, it gets *cold*. I'm not talking about the kind of cold it might have gotten back where you moved from —this is *real* cold. So, just a word of advice—next time you head out for the day, and it could be dark when you're heading back, I'd really recommend you bring a coat."

The stranger considers this. "I appreciate that," he says. "But my car's right outside."

"I expected it was," Georgia says. "You should still bring a coat."

"I'll keep that in mind," the stranger says, then leaves the building.

The teen is still trying to race to the end. Georgia sees him. "Take your time," she says. "I'll stay open for you."

"Oh, thanks," he says, surprised. "I appreciate that." He sucks his teeth. "Were you just trying to get rid of the old guy? I didn't like him, either. Too loud. Real creepy vibes."

"Yeah," Georgia says, wandering over to the window. She sees his headlights come on as he starts his engine, and then the stranger drives away. "That's what it was."

15

They dumped the car they took hours ago blocks away, then continued on foot. Keith knows the streets better than Charlie or Kayla, so they follow his lead. He takes them down side streets and quiet roads, places that have less traffic and cameras. Keith notices how Kayla sticks close to him. He's a familiar face from back at the explosion. Probably the only familiar and friendly face she's seen since then. Charlie is near, and he's helping out, but it seems, as far as she's concerned, the jury is still out on the Brit.

They hide down an alleyway, peering out. It's mid-morning. The city has well and truly come to life now, though subdued, Keith thinks. More subdued than it ordinarily would be, had there not been a bomb set off yesterday, and the Vice-President of the United States had not been killed.

"Well," Charlie says, grinning at them. "If we weren't in trouble before, we probably are now."

"How long have you held back on saying that?" Keith says.

"Figured until the adrenaline wore off," Charlie says. "Give everyone a chance to calm down first. Tell you what, mind, when

I came to America, I didn't expect to become a fugitive within a few days."

"You don't live here?" Keith says. He'd assumed Charlie was an ex-pat. Charlie shakes his head. "Why're you here? Vacation?"

"I'll tell you later," Charlie says, looking out at the road. "When we're not busy running and hiding." His eyes zero in on something on the other side of the road. Keith follows his gaze. It's a parking lot. Charlie raises his head, looking around for security cameras.

"Just the one," he says, pointing. "And it doesn't cover the whole lot."

"Are you suggesting we *steal* a car?" Keith says.

"We can hardly go buy one," Charlie says. "First of all, I've got loose change, and I reckon it's the same for you and the young'un here. Second of all, we've probably got cards on us, aye? Well, if we use them, it's gonna alert them to where we are. So even if we wanted to, we *can't* go buy a car. So, *yes*, I was thinking that we're gonna have to take one. Or, look at it this way —borrow it for a while, then leave it somewhere it's easily found."

Keith watches him with narrowed eyes. "And you just happen to know how to hotwire a car?"

Charlie pulls a cheeky face and winks at Kayla. "I may have dabbled back in my misspent youth."

Keith shakes his head. "This is ridiculous. The cops are already gonna be after us for breaking out of jail. We don't need to add grand theft auto to our list of larcenies."

"Well, in fairness, it certainly did look like they were trying to kill the young'un here." Charlie tilts his head toward Kayla.

They both look at her. She stares at the road, her face pinched. She's heard them, heard everything they've said, but she can't look back at them. Her mind is racing. Her confusion at everything that has happened since yesterday is evident on her face.

"Speaking of," Charlie says, getting her attention. "You got any idea what that was all about?"

"Who knows why a couple of Nazis would try and make a grab for her," Keith says. "I can imagine they had some sick things on their mind, and we don't need to discuss them now."

"I'm not talking about them wankers," Charlie says. "The bigger question is why they would put a young lass in a cell with them in the first place. No, I'm talking about that agent. The one that was taking her away, with them two cops that were all too eager to start shooting at us. You got any ideas, pet? They say anything that gave you any kind of clue where they were planning on taking you?"

Kayla looks at him and blinks. "Pet?" she says.

Charlie chuckles. "It's colloquial. It's a term of endearment. Why, unless the person saying it sounds angry. There'll be a different kind of emphasis on it, then. You haven't answered the question."

Kayla shakes her head. "No, no…" She looks dazed. "They didn't… they didn't say anything…"

Keith places a hand on her shoulder and squeezes it. She looks like she needs comfort. His hand will have to do for now. He looks back at the parking lot. At the one security camera. "So, if we take a car, and it's a big *if*, then what?"

"Reckon we should probably work something out before we cross the road," Charlie says. "We need some kind of plan."

"I'm open to suggestions," Keith says.

"Well, personally, I'm gonna try and get back to England," Charlie says. "Keep my head low and find a way to get smuggled out of the country. No way I can show my face at an airport, not if they're looking—and I reckon we go off the assumption that they *are* looking."

"So your plan is to escape the country?" Keith says.

"That's exactly right."

"You aren't gonna try and clear things up?"

"Why would I? I don't need to come back here. Besides, I know I didn't plant the damn bomb—when they find who did, they aren't gonna care about the likes of us slipping through the cracks."

"And all the chaos back at the police station?"

"Who gives a shit about a couple of Nazis?"

"I'm talking more about the gunfight and the stolen vehicle."

"That's on them. *We* didn't pull any guns."

"I want to go home," Kayla says suddenly.

Keith and Charlie look at her. She's still avoiding their gaze.

"I want to know if my mom's all right," she says, her voice low. "I want to see my dad. I want them to know *I'm* all right. I just… I just want to go *home*."

Keith looks at Charlie. They lock eyes, and Keith can see that they're both thinking the same thing. Charlie sighs. "All right," he says. "So, first thing's first. We get the car, and then we take Kayla home. And then I can drop you—" he nods at Keith, "—wherever it is you want to be, and then I can get out of here."

"That's as good a plan as any right now," Keith says, though he's wondering where it is he *will* want to be after they've dropped Kayla back with her parents and explained the situation to them. He isn't sure. He supposes he has a little time to think about it. He should probably lay low and wait until things have blown over, like Charlie said. Wait until they catch the person who *is* responsible. By then, they'll be so caught up in their victory that they won't be thinking about the three that got away.

The negative part of his brain reminds him that they haven't caught any of the ARO yet. But, he reminds himself, the ARO hadn't killed the vice-president before. Everyone is going to be on this. No one's going to rest until the person responsible has been captured.

He thinks about Dom. They work together at the diner. Dom

is a good friend. Dom will cover for him and give him a place to stay as long as he needs. Dom is probably his best option.

"Howay then," Charlie says. "Let's get a move on. Here's what we'll do. Two of you wait here. I'll go grab a car. I'll circle back around and pick the both of you up. In the meantime, keep your heads down. All right?"

Keith nods. Charlie turns, pulls up his collar, and leaves the alleyway. He keeps his head lowered, as he has advised them to do, and his hands shoved deep into his pockets. Keith watches him go.

"He's actually going to steal a car?" Kayla says.

"Uh-huh. He sounded like he had his mind made up about it." Charlie crosses the road and hops the wall into the parking lot. It seems like he already has a vehicle in mind. He goes straight for a silver Ford. He doesn't look up, doesn't look around. Goes straight to the car as if it's his, and the keys are right in his pocket.

"He's crazy," Kayla says.

"Uh-huh," Keith says again. "I'm certainly starting to wonder about that."

"What if…" Kayla trails off. Keith looks at her. Her features are strained. She looks older than seventeen right now. "What if he doesn't come back for us?" she says, finally.

An alarm goes off. Keith's head snaps around. It's coming from the parking lot. The Ford that Charlie has broken into. Its signal lights are flashing, and its alarm is whirring. Its driver's door is wide open. There's no sign of Charlie. Then, the alarm silences, the lights stop flashing, and Charlie sits up behind the steering wheel. He pulls the car out of the parking space and heads toward the exit.

"Well, if he doesn't," Keith says, "we'll find another way to go find your parents. How you holding up, anyway?"

She chews thoughtfully at the inside of her lip. It's a while before she speaks again. "He made a point," she says. "Charlie.

When he asked why I was put in with those guys. I shouldn't have been, right? They shouldn't have put me in the cells."

"No, I don't think they should have," Keith says. Something felt off about the situation. He doesn't say this to her, though. He doesn't want her to overthink, doesn't want her to worry. "But I guess we'll never know," he says.

"That's him," Kayla says, nodding her head down the road.

Keith peers out to check. It's Charlie. He pulls to the side, waiting for them to join him.

"Hop on in, lads and lasses," he says, the window down.

Keith gets in the front, and Kayla in the back. Charlie pulls away before they have a chance to pull their doors all the way closed.

"I'm gonna need directions," Charlie says. "Because I don't have a clue where I'm going right now."

16

Georgia didn't sleep much again last night. At one point, at about two in the morning, her security light went off. She saw it through the gap in the curtains of her living room. She braced herself, expecting something to follow up this sudden light. Nothing did. She went to the window and peered out just as the light was turning itself off. There was no sign of anyone. She watched for a while. Stood perfectly still and held her breath. Watched for movement. There was none. She told herself it could have just been an animal, but she wasn't so sure. Things have felt off lately. Her paranoia has been in overdrive.

She reminds herself that finding footprints in the snow near her property, not to mention the tire tracks, doesn't mean she's paranoid. It means someone could be looking for her.

She did her usual morning routine—her workout and her run —but on her run, she was extra cautious, expecting someone to jump out at her at any moment. In her mind, this phantom always has the face of the stranger from the library. No one does, though, and she takes a shower and gets dressed, and drives into town. She's not alone today. Camilla is in, too, though she only stays until midday.

"Glad you came along when you did," Camilla told her, not for the first time. "I just can't do full days the way I used to. If you weren't here, we'd probably only get open about three days a week, and those days would be halves, at that."

"Happy to help out," Georgia said, keeping an eye on the windows, on the road, and the parking lot, expecting the stranger to turn up. He hasn't yet.

Camilla went home about an hour ago. Georgia is not alone, though. The library is busy. The dramatics of the last couple of days haven't entirely faded, but people feel more prepared to go about their daily lives. Georgia busies herself with her work. She stamps books. Puts away returns. Finds titles for people.

Keeps one eye on the door.

Every time she walks by the window, she looks outside. She hasn't seen any sign of the stranger yet, but she doesn't doubt that he's out there. He could be watching the building, waiting for her to leave.

When the library closes, Georgia doesn't hang around. She leaves the building and goes straight to her truck. She looks around on her way. She's casual about it. Shakes her hair. Brushes a lock behind her ear, covering her roving eyes with her hand as she does so. There are plenty of cars around, but they all look empty. This doesn't calm her. Her paranoia remains high. Inside the truck, she watches her mirrors. All the drive home, she watches them.

Halfway back, she catches a glimpse of something. A car following but staying back on the bends, trying to keep out of view. To someone lesser, someone untrained, someone unexpecting, they *would* be out of view. They *would* be unseen.

But Georgia sees them. She watches them as she goes. She doesn't alter her speed. Doesn't speed up or slow down. Then, close to him, they're not following her anymore. She keeps going, watching still, and then pulls over. Stops. Watches and waits.

They don't come back into view. There's nowhere else to go around here. Nothing else down this road. She realizes it has stopped in the same place where she found the halted tire tracks the last time.

Georgia drives on and returns home. She checks the area around her house. There are no signs that anyone has been on her property. She goes inside and makes food, eating by a window so she can look out across the snowy grounds into the trees. There's nothing to see. After eating, she dresses warmly and goes outside. She doesn't run. Just walks. Making out like she's out for an early evening stroll. She heads through the trees, circling around, and heading back to where she estimates the car that was following her has stopped.

She takes her time walking. Her footsteps crunching the snow are the only sound. No birds. No small animals. Just her. She looks around, but like outside the library, she's subtle about it. She looks, and she listens. So far as she can tell, there's no one else in the woods.

The road comes into view. The car is there, parked up, as she suspected. The engine is running, likely to give its occupants warmth. Georgia conceals herself behind a tree. She can see the two men sitting up in front, but they're not looking her way. There might be men in the back of the car, too, but it's hard to tell. The windows are tinted. She notices how the passenger turns back and speaks as if he's communicating with people back there.

She sees the driver. She recognizes him. He's the stranger from the library. The man who asked for books about the local area. The supposed newest arrival to the town. He's staring down the road, looking toward her house. When the passenger turns back, laughing at something someone in the back has said, he looks the same way.

There is nothing else down that road, only Georgia's home and, as far as those men must be aware, Georgia herself.

17

They've sat at the end of the road for hours. Keith won't allow them to go any closer, not yet. Not straight away. Charlie understands, but Kayla does not. She doesn't protest, but it's clear she's agitated about being so close to home and yet not allowed to go to it.

Charlie watches the houses opposite. Checks the windows. They're empty. He doesn't see anyone watching the house Kayla has pointed out to them. It's an affluent neighborhood with manicured lawns and expensive cars.

The driveway of Kayla's home is empty. Neither of her parents' cars is there. Keith told her they were probably out trying to find her.

"Are you friendly with your neighbors, Kayla?" Charlie asks, looking at her in the rear-view mirror.

She meets his eyes in the glass when he speaks, then turns away and looks out the window, resting her chin in her hand. "Not particularly," she says.

"How about your parents? They get on with them?"

Kayla shrugs. "I guess so… They don't really talk about the neighbors."

"That's fair enough," Charlie says. "I don't really get on with my neighbors back home. Well, I mean, I don't have anything against any of them. I just don't wanna be their best friend, either.

"You have any school friends who live nearby?" Keith says to Kayla.

"No," she says. "They all live elsewhere. I don't really know anyone on the street. Why are you both asking? Are you wondering if anyone might see me in the car?"

"That was part of it," Charlie says. "But mostly, I was just making conversation."

"Just conversation," Keith says.

"How long do we have to sit here?" Kayla asks. "My house is *right there*. Can't I just go to it?"

"You can," Keith says. "Once we're certain."

"Certain of *what*?"

"That there's no one waiting here looking to grab you. When we're sure that your house isn't being watched."

Kayla sighs, but she doesn't protest. She trusts Keith; that's clear. Charlie imagines she's probably not so sure about *him*, but that doesn't really matter. They won't know each other long enough for it to make a difference. Soon, she'll be back in the safety of her home, and Charlie will be finding his way back to England. Back to Newcastle. Most importantly, back to Niamh.

"Do you think anyone would?" Kayla says.

"We don't know if they *would*," Keith says. "But it's better to be safe."

"How would they even know where I live?"

"Because they're the government, pet," Charlie says. "And for whatever reason, they seemed to be interested in you."

He sees in the mirror the way her brow furrows at this. "Do you…do you see anyone? *Is* anyone watching my home?"

"Don't see anyone yet," Keith says. "But we're gonna be thorough."

Kayla nods, but she's still frowning. She starts to yawn, the events of the two days catching up to her. Her adrenaline probably wore off a long time ago. She blinks repeatedly.

Keith notices, too. "Take a nap if you need to," he says. "We ain't going anywhere. We'll wake you when we're sure it's safe."

Kayla nods then settles back down in the backseat, turning onto her side and curling up into a ball. It doesn't take long before her breathing deepens, becomes shallow, and she's asleep.

Charlie admires how well Keith handles her. He's patient. He's friendly. He's caring. The two of them only met yesterday, but already he has her best interests at heart. He's looking out for her. Determined to make sure she's all right and that she gets home safely. "You got kids, Keith?"

Keith shakes his head. "No. Been a while since I last had someone I'd be interested in having them with, too. How about you? I see you're married."

Charlie glances down at his wedding ring. "Aye," he says. "No kids, though."

"No interest, or…?"

"Well, Niamh's after a couple, but… I'm just not so sure, myself. Not sure I'm ready yet. But they say you're never really ready, don't they?" He shrugs.

He turns to Keith. "You military?"

Keith looks back at him. "That was a sudden topic shift. Why do you ask?"

"Just curious. The way you react, how you handle yourself, some of the things you say."

"I get the same vibe from you, man."

Charlie laughs. "Are you?"

"I *was*. Navy Seal."

"Impressive," Charlie says.

"Yeah, well, these days, I'm a chef in a diner. So what about you?"

"Just regular old British Army, mate." Charlie holds back on telling the whole truth, and he can see in Keith's face that he knows this is the case. Keith doesn't press, though. "And that was in a past life, too. These days I do security consulting. That's why I was over here."

"Someone over here was prepared to hire a regular old British Army soldier to be a security consultant, huh?"

Charlie grins. He isn't going to tell the truth, but he doesn't see any point in lying further. "Can't talk about it, mate."

Keith cocks his head. "SAS?"

Charlie doesn't say anything, but he raises his eyebrows. "Like I said—can't talk about it."

Keith chuckles, turning back to Kayla's house. "Well, aren't we a pair?"

"Aren't we just?" Charlie says. He looks at the empty drive-way. "Taking their time coming back, aren't they?"

"If it was my daughter who'd gone missing during an explosion, I'm not so sure I'd come back either, not until I knew what had happened to her." He bites his bottom lip and adds, "One way or the other."

"Aye, well. If they hurried up about it, they'd find a pleasant surprise waiting for them, wouldn't they?" Charlie looks at the neighboring houses again, the houses opposite, and the cars parked up and down the street.

"It looks clear to me," he says. "And it's looked clear this whole time. How much longer do you wanna give it?"

Keith glances back at Kayla, still sleeping. "Another half-hour so she can rest," he says. "Then let's go on up."

"We're going with her?"

"Figure we should, seeing as how her folks aren't home. You don't have to if you don't want. You can stay right here."

"I'll come with," Charlie says. "I get bored too easily when I'm left on my own."

Keith laughs at him and shakes his head.

They wait another half-hour, and then Keith gently wakes Kayla from her nap. "It's clear," he says. "You ready to go on up?"

Kayla looks at him, still half-asleep, blinking through bleary eyes. "Mom?" she says. "Dad? Are they back?"

"Not yet," Keith says, his voice gentle. "But they've been gone a while now. They're bound to come back soon. Come on—Charlie and I are gonna come up, too. We'll wait with you until they come back. We'll help explain everything that's happened."

Kayla looks grateful at this. She nods, then rubs at her eyes.

The three of them get out of the car. Despite how long they've been watching, Charlie remains vigilant. He imagines Keith does, too. He continues to watch the street as they make their way to the house, but even up close, there's still nothing to see.

They reach the house. Kayla starts patting her pockets. "Oh, no," she says. "I just realized, I don't have my key. I must've lost it somewhere since yesterday."

Charlie rings the doorbell. "Just on the off chance."

"Do your parents keep a spare lying around?" Keith asks. "Hidden somewhere—under the mat, a plant pot, a rock, something like that?"

Charlie looks down. There is no welcome mat. He looks back at the lawn, up the pathway they've just walked. There are no plants or rocks. It's very plain. He assumes Keith could be assuming there might be more going on around the back. Charlie looks at the other lawns. A lot of them are plain and well kept, but most of them have some kind of feature—a small tree in the middle, or a flowery or rock border, something like that.

Kayla frowns and shakes her head. "No—no, I, I don't think so. They've never mentioned it to me."

Charlie looks back at the door. No one answered the bell, but he didn't expect them to. On a whim, he tries the handle.

It's unlocked.

He looks back at Keith and Kayla. Keith raises his eyebrows. Kayla stares inside the house. She attempts to squeeze past Charlie, calling out, "Mom? Dad?" but Charlie holds her arm, restraining her.

"Don't go straight in," he says. "Just...just hang tight, all right? You wait here with Keith."

Keith places a hand on Kayla's arm. His face looks solemn. He has the same concerns Charlie does—that someone may have already been here. That they could be walking into something they won't want Kayla to see. Charlie goes inside, wishing he had a gun or any kind of weapon. He takes his time, alert, listening to the sounds of the house. It's very still. He doesn't feel like there's anyone else in it. He's all alone. He's had it before, sweeping a house. There's a vibe when someone else is present. Something about the way they breathe, perhaps, or even the way they hold their breath. The way they hunch, either desperate to conceal themselves or ready to launch an ambush.

The hallway is long and leads back into the kitchen. There's a staircase to his left and what he assumes to be the living room to his right. The door is closed.

There's a dresser near the foot of the stairs. There's a bowl of potpourri in the middle, and he catches a faint whiff of its flowery scent. On either side of this bowl, there are framed pictures. Charlie gets closer. The one on the left is whom he assumes to be Kayla's parents on their wedding day; he is in a suit, and she is in a white dress, holding a bouquet of flowers, both of them smiling. On the right, there's a picture of them with Kayla as a child. Kayla is small between them, holding both of their hands and laughing as she kicks through some dead leaves in a woodland setting. She looks to be about seven or eight. Her parents look similar ages to those in their wedding photo.

Charlie moves on to the living room. He's careful opening the door. He peers inside, checking that it's clear. It is. There are no bodies here. No blood. No signs of a struggle. It looks calm. It looks normal. Two sofas angled toward a television. A bookcase with no books against the far wall instead filled with what looks to be jazz records and a handful of DVDs. A framed picture of Kayla on the wall opposite, older now, looking about twelve. It looks like it might be a school portrait.

Charlie keeps going. He gives the kitchen and the backyard a quick glance. They're both clear. He notices, though, that the backyard is just as plain as the front—no flower beds, no plant pots, no water feature, nothing. Charlie doesn't think much about this. Some people don't like gardening. He's one of them.

Upstairs is much the same. There are three bedrooms. One of them has a desk and a computer, a home office. The main bedroom must belong to the parents. The bed is made drum tight. There are more pictures here. Mostly of Kayla at various ages. Charlie checks a wardrobe and the drawers. They're full of clothes. It doesn't look like anything has been packed in a hurry.

Kayla's bedroom is next door and much smaller. A single bed, with a small television at the foot of it. Her bed is unmade. There are some clothes strewn about the floor.

Charlie goes back downstairs to the front door. "It's clear," he says to Keith.

"Are they home?" Kayla says. "I was telling Keith they never leave the door unlocked."

Charlie shakes his head. "There's no one here."

Kayla steps past him into her house. She pauses in the hall, looking around, blinking. She shakes her head and rubs at her eyes.

"Are you all right?" Charlie says.

"I'm just tired," she says, waving a hand. She goes upstairs, presumably to her room, or else to verify for herself what Charlie has already told her.

Keith goes into the kitchen. He looks around. "You see any signs of trouble?" he says, keeping his voice low despite Kayla being upstairs.

"No, nothing," Charlie says. "Granted, it hasn't been the most thorough of looks, but nothing's leaped out at me."

He tells Keith, too, about how he checked in the main bedroom upstairs for any signs of flight, but saw nothing out of place.

Keith nods, then checks in the cupboards and the refrigerator. "The place is still stocked," he says. "Chances are, they probably *have* just gone looking for their daughter."

"We should try and find a way to get in touch with them," Charlie says, leaning back against a counter and folding his arms. He looks off into the corner of the room, and something catches his attention. Something he didn't spot earlier when he was just in the doorway. It's another door. He straightens and goes to it, trying the handle. It's locked, but the key is in it.

Keith steps closer to him. "I assume you haven't been down the basement?"

Charlie shakes his head, then turns the key. "Kayla still upstairs?"

"I haven't heard her come down."

Charlie opens the door, then peers down into the darkness. He expects a musty smell, but that isn't what greets him. Instead, it smells like wood and varnish.

Keith points out the switch to him, and Charlie flicks it. The staircase is illuminated. They both go down. Charlie is expecting to find tools, gardening equipment—a lawnmower at the least—maybe, judging from the wood smell, a work area with a bench.

That's not what they find.

"Holy shit," Keith says.

"You never seen anything like this before?" Charlie says. He's not used to being in houses with basements. He thinks they're more common in America.

"I've never seen one in a basement, that's for sure," Keith says, stepping closer to the construction in the center of the room that takes up most of the basement's floor space.

It reminds Charlie of a Wendy house, but bigger and with a flat roof. A small wooden hut with a couple of windows on the side and a door at the front. The windows show that the inside is bright pink in color. The door is pointing toward them. Keith goes to one of the nearest windows and peers in.

Charlie hears him mutter to himself, "What the hell?"

Charlie goes closer, glancing around the rest of the basement. There isn't anything else down here. There isn't space for anything else. He notices, though, electrical cables that run from the ceiling down the wall and along the floor, feeding into this little wooden house. Keith opens the door. Charlie doesn't bother looking into the window. He follows Keith inside.

It's small inside and just as pink as it looked through the windows. Opposite them, on the ground, there is a thin mattress from a single bed, and it's strewn with tatty teddy bears. There is a thick duvet, also pink, and a couple of pillows at its head—again, pink. The bedding looks much cleaner and better kept than the bears. On the ground, at the head of the bed and bolted into the concrete below, there is a shackle. It lies open. They can see another on the other side of the bed, lying atop the pink duvet. At the foot of the bed, there is a television screen. Next to the television is a small stereo. Charlie and Keith exchange looks.

"What the hell is this?" Charlie says.

Keith doesn't answer. He goes closer to the mattress and looks it over. He turns to the television. Charlie can see that the cables he spotted outside run to this and to the single lightbulb hanging overhead, which presumably came on when he flicked the switch at the top of the stairs. Without a word, Keith turns on the television. It plays static. He flicks through a couple of channels, but they're all the same. More static. He turns to the stereo. There's a CD inside. He hits play. He promptly turns it back off. If it was playing music, it was the musical equivalent of the static on the television, but louder. It was turned up to a deafening level. Wincing, he crouches down and picks up a teddy bear, and looks into its face. It's missing an eye.

There's nothing else in this strange little cabin. A rug on the floor next to the bed, again pink, likely to soften the hard floor. There's barely any space to move. Whoever was in here—and it looks very much like a children's space—could only sit on the bed and stare at a television that seemingly doesn't work or listen to some ear-splitting noise, with only some old teddy bears for company.

"I'm not gonna lie," Charlie says, "this is making me feel a little queasy."

Keith grunts and straightens. "Me too," he says. He motions that he wants to leave the cabin, and they both step outside, closing the door after them. Keith's brow is furrowed. After a moment's thought, he says, "What did that look like to you?"

"It looked like somewhere you'd keep a kidnap victim," Charlie says. "And it looks like it's decked out for a fucking *child*."

Keith nods along. "There's no sign of the parents. Potentially they found out Kayla was being held in jail, and they split, worrying the cops might turn up and search the house and find *this*? I'm just spit-balling ideas here."

"That would be an extreme reaction. Why would the cops come *here*? I suppose, maybe, they've heard we escaped. *That* would be cause for alarm. That might bring the cops looking."

Keith looks at the ground with a finger curled over his lips while he thinks.

"I don't think Kayla knows about this," he says. "If she were aware, I don't think she'd be all right with us coming inside. *You* came in alone—she had no idea whether you'd check the basement or not."

"There's a darker alternative," Charlie says.

"What's that?"

"That it's *for* her. A kind of weird punishment area."

Keith considers this. "Again, I have to question whether she'd be all right with us finding this."

"So, what do we do?"

"I say we get out of here. Find somewhere to lay low. You can keep going, get on to England, but I'll take Kayla with me. We'll keep her heads down until the explosion stuff blows over, and then…"

"Then what?"

Keith looks back at the strange little cabin. "I'll have to think about that. I'm not so sure this is the best place to bring her back to. Come on, let's get back upstairs before she comes down."

They go back up to the kitchen, turning off the light and locking the door after themselves. They hear Kayla coming down the stairs. "Keith?" she says. "You there?"

"We're in the kitchen," Keith calls back.

Kayla comes down and joins them. Her hair is wet and tied back from her face. She's had a shower and changed her clothes. "I tried calling for you earlier," she says.

Keith doesn't answer straight away, and Charlie glances at him. He can see him thinking, deciding what to say. Charlie decides to address things. "We were in the basement," he says.

Kayla frowns. "Basement?"

"We were thinking we should get out of here," Keith says, shooting Charlie a look that tells him not to push things too far. "All of us."

"But, my parents—" Kayla says.

"Aren't here," Keith says. "And we're not sure waiting around is the best thing. We'll find somewhere to lay low, and we'll find a way to get in touch with them when we can. Okay?"

Kayla continues to frown, thinking on this. "Do you think that's the best idea?"

Keith nods. "I do. We don't know how long they're going to be gone. We don't even know where they are. Maybe…maybe you should pack a bag, huh? Grab some clothes, and we'll find somewhere we can lay low. But don't worry—we'll find a way to get in touch with your parents. I promise. But until we do, I'm not sure this is the best place for us to leave you."

Kayla deliberates a moment longer, but then she nods and turns, leaving the kitchen and heading back upstairs.

When she's gone, Charlie points at the basement door. "You saw her, aye? She sounded like she didn't even know they *had* a basement. How's that possible, man? It's right there."

Keith shakes his head, not having an answer. "Whatever weird shit her parents might be doing, whatever illegal things they're getting up to, it doesn't seem like Kayla has any knowledge of it. Let's not push her on it, all right? Let's just get out of here and find somewhere me and her can hide out."

Charlie looks at the closed basement door again. He shakes his head, but he'll do as Keith asks.

18

James and Shira are making dinner. They came home after they got the footage to him earlier in the day. Hours have passed since then. It's early evening now. They're making spaghetti. Matt calls. James answers quickly. Shira stands near him to listen in.

"Matt," James says, answering. "Is the footage any good?"

"Well, it's nice to hear your voice, too, James," Matt says. "And to answer your question, I don't know yet. The techies seemed happy enough with it when I handed it over, and they first looked at it, but I don't know for sure yet. They've been working on it since, so we might know something soon. I was calling to check how you're doing."

"Oh, sorry," James says. "I appreciate you calling. I'm doing well. The arm's fine. I'm just hoping this footage is a break-through, y'know?"

"Well, it's the best breakthrough we've had yet—other than the ARO actually coming out and claiming responsibility."

"Imagine if you could actually catch one? Hell, that would change everything. Finally find out who and *where* these bastards are. Put this bombing bullshit to bed."

"Yeah, that would be something. You done any more sleuthing today?"

"No, we came home after the footage. We got what I went looking for. How are you doing, anyway?"

"Well, as you can imagine, work is nonstop. I think I've had about three hours sleep since yesterday. I'm on a break right now, out in my car. Figured I'd check in."

"How *are* things in the White House?"

Matt lets out a long, heavy sigh. "I can't talk about it too much. But, y'know, there are a few things I can say to a trusted friend that isn't going to get me into trouble. And you *are* a trusted friend, aren't you, James?"

"You know I am," James says. "I avoid reporters every chance I get. Wouldn't dream of relaying to them anything you might be about to tell me."

"Good," Matt says. "The president isn't taking it too well. He and Jake weren't just running partners; they were friends. They went way back. Not to mention the fact that the hospital, which was a passion project of both he and the first lady, has been so badly damaged. Zeke Turner has stepped up. He's helping Frank through."

James knows the name. Zeke Turner, the Speaker of the House. Third in the line to the presidency, should anything have happened to either the president or the vice-president. Now second in line. "I'm glad he's got someone helping him out."

"Zeke's been a big support to him. That's plain to anyone. Things are busy, as I'm sure you can imagine, but whenever Frank gets a quiet moment in the Oval Office, he's usually in there with Zeke."

"Oh, yeah? How's the first lady doing?"

"Louise is upset, to be sure. As I said, the damage to the hospital has them both distraught, but the fact that so many people have been killed and hurt just because they came along to see it get opened… I think she feels some kind of responsibility."

"She shouldn't."

"Yeah, but you know how these things can affect people." Matt sighs again. He sounds tired.

"How long you got left on your break?" James says.

Matt laughs. "Not long enough. Oh, hey, I'm getting another call. Let me take this."

"Sure," James says as Matt hangs up.

He knows that if it's important, Matt isn't going to call back. It's probably a call to hurry back to work. Something has come up. James slides his phone back into his pocket and looks at Shira.

"Well," he says. "Nothing noteworthy."

"*Mm*," Shira says. "Zeke Turner, he's the speaker?"

James nods.

Shira nods back.

James raises an eyebrow. "Why?"

"No reason," she says, though something in her tone throws James. "Just remembering who he is."

James is about to push further when he feels his phone ringing again. He pulls it back out of his pocket and checks the screen, surprised to see that it's Matt again. "You miss me already?"

"I got news for you, buddy," Matt says. "That was a tech. The footage *is* good. They've managed to get it cleaned up. I thought you'd wanna know."

James feels his heart rate quicken. "Can you see the bomber? Is it a decent shot of them?"

"I haven't seen it personally," Matt says. "But yeah, from what I've heard, the bomber is real clear."

James looks at Shira and raises his eyebrows.

"Keep an eye on the news," Matt says. "I was told there's gonna be a big update real soon. You did good work, man. And all while you're supposed to be on sick leave." He laughs.

"I just wanted to help out," James says.

"And you did. Now I better get back inside and take a look at this footage. I'll talk to you soon."

James puts his phone away and looks at Shira. She speaks before he does. "We better go get the TV on," she says.

Dinner is forgotten as they hurry through to the living room and wait to see the face of the person who has caused so much chaos.

19

Kayla doesn't really understand why they insisted they should leave her house, but she trusts them enough to believe they have her best intentions at heart. They're *their* best intentions, too. They're all in the same boat, after all.

They've returned to the city. They got rid of the stolen car. Charlie left it in a different parking lot, a few blocks away from where they are now. They've come to a diner for food. They sit in a booth at the back, away from the windows. They keep their heads low. Kayla didn't feel particularly hungry, but Keith insisted that she eat, so she ordered a chicken salad. Charlie and Keith both ordered burgers.

She can't help thinking about her parents. Where they might be right now. How worried they must be.

Most of all, she thinks about her mother. Worries about her. She was there when the bomb went off, too, and Kayla hasn't heard anything about or from her since. Could that be why her father wasn't home? Maybe he was in the hospital with her, or... or in the morgue.

She tries not to think about this last option. She hopes it isn't true. Instead, she chooses to believe that her mother got home and that she and her father have ventured out in search of her. It keeps her hopeful. When she's not hopeful, she feels close to a breakdown. Her chest and throat get tight. She feels like she can barely breathe. Her eyes fill with tears. She can't fathom the thought of never seeing them again.

So she doesn't think about that. She clings to the belief that she'll see them again and that she'll see them again *soon*.

To distract herself, she looks around. The diner isn't busy. They are the biggest group in it. Everyone else is by themselves. One other booth is occupied by a woman on her own, and two men sit apart from each other at the counter. There's only one waitress working. In between having to do anything, she stands behind the counter and stares up at the television. It plays the news. All it can talk about is yesterday's explosion on a continuous loop. She looks to the windows. Outside, it's raining. The drops pound against the glass, and an occasional wind rattles it in its frame.

"Didn't expect you to still be with us," Keith says to Charlie. "Thought you'd be trying to get back home now."

Charlie glances at Kayla, a look she doesn't understand, though she thinks it might be concern, then says, "Figured I could hang around long enough to eat. Been a while since I last did. Since right before the explosion, in fact."

"Well, England isn't going anywhere," Keith says. "It can wait while you eat."

"Aye," Charlie says. "Didn't you say you worked in a diner?"

"Not this one," Keith says.

Kayla takes a sip of her soda. Ice clinks against her teeth. "What's it like, where you live?" she says to Charlie, putting her glass back.

Charlie chews on a fry. "What, Newcastle?"

Kayla nods.

"Best part of England," Charlie says, winking. "You should visit it sometime."

"What's to see?"

"It's got some canny bridges. There's the architecture, the castle. The people are nice there, too, not like in some of the other cities."

"Do they all talk like you?"

"Aye."

Kayla looks at Keith and smirks.

"I saw that," Charlie says. "There's nowt wrong with the way I talk."

"I still struggle to understand you most of the time, man," Keith says, chuckling.

"We can't all speak like we go to boarding school," Charlie says. "I'd rather sound the way I do than like some poncy prat from down south."

Kayla isn't sure why this is funny, but she finds herself laughing at it. There's something about the way Charlie says it.

Keith joins in with her, perhaps finding her laughter contagious. Charlie doesn't look impressed. He watches them with a raised eyebrow, not enjoying being their figure of fun. He waves a hand at them and then picks up his burger.

The television behind and above the counter gets bright. Something flashes up on the screen. It catches Kayla's attention. It seems to have gotten the attention of most people in the diner. There's breaking news. The president will be hosting a press conference soon. Kayla wonders what this means. She guesses that perhaps something has happened— maybe they've caught whoever planted the bomb? Kayla hopes so.

One of the men at the counter calls to the waitress. "When'd they say that's happening?"

"Ten minutes," the waitress says. "Something must be up, huh?"

The man nods, leaning forward on the counter with his hands clasped in front of his mouth. His eyes are glued to the screen. He's settled in. He's waiting for the press conference. All eyes have drifted toward the television. Everyone is interested in what the press conference is about.

Charlie has turned to see what everyone is looking at too, and Keith is watching. Charlie turns back around. "Could be something big," Keith says.

Charlie shrugs one shoulder. "Could be," he says, then takes another bite of his burger. "Unless it's something that can help us out, I'm not that interested. Let's be honest, it's probably just gonna be some rousing speech about refusing to give up, right? Some morale booster, without actually saying anything at all."

"Guess we'll find out soon enough," Keith says, picking up his own burger.

Kayla eats another piece of chicken, then puts her fork down. She hasn't finished her salad, but she doesn't feel hungry. She sips from her soda instead and watches the television. She can't hear it from where she is, but she can see a circle of talking heads, presumably discussing what the press conference could be about. They all have somber faces and nod thoughtfully at each other.

The minutes pass by. No one leaves the diner. Charlie finishes eating and sits back with his glass of water. Keith is still eating as the press conference begins.

"Turn it up, darlin'," the guy at the counter says.

The waitress does so. She turns it up so the volume reaches the whole diner.

Frank Stewart, the president, is already in position behind his podium as the studio cuts to the conference. He's looking straight into the camera. Kayla can see his steely eyes. His face is usually chiseled and handsome, but now he looks tired and haggard. He's broad, though, and no matter how tired he may be, he still looks strong and authoritative. Charlie turns in his seat so he can see the television. Keith continues to eat while he watches. Kayla feels like the president's eyes are boring right into hers. She imagines it probably feels the same for everyone present.

The diner wasn't loud, to begin with, but a hush falls over it as the president starts speaking. "Yesterday, our nation was rocked by a heinous attack, perhaps the worst in our history. Our vice-president, and my good friend, Jake O'Connelly, lost his life in this attack." He looks pained as he says this.

His voice never wavers, though. It is deep and carries far. Kayla imagines a man couldn't get to his position without first being a good public speaker. "I promised you all that this attack would not go unpunished. A domestic terrorist group calling themselves the Anti-Right Outreach has claimed responsibility. We don't know who they are or where they're located. We don't even know what they want. They have refused to make their aims clear, and thus we can only assume their goal is to sow chaos and anarchy in our land."

He takes a moment and looks down at his podium, and shuffles his papers. "But we won't break. We're a proud people, and it will take more than bombs to break us." He waits a beat, staring defiantly into the camera. "Recently, we obtained footage taken from near yesterday's explosion. It shows a person we believe was responsible for yesterday's attack. I ask all of you watching to look closely at this footage to study the face of the person we're about to show you. If you know who they are, know where they are, please, contact us. Any information will be greatly appreciated.

"And, if you're the person in this footage, if you're watching, I give you this opportunity to give yourself up. Wherever you are, whoever you are, we *will* find you. I guarantee you of that.

"Again, to everyone else, if you have any information that

may help us, no matter how small you may think it is, please, get in touch."

The screen fades to black. There are some mutterings in the diner, mostly from the men and the waitress at the counter. Charlie doesn't turn around. Keith continues eating his burger. He's almost finished it now.

The footage begins to play. It's brief. It shows a person coming into view from around the side of a building. It pauses before the explosion occurs. The screen zooms in. The blurred face begins to clear. They're looking right at the camera, almost as if they've realized, at the last moment, that it is there and pointed directly at them.

Kayla feels her heart leap into her throat. She clenches her jaw. She feels herself begin to shake.

Slowly, Charlie begins to turn. Keith has put down the remnants of his burger. They're both looking at her.

The face on the screen, while slightly distorted, is undoubtedly hers.

Kayla tries to swallow. She tries to shake her head. She hears voices rise from the other occupants of the diner, discussing what they have just seen. Behind the counter, the waitress is frowning, recognition creasing her features. She begins to turn.

Kayla lowers her head. "It's a mistake," she tries to say, but her words catch in her dry throat. "That's not me. It can't be me."

Images flash through her mind. She sees herself, the last place she remembers before she found herself outside after the explosion. She was in a changing room. Looking at herself in a mirror. She was trying on a new sweater. But then there was a flash—she wasn't in a changing room. She was in a place she didn't know. It looked like a parking garage. But then, no, she was in the changing room, looking at the sweater. She'd never left. Did she buy the sweater? Did her mother purchase it as a gift for her?

What happened next? Where did they go? How did Kayla get outside?

She feels sick. The blood in her temples is pounding. She can't hear anything. She presses her hands to the side of her head and squeezes. Her eyes are tightly shut. She feels herself shaking.

She can't remember how she got to the city. Her mother must have driven them. She must have. Right? Where did they park? What did they talk about on the way in?

Where is her mother now?

What happened to her after—during—before—the explosion?

"Kayla?" It's Keith's voice, managing to break through the noise in her head. She forces her eyes to open. They're burning. She feels like she's going to be sick.

Kayla shakes her head. "I didn't do it," she says. "It wasn't me."

"Kayla, we need to—"

Keith reaches a hand out to her. Kayla twists away from it and slides out of the booth. She pulls up her hood and flees from the diner. She's sure she sees heads turn as she goes, but no one calls after her. No one tries to grab her. The waitress watches her go, wondering if she's sure the girl she earlier served is the same girl who was just shown on the television.

Kayla runs out into the rain. It hits her in the face. It soaks through her clothes. She runs, and she keeps running, feeling sick. Feeling confused. Seeing images flash through her head—real or imagined, she's not sure. The footage from the television is frozen in her mind. Kayla's own face stares back at her, her eyes empty.

It wasn't her. It couldn't have been her. And yet why, now, can she see herself in the multi-story, crouching, connecting wires? Planting something. Something that looks like a bomb. These images, they look—they *feel*—so real. But they can't be. It's just her mind running wild after seeing the girl who looks so much like her. The real bomber.

Kayla stumbles and falls. She lands in a puddle. There's a homeless man nearby, taking shelter in a doorway. He says something to her, but she doesn't hear what it is. Dripping water, she pushes herself up. She looks back at the diner.

No one is following her.

20

Keith makes to follow Kayla, but Charlie reaches out and stops him. "What are you doing? Just let her go, man." He leans forward and keeps his voice low. He's wired after seeing the footage, Kayla's face. "You saw what she fucking did, man! And we broke her out of jail. Jesus *Christ…*" He lets go of Keith's arm and sits back.

"We don't know that for sure," Keith says.

"I think we *do*," Charlie says. "You saw the video. That was her, right there on the screen, on the scene, clear as day. She set the fucking bomb, Keith. *She* did. I mean—" Charlie throws up his hands. He isn't sure what else he can say. He shakes his head.

"She's just a kid," Keith says.

"I don't know about you, mate, but I've seen kids do some messed up things."

Keith has, too. He looks at the window, at the rain battering against it, running down. He sees how the waitress, and the guys in the counter, keep looking their way, likely wondering why the young girl who was sitting with them has run out into the storm, and neither of them has followed.

He looks back at Charlie. "Remember what we found in her

basement. What if…what if they were holding *her* down there. What if they messed up her mind, and it made her lash out—what if she didn't even know what she was doing?"

Charlie raises an eyebrow. "That's a stretch, and you know it. Look, for whatever reason, you think you've gotta look out for her—why? Because you found her after the explosion? Well, it's really looking like she was the fucking *cause* of that explosion." He whispers this last, and it makes his words sound harsher. "You don't owe her anything, mate. Neither of us does. In fact, it sounds like she owes *us* a hell of a lot—maybe starting with an explanation. We've put our lives at risk for her, man."

Keith stares out at the rain. "I'm going after her," he says, beginning to stand. "You ain't gotta if you don't want to, but this is what I want to do." He grits his teeth. "What I need to do." He leaves. Charlie doesn't try to follow. He remains behind, in the booth, deliberating. He isn't watching Keith go.

The rain lashes hard against Keith's face. He narrows his eyes against it, searching out Kayla. He makes her out in the distance, running down the block. He follows. Keith has to jog. He pulls up the side of his jacket to protect his face, though it doesn't provide much shelter.

Kayla disappears around a corner up ahead. Keith hurries so as not to lose her. When he gets around the corner, she's gone from view. The rain isn't whipping him in the face here. The buildings block the worst of it. Keith looks around. He can't see her. He jogs down the block, wiping rain from his eyes. He manages to find her near the end, taking shelter in a doorway. She sits with her knees drawn up, her arms folded atop them, and her face buried into them. Her hood covers her hair. He knows it's her, though. She recognizes what she's wearing.

Keith doesn't get too close. He doesn't want to spook her, to set her off running again. "It's raining pretty hard," he says. "Mind if I join you?"

Kayla looks up. He thinks she's crying, though it's hard to tell through the rain. She doesn't say anything.

He thinks about when he first met her. She'd stumbled through the haze, and she'd come from the same direction as in the footage he just saw. She came from the direction of the multi-story parking lot where the bomb was planted.

"I'm gonna take a seat," Keith says.

The ground isn't dry, but at least he's out of the rain. He leaves some space between himself and Kayla. He doesn't want her to run again, but at the same time, he wonders how concerned he should be about her. He watches the rain coming down hard, splashing on the sidewalk. A taxi rolls by, taking its time along the slick road.

"I didn't do it," she says.

"Okay," Keith says.

"I'd—I'd remember if I did something like that, right?"

Keith looks at her, raising an eyebrow. Thinks how that was a strange way for her to phrase herself.

She sees the look he gives her. "I can—I can picture things—it—it looks like I'm in a building, maybe a parking lot, I'm not sure. But that can't be real. I'm just—it's just my imagination, after the footage. Could that footage be doctored? It could be fake, right? And now it's just got me all confused. It's got me imagining things that never happened, places where I never was…"

"Where *were* you when the explosion happened?" Keith says.

Kayla frowns. She wipes rain from her face. "I—I don't remember. The last thing I remember, I was in a changing room. I was trying on a sweater, and my mom was waiting for me outside, and then—and then—and then—"

She's stuttering. It sounds almost like a machine glitching.

She shakes her head. "And then I was outside. In the smoke and the noise, and then I found you. I don't know… I don't know how I got out there. I don't know what happened between leaving the changing room and being outside. My mom never said we were going to the hospital's opening. She never—she never mentioned it. I don't… I don't *think* she did. I don't think she said anything about it at all. I'm not…I'm not sure I knew it was happening—I'm not—I'm not—I'm not—"

It's like she's glitching again. "It's all right," Keith says. "Take your time."

She straightens her spine and takes a deep, shuddering breath. She exhales it out. "Maybe…maybe the explosion gave me amnesia? That's all I can think… And - and maybe that's why I'm seeing all these things—all these images of things I didn't do— maybe I hurt my brain somehow. We were never in the parking lot. We didn't park there."

"Where *did* you park?"

Kayla's face goes blank. She blinks over and over. "I don't—I can't remember."

Keith thinks about the little cabin her parents kept in their basement. He thinks about the shackles. He tries to see her wrists and if there are any pale scars that may have been left by them, but she has her sleeves pulled up over her knuckles.

She turns to him suddenly. "You believe me, right? I didn't do it. You believe that, don't you?"

Keith grits his teeth. "The best thing I think you can do right now," he says, "is hand yourself in. Work with the police, and try and get things cleared up. If you didn't do anything, this is the best way to prove it."

Kayla's brow furrows. She looks terrified. "I can't go back there. They tried to kill me."

Keith looks at her, remembering every conversation he's had with Charlie about what the NSA agent might have been attempting to do by putting her in a jail cell with a couple of Nazis—not to mention everyone else who was in there. A young girl like her, no matter what they thought she might have done, shouldn't have been anywhere near those cells. And that was before they'd released the footage.

"I just want to go *home*," she says, covering her face with her hands.

Keith wants to reach out. He wants to comfort her. To place a hand upon her arm or wrap it around her shoulders. He can't bring himself to do it. He doesn't know how much he believes in what she says. She could have been lying to him this whole time. Manipulating him from the moment they first met.

Then he remembers when he tried to make his one phone call, and the line was hijacked. *Keep the girl safe*. Who told him this? *Why*? Was it all part of the manipulation?

He watches her trembling shoulders. The way her body convulses with her tears. It all looks so real. She's upset. She can't even bring herself to show her face.

Keith opens his mouth, but he doesn't have anything to say. Finally, he reaches for her. She's just a young girl, all alone, out in the cold and the wet. Whomever she may really be, and whatever she might have done, at this moment, he can give her some comfort.

Before he can reach her, he hears a car rolling along, coming from their left, getting closer to them. He sees its headlights illuminate the sidewalk in front of them. It stops near them. Keith peers out from the shelter of the doorway. He sees the car—a black Chevrolet. The passenger window is down. An arm juts out the window, clutching a Glock.

"Jesus!" Keith cries as he throws himself back, grabbing Kayla and pulling her closer to the wall as a bullet tears through the space where his head had been just a moment ago. He hears further gunshots. They impact the side of the building where they're sheltering and rip chunks out of the archway. Kayla cries out, clutching at Keith.

The gunshots stop, but he hears the car coming closer, looking to get a better shot. Keith scoops Kayla up and throws her over her shoulder. He jumps out of the doorway and twists left from the direction where they came, and he starts running. He hears an alarmed shout from inside the Chevrolet, and then it frantically tries to turn in the middle of the road, its engine roaring and its tires screeching.

Keith gets them down to the corner and then puts Kayla down. He keeps hold of her hand. "Run!"

He can hear them speeding to catch them up. Glancing back, he sees it gaining on them. He and Kayla run, splashing through the rain, trying their best not to slip and fall. A couple of times, Keith has to prevent Kayla from doing just that. He hauls her up and keeps her on her feet.

He hears a gunshot. It whistles through the air, but he doesn't see where it lands. It doesn't hit him or Kayla. They reach the corner of a building and round it, keep going. Keith spots an alleyway. The car can't pursue them down it. He drags Kayla with him. There's a dumpster at the end, a chain link fence behind it. He lifts Kayla, puts her on top of the dumpster, then pulls himself up as she climbs over the fence. He waves for her to keep running as he follows her over.

The Chevrolet screeches to a halt at the end of the alley. There's a gunshot. Keith throws himself over the fence and takes cover behind a dumpster. There are a couple more gunshots. One rattles the fence. Another thuds into the dumpster. He hears footsteps pounding down the alley, heading to the dumpster.

There's a trashcan in front of Keith and a couple of waste bags that didn't fit inside piled up beside it. Behind him, he hears their pursuers clambering up the dumpster. He grabs the trashcan, raising, spinning. The man at the front has the Glock. He's raising it toward Keith. Keith swings the trashcan up, slams it into his face, and knocks him back into the man behind him, sending both of them tumbling off the dumpster. Keith instantly turns and starts running again, following Kayla.

Before he left, though, he got a good look at the three men coming after them. He recognized them all. The NSA agent and the two cops from back at the police station. The men who put Kayla in the cell with the Nazis. The men who attempted to transport her from the station before Keith and Charlie caught up to them.

He sees Kayla up ahead and races to catch up to her while wondering how the three men he's left behind managed to find her. He takes Kayla by the wrist. To their right, there's an apartment block. Someone is leaving; their raincoat is pulled up over their head to protect them against the rain. Keith grabs the door before it can swing shut. He pushes Kayla inside ahead of him. He drags the door shut and looks out. The two cops and the NSA agent are coming over the road after them.

"*Shit,*" Keith says.

He's unarmed. All he can hope to do is outrun them. Find somewhere to hide and wait them out. Already, he feels his chest tightening. His breath is beginning to catch in his throat. He tries not to think about it.

Kayla sees them coming, and she recognizes them too. "What now?"

Keith looks around. Spots the door that leads through to the building's stairwell.

"Up," he says, pointing at the door.

The men outside fire at them through the door. The glass in it shatters. Keith ducks down, and he and Kayla burst through the door into the stairwell.

"*Up!*" he repeats.

21

Charlie, against his better judgment, went after Keith. He deliberated on it in the diner for a while first. He balled his fists and clenched his jaw, staring out the window at the rain. He felt himself growling as he pushed himself to his feet, then ventured out into the storm.

He'd left it a little late to follow, and he was struggling to catch up to where Keith and Kayla had gone. The gunshots drew him.

Ordinarily, his instinct is *not* to run toward gunfire—not these days, when missions and action are supposed to be a thing of the past. This time, however, he knows they are where he needs to be. So he runs, but he's not careless about it. He reaches the corner of a building and peers out in time to see Keith and Kayla disappearing around a corner up ahead and a black Chevrolet spinning in the middle of the road, going after them.

Charlie follows, keeping a safe distance. Unarmed, there isn't much he can do to help. He follows, seeing Keith and Kayla disappearing down an alleyway and the Chevrolet halting at the entrance to it, the men inside getting out to follow. Charlie recognizes them instantly. The NSA agent and the two cops from back at the police station. His mind races, wondering what they're doing here, how they were able to track them down. They've been careful and done their best not to leave any kind of trail.

Through the wind and the rain, Tom hears a commotion in the alley. A clattering, someone crying out like they've been hurt. It didn't sound like either Keith or Kayla.

He hears someone bark, "Get up! Get after them. Let's go!"

Charlie goes to the alley, but he doesn't follow, not straight away. He pushes his rain-slick hair back out of his face.

There's a gunshot. The sound of breaking glass. Both noises are distant, though. He peers around the corner. They're gone from view, all of them. Charlie follows, climbing up the dumpster and using it to get to the other side of the chain link fence. At the end of the alley, looking out from the cover of the building, he sees the NSA agent and the two cops going into an apartment building. Inside, they bolt to the right. Charlie goes after them. The door has fallen shut, but he's able to get it open, reaching through broken glass.

To his right, there's a door slowly falling shut. He catches it before it can close all the way and peers inside. It's a stairwell. He hears footsteps pounding, heading up. Charlie continues to follow but keeps his business. He looks up, watching them go, seeing if they might split off on one of the floors. He notices how one of the cops is lagging behind. He's not in as good shape as the other two. Charlie speeds up, keeping his footfalls as quiet as he's able. It doesn't take him long to catch up to the lagging cop. His shoulder is pressed up against the wall for support, propping him up. He's breathing hard, panting. He's carrying a Glock, hanging down by his side in his limp right hand.

Charlie holds back, waiting for his best moment to strike. A couple of levels up, the NSA agent calls back. "They're heading for the roof! Hurry your ass up!"

Charlie strikes. It doesn't take much for him to deal with the slow cop. He gains on him and slams the side of his head into the wall. He goes down without protest, with barely a sound. He's not unconscious, but he doesn't have any fight in him. The slog up the stairs has taken it out of him. He almost seems grateful for the excuse to rest.

Grabbing the Glock, Charlie speeds up, heading for the top, for the roof. He would have liked to hold back, to question the fallen cop, find out how they were able to get here so fast and what their intentions were back at the jail. There's no time, though, not right now. Two armed men are gaining on Keith and Kayla, and they don't have any weapons. Questions will have to wait.

At the door to the roof, Charlie pauses. He doesn't hear any gunshots outside, but he can hear voices. He opens the door a crack and looks out. He can't see Keith or Kayla, but the cop and the agent are nearby. They both have their handguns raised. The agent is speaking, calling out.

"Come on out and give yourselves up," he says, breathless. He breathes deeply before he continues. "Don't make this any harder than it's already been. There's nowhere you can go where we won't run you down."

The cop taps the agent and points to the edge of the building. Charlie has to twist to see what he's indicating. A fire escape. Keith and Kayla have likely attempted to make their way down it. The cop and the agent start making their way over.

Charlie breaks from the cover and runs down the cop. He knocks the gun from his arm, then clamps an arm across his throat and presses the Glock into his temple. The agent spins.

"Keith!" Charlie calls. "It's me! I got them covered."

The NSA agent's eyes blaze angrily, and he doesn't lower his weapon.

From the fire escape, Keith and Kayla raise their heads. Keith is in a bad way. He has a hand pressed to his chest. Kayla is holding his shoulders, looking concerned. It's hard to tell what might have happened to him. He doesn't look like he's been shot. He *looks* like he's having a heart attack. He's in good shape, though. Those stairs, no matter how many of them there were, shouldn't have been too difficult for him—especially not as an ex-Navy Seal.

"Don't look at them," Charlie says to the agent. "You don't have to worry about them. Look at *me*. Worry about your buddy here."

The agent's lips are pursed. His mouth is a thin slash across the bottom half of his face. Rain gets into his eyes, and he blinks it out.

"Drop the gun," Charlie says.

The agent doesn't. He raises it. Charlie curses as the agent fires at him. He feels the bullets, three of them, hit the cop—his human shield. Charlie falls as the impact is driven back into him. He hears Kayla cry out. On the ground, he quickly pushes the shot cop off and scrambles out from under him. The agent is gone. He sees the door to the stairwell falling closed. He's escaping. Charlie scurries to his feet and makes to follow. He pulls open the door. He's about to go after when Kayla calls to him.

"Charlie!" He looks back. The rain is streaking down her face. Her hair clings to her head and her cheeks. Keith is beside her. He's on his back, both hands clutching at his chest now. "I need you!"

As she screams this last, Charlie hears distant gunshots on the way down the stairwell. Three, a couple of levels down. The other cop? It sounds like it came from where Charlie left him fallen. Why would the NSA agent shoot him, too? Why would he shoot both of the cops? The one on the ground, his blood mixing with the rainwater on the roof, is clearly dead. He lies stone-still. Steam rises from his corpse.

None of these things matter right now. Again, the questions

can wait. What can't wait is Keith. Charlie runs to him. "What happened?" he says, dropping to his knees, casting his eyes over Keith's body to try and find anything that could have harmed him.

"I don't—I don't know!" Kayla says. Charlie realizes she's crying. It's hard to tell through the rain. "He just—he was breathing hard, and then, in the fire escape, he couldn't go any further. What's wrong with him?"

Charlie can hear Keith's gasping breaths. He reaches out. Charlie takes his hand. Keith grips it tight. He manages to swallow. He's trying to say something. Charlie puts an ear close to his mouth. Keith keeps stammering the same letter, over and over— "*P-p-p-p*," and then finally, he's able to get it out: "*Panic attack.*"

"Panic attack?" Charlie says, coming up. He looks at Kayla. "He's having a panic attack."

He turns back to Keith. He places a hand on the side of his head. He needs to soothe him. Needs to calm him to a point he's able to take a deep breath. To fill his lungs. The panic is making it difficult for him to breathe. Not being able to breathe will make him panic further.

"It's all right, big lad," Charlie says. "Come on, stay with me, now. Nice and calm. Think about the rain. It's nice and cold, isn't it? Feel that on your face, on your skin. I bet it's soaking through your clothes, isn't it? It'll be all the way through your jacket and your shirt, lying down like this." Charlie laughs. "When I was little and I'd been playing out and got caught in the rain like this, I'd come home and my granny used to say I looked like a drowned rat. She also used to say—you see how the rain is bouncing off the ground like this? You see it? When it was raining so hard like this, and the rain would bounce off the ground, she'd say '*the fairies are dancing*.' You see that? Look how it bounces —looks like dancing fairies, doesn't it?"

Keith blinks. His nostrils flare. Charlie sees his chest expand, his lungs fill.

"That's the way, big lad. Keep it up. Nice and easy—nice and long and slow, deep breaths, come on now. Come on, that's feeling better, isn't it?"

Keith starts to cough. He tries to sit up. Charlie and Kayla help him. Keith wipes rain from his face with an already-soaked jacket sleeve. It doesn't make much difference. He looks up at Charlie. "I have... I have PTSD."

Charlie pats his back. "That's all right, mate," he says. "I won't hold it against you. Keep us out in this rain any longer, though, and that's gonna be a different story."

Charlie and Kayla take an arm each and help Keith into the stairwell. Charlie goes in first, Glock raised, making sure the maniacal NSA agent isn't waiting for them. He isn't. Charlie looks down and can see the cop he left fallen, lying dead, bullets through his chest and head.

"Howay," Charlie says. "We need to get out of here. We can't hang around. All this gunfire and people live here. More cops are gonna be coming." He goes to take Keith's arm again, but Keith waves him off gratefully, signaling that he's all right.

"Where do we go?" Kayla says. "We don't have a car—we don't have anyone that will help us—"

"We find somewhere to lie low," Charlie says. They're heading down the stairs, past the body of the dead cop, being careful not to step in his pooling blood. "And then we need to try and figure out what the fuck is going on here."

"But *where*?" Kayla says.

"We'll figure it out!" Charlie says, growing impatient. "Right now, we need to get out of this fucking building."

"I know somewhere," Keith says, gasping. Kayla still has his left arm over her shoulders, and his right arm is stretched out, his hand pressed to the stairwell's wall for support. "It's nearby. We don't have to go far. We don't even need a car to get there."

22

Georgia returned home after she found the car. She didn't sleep much again last night, but no one approached her house. She stayed alert. She checked out the window, being careful to make sure no one could see her. The security lights were never set off. She didn't hear any footprints in the snow. This morning, when she left, she checked the area and found no fresh prints.

On the way in, in her truck, she watches her mirror. It has always been a part of her life, but lately, its importance has grown. She turns her head when she passes the spot where she saw the car parked. It's no longer there. She can see the tracks where it was pulled over, though. She wonders where it is now. In town, perhaps. Waiting for her. Always waiting for her.

Passing through town, going to the supermarket before she carries on to the library, it's quiet. When she gets out of her truck, she feels a change in the air again. It's like a couple of days ago when the bomb went off in Washington, DC. There's a similar vibe. Inside the supermarket, she soon finds out why.

The store is empty. Georgia begins to wish she'd had the radio on in the truck. There may have been news, important news, following up on recent events. She was distracted. The stranger, and his car full of buddies, occupy her every thought now.

There is one cashier working. A young woman who looks like she's not long out of high school. Georgia notices she's pregnant. She's at her till, but she's not doing anything. She's staring down at her phone, engrossed, her other hand resting atop her bump. The phone's glow shines up into her face. Her eyes are narrowed. Every so often, she shakes her head. Georgia grabs a sandwich, then goes to the cashier.

"What are you watching?" she asks.

The cashier is startled, having not realized anyone else was in the store with her. "Oh," she says. "Hello." She reaches for the sandwich to scan it through.

"What are you watching?" Georgia says, nodding at the phone. "Has something happened?"

The cashier looks shocked. "You don't know?"

Georgia shakes her head.

"It's been on the news all night!" the cashier says.

"I went to bed early."

The cashier turns her phone. She's playing the news. There are talking heads gathered around a table, animatedly discussing something. "They got footage of the bomber!" the cashier informs her enthusiastically.

Georgia feels a cold chill run down her spine. "That so?" she says. "Are they going to show him?"

"*Her*," the cashier says.

Georgia hoped this wasn't the case.

"And they're bound to show her in a minute," the cashier says, turning the phone back around so she can see. "They've been flashing it up *constantly*."

"How do they know she did it?" Georgia says, paying for her sandwich.

"She came away from where the bomb was planted," the

128

cashier says. "There's footage. She walks away from where she plants the bomb, then dives into cover right before it goes off. Oh, here she is!" She turns the phone back around so Georgia can see.

Georgia studies the face. A young girl, maybe sixteen or seventeen. Brown hair frame her face. Empty eyes, looking up at the camera that has caught her image. *Empty* eyes. Void of all feeling, all emotion. Georgia recognizes those eyes. She's seen them before, so many times. She sees them in her dreams. She sees them in her mirror.

"They don't know who she is, though," the cashier says. "They can't find any record of her, even though it's a pretty clear image, right? But yeah, they've said it's like she doesn't even exist. They can't track her down. Freaky, huh?"

"Yeah," Georgia says quietly, absently. "Freaky."

"I mean, a picture like that, you'd think they at least know her *name*, right?"

"Her name is Kayla Morrow," Georgia says, muttering it, looking off into the past.

"What was that?" the cashier says.

Georgia shakes her head and looks back at her. "Nothing," she says. "I was just…just wondering what her name could be."

The cashier doesn't appear to have heard what she actually said. She nods along. "Yeah, a mystery, huh? It's crazy, right? But they're asking everyone to be on the lookout for her. I figure we should be careful up here, right? I know we're far away from Washington and everything, but Alaska's an easy place to disappear, isn't it? My dad used to say everyone came here when they were trying to get away from something. He said, all over the state, there were fugitives and runaways that no one would ever be able to find."

"He sounds like a smart man," Georgia says, feeling a hole in the pit of her stomach.

She holds up her purchased sandwich, nods her thanks, then

leaves the store. She goes to her truck and takes it to the library, but she's distracted, her mind pulling in a million different directions.

Camilla is supposed to be there already, but as Georgia gets close, she sees the building remains in darkness, and the door is closed. When she goes to it, she finds it's locked, still. Georgia pulls out her key, figuring Camilla is either ill or, more likely, she's engrossed in the news following this latest development. She remembers her reaction just a couple of days ago, after the explosion. She'll likely be the same again today, and the library, the whole town, will perhaps be just as it was that day. It'll be quiet.

Georgia pauses before she turns on the lights. She sniffs. There's a familiar scent in the air. She braces herself as she turns on the lights, but there's nothing to see. The smell persists. Georgia breathes deeper. *Blood.*

She looks around the room. It's clear. Georgia remains careful as she crosses the ground, looking down the bookshelves as she goes. She heads for the back room. The staff room. The smell of blood gets stronger as she gets closer to it. She still can't see its source. There isn't any on the floor, seeping under the door. Nor any splashed upon the walls or the ceiling.

She stops at the staff room door. Wraps the handle in her hand and braces herself. She pushes it open.

Here the blood is on the floor. *Here* it is on the wall and the ceiling.

It's coming from Camilla. She's been bound to a plastic chair in the center of the room, wrapped in tape to hold her in place, and her throat has been cut. It's been cut deep, all the way down to her spine. Georgia can see bits of bone poking through the mess of gore. The color has gone out of Camilla. The front of her clothes, and the ground below her, are soaked with her blood.

Georgia grits her teeth. Camilla was a colleague. She

wouldn't call her a friend, but they were close. Camilla gave her the job here at the library. She'd always been good to her. Georgia goes to her, avoids stepping in her blood, and presses the back of her hand to her cheek. She's icy cold. Georgia has no way of knowing when this happened—if it was last night or early this morning.

She hears the door to the library open and close. Georgia leaves the staff room, closing the door behind her. She sees who has entered. The stranger, who has been following her around town, who came in and spoke to her directly about books on local history. There are three other men with him. Georgia recognizes one of them as the passenger from the car last night. The other two she has never seen before. One of them locks the library's door.

The stranger steps forward. He's smiling. "What are you calling yourself these days?" he says. "Is it Georgia?"

Georgia doesn't answer. She looks the four men over. The passenger is smirking. He stands to the stranger's left. The other two are behind them both. One of them has dark hair, and the other is blonde. They have steely eyes and hard faces. All four men are big and bulky. They're muscle, here to keep her under control. The stranger is the oldest of them all. He's clearly in charge. The three others are young. The two at the back could pass for college boys.

The stranger's smile doesn't falter. He looks at her in an almost fatherly way. "It's time to come home, Georgia. You've been gone for long enough."

"This is my home," Georgia says.

"This is your hideout," the stranger says.

"You killed Camilla," Georgia says.

"Camilla?" the stranger says. "Oh, the woman in the back there, right behind you?"

The passenger chuckles. He pulls out a switchblade and holds it up for her to see. "Cleaned it, since," he says. "Old bitch was all cartilage. It was tough going. My arm still hurts a little."

These words are likely to rile her up, but Georgia maintains her composure. She keeps her eyes on the four men. She notices how the two in the back are slowly spreading out. They're going to attempt to encircle her. To subdue her. To restrain her. To bundle her in the back of their car outside and take them to wherever their headquarters might be these days.

"I've seen the news," Georgia says, eyes flicking around the room, searching for anything that might be of use.

There's a trolley nearby. There are a couple of books on top of it, waiting to be returned to their shelves. One of them is a thick Stephen King hardback. She keeps it in mind. "You're making moves. Big moves. The vice-president is dead. Has the time come?"

The stranger doesn't answer this, though his smile does not falter.

"So, what's your next move?" Georgia says.

The blond and the brunette are getting closer, the blonde to her right, near the trolley, and the brunette to her left, behind a table. Georgia starts making her own subtle forward movement. "Killing the vice-president is a pretty big deal. I can only think of one person you could kill that would make it a bigger deal. Is that why you've come to find me? I can't imagine any other reason you'd come here."

The stranger responds to this. "You were hard to track down," he says. "It's been *years* now, *Georgia*. But you should know, you should know better than anyone, that we always find who we're looking for. We'll always find one of our own."

"I'm not yours."

"You sure of that?"

Georgia swallows. She watches his mouth closely.

He can see what she's doing. "Not yet," he says, holding up a finger. "First, I'm going to give you an opportunity. This will go so much easier for you and so much *better* if you come along voluntarily. Hell, we'll even let you keep the name. *Georgia*." He glances to the passenger, still beside him. "What was the surname she chose?"

"Caruso," the passenger says, grinning.

"Georgia Caruso. It's an interesting choice," the stranger says. "You pluck it at random?"

Georgia doesn't tell him why she chose her name.

The stranger doesn't care. "Come with us, nice and quiet, and we'll see you keep your name and whatever meaning it might have for you. We can't do fairer than that, now, can we?"

He waits a beat for Georgia to give some kind of reaction or perhaps acknowledgment.

When she gives nothing, he continues. "You know what I can do if you won't. You know what I can *say*."

Georgia balls her fists.

The stranger takes his time. He steps forward, looking around. He's giving her time to think, to make a decision. All the while, the blond and the brunette are getting close.

"It's an interesting choice," he says, circling a finger in the air, indicating the building that surrounds them. "A library. This isn't where I thought we'd find you. I mean, don't get me wrong, the cabin all alone out in the wilds, on the outskirts of town, *that* is exactly how I expected it. You like reading or something? I can't imagine this pays too much. *Ah*, but let me guess—you don't do it for the money. That right?"

Georgia says nothing. She stares a hole through him while keeping the blond and the brunette in her peripheral view.

"Who's your favorite, Georgia? Come on, now. You can tell me that, at least."

"I'm not going to tell you who my favorite authors are," Georgia says. "What I'm going to tell you is this—you can get out now while you can, or you can stay here and get hurt. I will hurt you because you came here because you found me. Because you're going to try and force me to come back with you. I will hurt you because you killed Camilla. I will fucking *end* you. That is your one and only warning."

She stares at the stranger. For the first time, his smile falters. He takes a deep breath and sighs it out of his nostrils. He lets his shoulders sag. It's all a big show. "That *is* a shame, Georgia." He looks into her eyes, and his smile is full once again. It has become something more. There is no mirth in it. There is malice. He opens his mouth. "West," he says. "Clementine. Buds—"

Before he can say another word, Georgia screams, drowning him out. She darts right, to the trolley, and shoves it toward the blond, driving it into his knees and knocking him down. She scoops up the big Stephen King hardback, spinning toward the brunette. He's close, and he's big, his bulk blocking out the light. Georgia lashes out with a kick, burying her heel into his solar plexus with a side kick, driving the wind out of him and knocking him back. She follows him on the attack, still screaming, though she thinks the stranger has stopped speaking by now. His words didn't get through, didn't manage to penetrate her scream.

She slams a forearm into the brunette's exposed throat, then follows up with the point of her elbow, cracking the bridge of his nose. She turns. The blond is back up and coming for her. The passenger is, too, the switchblade drawn. Georgia twists out of the blond's lunge and slams the heavy hardback into the back of his skull. She keeps moving. She's not screaming now. She doesn't need to. The passenger slashes at her. Georgia uses the book to block and parry him. He stabs for her face, but Georgia raises the book in time. The tip of the blade protrudes out the back, inches from her face. She twists the book and wrenches the switchblade out of the passenger's hands.

As his body twists, going down in the direction of his knife,

Georgia jumps and slams her knee into his face, knocking him back over one of the tables. He's down. To her left, the brunette is on the ground, holding at his throat and gasping. The blond is trying to push himself up. Georgia kicks him in the side of the head, a swift, flat-footed punt just below his ear that rolls him over and keeps him down.

She looks in the direction of the stranger, but he's gone. It doesn't take long for her to find out where he is. His arms wrap around her from behind, pulling her close to him and squeezing the air from her lungs.

"Impressive," he says. He spits the words through gritted teeth. His grip is strong. Georgia struggles, but she can't break it. He starts talking again, right into her ear. "West," he says. "Clementine."

"No!" Georgia screams, attempting to drown him out. He's too close. His words get through no matter what kind of noise she tries to make.

"Buds. Harvest."

There are only three more words. Just three more words he needs to say.

"Red."

Georgia throws her head back. Her first shot connects with the side of his face, but it's enough to surprise him, to silence him. She does it again, and this time the back of her skull buries into the center of his face. Something cracks—hopefully it's his nose. His arms loosen. His grip isn't so tight. Georgia keeps throwing her head back into his face. She feels sharp pains digging into her skin, but she ignores them and perseveres until the stranger's arms have fallen from her completely. He's stumbled back, fallen to a knee. Georgia turns. She sees the damage she has done to his face. His nose is broken. His lips are swollen, and all cut up, and his teeth are cracked and chipped. It was likely these that caused the sharp pains in the back of her head. She'll have to check for shards later. To pull them out, make sure they don't get infected. Even now, she can feel blood trickling down the back of her neck.

The stranger looks up at her. His right cheekbone looks fractured, too. "Run," he says. He's still trying. Just one more word.

Georgia raises a leg and kicks him in the face with all her strength. "Shut the *fuck* up!" she shouts as he falls to the ground.

The stranger isn't moving. He lies very still with his eyes closed. His breathing is shallow. He's not going to be speaking any time soon. Not even just one final word.

She looks around the library. The other men are down. She hears a couple of pained moans.

She looks beyond these men. She looks to the shelves of books. To the walls and the roof, the building itself. Looks to the staff room where Camilla sits, dead. This place has been her home for so long now. It has been her escape. Her sanctuary. Now these men have come and destroyed it all, broken her peace.

She closes her eyes and takes a deep breath. In her mind, she sees the image of the young girl the cashier in the supermarket showed her. Kayla Morrow. The authorities might not know her name—yet—but Georgia does.

On the counter, where she put it down, she sees the sandwich she bought before she came here. There are a couple of drops of blood on its plastic packaging. She wipes them off, then takes it with her as she leaves the library, heading out to her truck. She needs to leave Minnow. To leave Alaska. It is hard to do, but she has always been prepared should this day come. She stands by her truck and looks out toward the town. She steels herself. It's time to leave. Time to return to the world. She's been drawn into a battle she thought she'd left long behind her. But it came to her door. It came for her. They brought it back to her.

She gets in the truck and drives away.

23

James barely slept again last night. Eventually, he got out of bed and came through to the living room, listening in to his scanner to hear if there was any further progress. Mostly, he wants to know if they have found out who the girl is yet. What her name is, where she lives, and how she was able to be radicalized to the point that the ARO persuaded her to plant a bomb that killed the Vice-President of the United States, not to mention so many Secret Service, local cops, and bystanders.

There were no updates, though, and James fell asleep with the scanner serving as white background noise. Shira wakes him, nudging his legs so she can sit beside him on the sofa. She's carrying two steaming mugs. She hands one to him, and James pushes himself upright, accepting it gratefully. It's coffee. Shira is drinking tea. She's already dressed—jeans and a black T-shirt tucked into them.

"Couldn't sleep?" she says.

James shakes his head, taking a sip and burning the roof of his mouth. He puts the mug down to one side and leaves it to cool.

"Let me ask you something," Shira says. "And this is curiosity, not criticism."

"Okay..." James says.

"All that has happened; why does it drive you so much? What are you hoping to accomplish?"

"I'm just trying to help out."

"I understand that, but there are plenty of people out there helping out. You have a broken arm. You've been placed on leave. You've been told to rest. Why aren't you resting?"

"People died—I can't just sit around and do *nothing*." His voice is rising.

"You're getting defensive," Shira says. "I told you, I'm just curious."

"Because—because—" James isn't sure how to answer. Because his arm was broken? Because he saw so many people get hurt and killed? "Because there was an attack, and I was *there*, and I saw the person who did it! I *saw* them, and it was my job to be looking out for people like that—and if only I'd seen them just a little sooner, maybe...maybe so many people wouldn't have been killed..." He trails off, shaking his head. He picks the coffee back up and takes another drink, not caring that it burns.

"It matters to you," Shira says.

"Yes, of course, it does. There was an attack—not just on my country, but on my *home*—and I was *there*. I was right there in the middle of it, and I could have died that day! I could be dead right now. I almost feel like... I almost feel like I didn't die *specifically* so I could bring these sons of bitches down. Does that make sense? Getting that footage, it felt like we accomplished something. It felt like we helped, *really* helped."

Shira nods once. "I just needed to know," she says. "Because if it matters to you, it matters to me. Do you plan on pursuing this further during your forced time off?"

James nods.

"Okay. I thought that would be your answer. With that in mind, I did not sleep much last night either. I was thinking—

thinking of ways I could help. Ways I could help you, specifically with your search."

James tilts his head. "How do you mean?"

"I may have left Mossad," she says. "I may have left Israel. But I still have friends there. Friends who are interested in what has happened here. Friends who would be willing to help us."

"Help in what way?"

Shira stands, the tea held in both hands. She begins to pace the floor in front of him. "I'm not sure you'll like it."

"Just tell me."

"I have a friend," she says, "and he's very good at what he does."

"Well? What does he do?"

"He speaks to computers," Shira says. "He speaks *through* them. He understands their language, and there isn't a single one of them—no matter where it might be in the world—that he can't communicate with."

"He's a hacker?" James says.

Shira nods.

"And you're saying…" James puts his mug down and stands. "You're saying…*what*, exactly? That he could hack into the…into the US government?" He starts pacing now, shaking his head. "Jesus Christ, Shira, is that what you're saying? Holy shit, should we even be talking about this?"

Shira stands still and watches him.

James stops pacing, too, and looks back at her.

"He can find where she came from," Shira says. "It doesn't have to have anything to do with the government—not if it doesn't need to."

James narrows his eyes.

"Security footage," Shira says. "He finds where the girl first turns up and traces her back. Finds out where she came from. We find out where she came from. We find out who she is."

James waits a beat, considering. His right hand rubs at his cast. His bones itch within the plaster, knitting themselves back together.

"This…this friend of yours," he says, his thoughts jumbled. He struggles to order them. "Is he with Mossad?"

Shira nods.

"And why…why would Mossad be interested in our extracurricular activities? If the US government wants their help, I'm sure Mossad is already willing to offer it. They probably already are."

"He's not going to help the US government," Shira says. "He's going to help *us*. Because I'll ask him to. He's my friend. That's what friends do."

"Have you…have you spoken to him already?"

"I've reached out via email. Don't worry. I know how to send it covertly. It won't be intercepted."

"Sometimes," James says, "I feel like I should ask you more about your past—about your time with Mossad—and other times…" He shakes his head. "Other times, I really believe I don't want to know."

"If you ask me anything," Shira says, "I won't lie to you. But you know there are some things I *can't* tell you."

James breathes heavily. He squeezes his cast and feels a twinge in his arm. "What did you tell him?"

"Just enough," Shira says. "Not everything. He doesn't need to know everything, not yet. First, I needed to speak to you."

James sits back down, running his right hand across his mouth. He chews the edge of his thumb. This is a lot to consider. His brain is fogged. This isn't how he expected his first conversation of the day to go.

Shira remains standing. She watches him. She finishes her tea. "I'll give you some time to think about it," she says. She starts to leave to go to the kitchen. She pauses at the sound of a faint buzzing. She looks at James. It's his phone.

James pulls it out. It's Matt. He tells her.

"Don't tell him anything we've discussed," Shira says.

"No," James says, "definitely not." He answers.

"Hey," Matt says. "How's your arm?"

Shira leaves the room. James isn't sure where she goes.

"Still broken," James says. "How are you? You manage to get a good night's sleep last night?"

Matt laughs. "You kidding me? After the footage was released? Seems every department in the country has been inundated with calls about our mystery girl."

"Yeah?" James perks up at this. "You know who she is yet?"

"You heard me say *mystery* girl, right? I mean, maybe, *maybe*, somewhere in these thousands of calls, *someone* knows something, but we can't say for sure yet. Every promising lead we've followed up on so far has been a dead end." Matt sighs. "But we'll get there. She can't hide forever. Everyone is looking for her."

"Good," James says.

"Speaking of," Matt says, "I was calling to thank you. The footage you found, that's a breakthrough."

"I just wanted to help," James says. "I *needed* to."

"Uh-huh. You planning on helping further? You're supposed to be resting, buddy."

James hesitates. "I just... I'll do what I can."

"What you *can* isn't very much. Rest up, James. Get better. Get back on the beat. *That's* how best you help. Getting this country back together, back to normal, that's the best way you can help. The country needs to heal, and getting back to normalcy is the best way to go about that."

James opens his mouth, but he doesn't have anything to say to this. He bites his lip.

"You still there?" Matt says.

"Yeah, I'm here."

"All I'm saying, buddy, is feel free to sit the rest of this out. You've done more than enough. More than anyone asked you to. Hell, when you get back from your leave when you're all healed up, I'll put in a good word with your department, recommend you get promoted up to detective. You've more than earned it. But for now, you can leave this to us."

James's silence draws out.

"James?"

James clears his throat. "Yeah, yeah, I hear you. Yeah, you're probably—you're right. You're right."

"Rest up, man," Matt says. "It's the only way you're gonna heal. Now I've gotta get back."

"Sure… Sure thing, man. I… I bet it's crazy over there."

"You've got no idea, buddy. Take care of yourself, James. Talk soon."

James sits back and runs his hands through his hair, then down his face. Shira returns. She stands in the doorway, her arms folded, leaning into the frame.

"Matt says I should let it lie," James says. "Said I should be resting. They can deal with it. Except…except…"

"Except what?" Shira asks though he's sure she already knows.

"Except if it wasn't for us, they wouldn't have the footage of the girl, would they?" He purses his lips and shakes his head. He looks at Shira. Holds her gaze. He deliberates. Shira doesn't move. She waits. Waits for him to make his choice. Waits for him to decide what they're going to do next.

James rubs his eyes. He takes a deep breath. He braces himself.

"Are you going to take Matt's advice?" Shira says. "Are you going to sit back and let them deal with it?"

James looks at her. "Make the call."

24

Kayla is in the bedroom. She's not sleeping. They know she's not sleeping, but she wants to be left alone.

Keith and Charlie are in the living room, watching the television, watching the news. Their faces are plastered across it now, too.

"Fucking hell, man," Charlie says.

The news says that they're accomplices to the unknown girl. Unlike with Kayla, they *do* know their names. They know their backgrounds. They're sharing everything about them—where they're from, what they do for a living. They don't mention that Charlie was SAS, though, or that Keith was a Navy Seal. They say they're ex-British Army and ex-US Navy, respectively.

They're not watching it alone. Sitting with them is Dominic Freeman. When Keith introduced him to Charlie and Kayla, he shook their hands and told them to call him Dom. They're hiding out in his apartment. Keith said he was a friend. That he trusted him. Without many other options, Charlie has had to trust that this is the safest place for them to hide out. Dom is friendly enough. Charlie thinks that he and Keith must be very good friends for him to put himself out like this, harboring three fugitives, especially when he's no doubt seen Kayla's face already and knows exactly what she's been accused of. There must be a deep kind of loyalty between them if Dom can trust the girl because Keith does, no questions asked.

Dom lives alone in the apartment. There's no sign of a partner or children. It's kept neat and ordered, and Charlie wonders if Dom is an ex-Navy buddy of Keith's. Perhaps another Navy Seal. His home is rigid and structured, and clean, as if he has military experience.

"It hasn't once mentioned that the cops had her in jail," Keith says. "And it hasn't once mentioned that we were there, either. It hasn't mentioned our breakout."

Charlie runs a hand across his mouth. "You sure about that?"

Keith nods. "Man, we've been watching this for a while now —they keep saying the same things, over and over, but they've never once said *that*."

"I've never heard them say that, either," Dom says. "To be honest, they haven't strictly said that the two of you are *wanted* wanted. Just that they'd like to talk to y'all, and that you've been seen with the girl."

"I've seen how they want to question us, mate," Charlie says. "And they're coming on a bit strong."

Keith grunts. "Shooting first and asking questions later—if at all."

"I'm not saying y'all should actually go and talk to them," Dom says, holding up his hands. "I'm just saying that's what *they're* saying. They're not putting as much pressure on the search for the two of y'all as they are for the girl." He glances back over his shoulder toward the spare room where Kayla is lying. "Speaking of, she okay? She's been in there a while now."

"She's just going through a lot," Keith says. "She needs a little time. A few days ago, she was just a regular teenager, and now her world is suddenly chases and shootings."

Charlie thinks about the hut they found in the basement of her parents' house, and he wonders just how 'regular' her teenage life actually was.

"And you say this guy, the NSA agent or whatever, he just gunned down the two cops that were with him?" Dom says.

Keith nods.

Dom whistles through his teeth. "Shit, son. The hell you gone and got yourself caught up in?"

Keith and Charlie exchange looks. "That's exactly what we'd like to know, mate," Charlie says.

Dom stands. He twists from side to side, stretching out. "Right," he says, "I'm gonna head out, check the lay of the land. See if I can find any answers for you. *And* see if there's a way we can sneak y'all out of the city—I'll check if I can call in any favors, too, if I need to."

"I appreciate you, man," Keith says, and they bump fists.

"I'll keep in touch," Dom says.

He's already wearing his boots. This isn't the first time he's gone out since they arrived at his apartment. He went down to the store and bought some burner phones so they could all keep in contact. He grabs his jacket and pulls it on.

"Good meeting you, Charlie," he says on his way past, patting Charlie's shoulder.

"Likewise, mate," Charlie says, watching Dom as he heads out the door.

He turns back to the television, to his own face on the screen. Once again, as his thoughts have so often over the last few days, he thinks of Niamh. No doubt this news has made it back home. It is probably all over the BBC. She'll see it, and she'll have no way of getting in touch with him. He could try and email her, perhaps, but it's too risky. He needs to wait until they're back on the move. They need to get out of the city. Dom's apartment is all right to lay low for now, but it's nothing more than a temporary hideout.

They need to get out of the city, maybe even the state, as soon as they can. As far as Charlie is concerned, he needs to get out of the country, but that's an issue he's not going to be able to resolve any time soon. For now, they need to get somewhere they can think. Plot their next move.

Charlie clears his throat. "We ain't had much of a chance to talk," he says. "Since the rooftop."

Keith strokes his jaw, more than likely knowing what Charlie is about to say. "Uh-huh."

"The panic attacks," Charlie says, "they a regular thing?"

It takes Keith a moment to answer. "They've been more regular lately," he says. "Explosions and getting shot at will do that."

"There an underlying cause? You have PTSD?"

Keith nods. "Why I had to leave the Navy Seals."

"Something happen there?"

"A *lot* happened there."

"Something specific."

Keith shakes his head.

"How well do you manage it?"

"You're asking if I'm going to be a liability."

"I'm sure you can understand why," Charlie says. "Things being what they are. And I'm trying to be a bit more polite about it."

Keith smirks. "I appreciate your manners." He takes a deep breath. "The truth? I don't know, man."

"You on medication for it or something?"

Keith shakes his head. "No, no medication. I've just gotta... I gotta *breathe* through it." He chuckles, but there isn't any humor in the sound.

"Does that help?"

Keith shrugs. "Sometimes. Look, Charlie, I know this isn't ideal, and I probably should've told you about it sooner. We just haven't had much of a chance. But I'll get through. Whatever we've gotta do, I can do it. I ain't gonna let this hold me back."

Charlie nods. He wants to believe Keith and hopes that he's right, but realistically, he knows that things aren't going to suddenly, magically change for Keith. His PTSD is one thing, but the panic attacks are another thing entirely—they're a problem, and they could cause problems. They could put Charlie at risk. They could put Kayla at risk. They certainly put Keith at risk. They slow him down. Charlie has seen them firsthand, and they almost killed him.

Charlie likes Keith. He's not going to leave him behind. These are genuine concerns, though. He has to keep them in mind, whatever comes next, whatever they decide to do.

Keith picks up the remote and mutes the television. "We need to talk some other things through, too. We need to try and figure out just what the hell is going on here."

Charlie nods, as grateful as Keith is to change the subject.

Keith points at the television. "They aren't telling the whole story. They don't have any reason to withhold any kind of information. There's nothing to be gained from doing that. They don't mention the jailbreak or the NSA agent tracking us down." Keith counts these off on his fingers. "And they don't mention the two dead cops that he killed. In fact, we've been watching the news for hours now, and there hasn't been any mention of them at all."

"And they've got to have found them by now," Charlie says. "One of them was killed on the roof, sure, and I'd guess that maybe they wouldn't have found him yet, except there's the guy dead in the stairwell, too. And that was an occupied building. The people living there would have heard stuff. And we know they called the cops—we heard the sirens when we got out. I mean, it's possible, but it's unlikely that they were heading anywhere else."

"So what are you thinking?"

"I'm thinking that whatever is going on here, that NSA agent has something to do with it."

"His name is Lloyd."

They both look up. It's Kayla in the doorway. She walks through to the kitchen, which is adjacent to the open-plan living room, to get a glass of water. She avoids their eyes. She's been quiet since the roof. Since the diner, in fact. Charlie isn't sure what she might have spoken to Keith about before the cops and agent rolled up on them and started shooting, if they got a chance to speak at all.

"The agent?" Keith says. "He's called Lloyd?"

Kayla turns and nods. She takes a drink. She looks to the side, brow furrowed while she thinks. "Lloyd…Nivens. I spoke to him at the station. He was…he was friendly."

She shakes her head, looking as if she feels foolish. Naïve, perhaps. Too trusting.

"Lloyd Nivens," Keith repeats.

Kayla finishes the water, then puts the glass by the side of the sink. She walks by them again, heading back to the bedroom.

"How are you feeling?" Keith says.

"Like I'm going to throw up," Kayla says, and then she's gone, back down the corridor, back to the room where she's locked herself away. They hear the door close after her.

"She's going through a lot," Keith says, turning back to Charlie.

"Aye," Charlie says. "Not every day you get chased by your own government for killing the vice-president."

"She says she didn't do it," Keith says.

"I'm sure she does."

"She asked me if I thought the footage could be faked."

"And maybe it is, but we still have to—" Charlie looks to the door, then leans in and lowers his voice. "We still have to entertain the notion that she *is* responsible, and we're here helping out a fucking terrorist. *And* we're on the fucking run because of it."

Keith chews his lip and stares at the mute television screen. "What if…what if there's a third option?" he says. "What if it's not so black and white as whether she *did* or *didn't* plant the bomb or whether the footage is real or faked?"

"How do you mean?"

Keith takes a deep breath. "Are you familiar with the Manchurian Candidate?"

Charlie blinks. "Aye."

Keith raises an eyebrow.

"You think—you think she's, like, a *sleeper* agent?"

"*Could* be a sleeper agent," Keith says.

Charlie snorts. "That's ridiculous."

"Is it? It's an option, it's an idea, and right now, we're short of those. Regardless of if it's outlandish or not, whether she's a sleeper agent, or whether she planted the bomb or she didn't, someone *has* released footage of her at the site of the explosion, and they *are* blaming her for it. Why her? Why *us*, for that matter?"

Charlie doesn't answer. He doesn't say anything for a while. He sits back in the chair and stares up at the ceiling. He tries to consider what Keith has suggested, but he can't take it seriously. He closes his eyes and takes a deep breath. Finally, he sits forward.

"Listen," he says, "if we wanna get through this, and get out of it, we have to approach it realistically. Put all that science fiction kind of nonsense to one side for now—"

"It's not science fiction," Keith says, "and it's not nonsense. It happened before. It happens still."

Charlie waves his hands. "Just listen, all right. But it all to one side—*for now*—and let's settle on the things we know and the things we *think* we know for sure. For instance, we know that this

NSA agent Lloyd Nivens *is* trying to kill Kayla and, by proxy, us. That's a fact. He's shooting on sight, and regardless of whether Kayla did plant that bomb or not, he shouldn't be doing that, right? So, that's something we know for certain. And how about, to get through this, we choose to believe unequivocally that Kayla did *not* plant that bomb. That the footage *is* fake. Now, we don't know why they did that, but that's something we can work on finding out. You with me so far?"

Keith nods.

"I mean, here's a hypothesis—we're asking why *us*, why Kayla. Maybe because of the same reason we were pulled into that police station in the first place—because we were *there*. And maybe Kayla was close enough to the explosion that they decided to scapegoat her. So, even if that answers that, it again raises the question of *why*? Why put the blame on us? Who *is* responsible? Is it the ARO, like they've claimed? If so, why does it feel like someone's trying to cover things up?" Charlie groans and gets to his feet, pacing the floor. "Jesus Christ, man, I sound like a fucking loony conspiracy theorist. This is nuts, man."

"But you're onto something," Keith says. "If we choose to believe Kayla, then we've picked a side. It's us against them. We need to know where we stand because it's the only way we're gonna survive."

Charlie stops pacing. He runs his hands down his face, then lowers himself back into the chair. He's kept the Glock he took from the cop. It rubs uncomfortably against his lower back now, and he has to shift to get back into a position where it isn't sticking into him. Keeping hold of a cop's gun probably wasn't a great idea, but not having a weapon when they're being pursued would be an even worse option.

"We need to talk to Agent Nivens," he says. "It's the only way we're gonna get any answers."

Keith nods. "I was thinking the same thing—the only problem

being I don't see how the hell we're supposed to get anywhere near him. We don't even know where he is."

Charlie's eyes narrow. "That reminds me—he seemed to find Kayla pretty easy last night after she bolted from the diner. You think that was a coincidence?"

"I've been wondering the same thing. Look, maybe we should just leave this for now. It's not going to get us anywhere. Let's sit tight, wait until we hear back from Dom. We should rest up and make sure we're fresh in case he manages to find us an opportunity. He does, we wanna be ready for it."

Charlie nods. "Aye, you're right." He rests his head in his hand and turns to the television. "Change it over. I'm sick of seeing my own face. Oh, and I need you to send Dom a message."

Keith looks at him.

"Whether he finds us a way out or not today, tell him to make sure he brings back some food. I'm starving."

25

J ames still isn't sure how comfortable he is with what they're doing, but he's agreed to it, and now they're following through.

Shira sits at the kitchen counter on her laptop. She's on the phone and speaking Hebrew. James doesn't understand. He stands to the side with his arms folded, watching. Shira isn't doing anything on the laptop; she's watching, too. She talks to her friend back in Israel. Noam Katz. He's a computer analyst for Mossad. It looks to James like he's also a proficient hacker, though perhaps the jobs aren't too dissimilar. He isn't sure.

Occasionally, Shira turns back to James and explains to him in English what's happening. "Noam has run the girl's face through facial recognition software, and now we're just waiting for a hit. He's going through all the security footage in the city, and outside the city, from that morning."

James bites his lip. "Surely...surely my government's already doing this, right? Like, the NSA, the FBI, the CIA—they've already gotta be doing this."

"Maybe they are," Shira says. "And, if they are, maybe

152

they're not as good, or as fast, as Noam is." She presses the phone to her chest so Noam can't overhear. "Are you having doubts?"

James looks at the laptop, at the images whizzing by on the screen. He grits his teeth. "They'll pass," he says, hoping this is true.

If they get something—if they get a hit, if they manage to find out who the girl is, or where she came from, or perhaps even where the ARO base is, then he'll not feel so bad. Then he'll be caught up in the moment, and all these doubtful butterflies will have been worth it.

Shira turns back to the screen, returns the phone to her ear, and resumes talking in Hebrew. James doesn't understand a word of it. He's always wanted to learn, for her. To impress her—to surprise her. But he's always so damned busy with work. He's never found the chance yet.

Shira perks up suddenly and points at the screen, motioning for James to come and take a closer look. "We have something," she says. "Do you see?"

The image pauses. It's a bus, stopped at some traffic lights. It's hard to tell where the picture was taken—a security camera by the side of the road or on a building, perhaps. "What am I looking at?" he says.

Noam must overhear. He draws a red circle around one of the bus's windows. James leans in closer.

"It's the girl," Shira says.

"Oh, shit," James says, seeing her now. "Yeah, yeah, that's her."

She sits by the window, staring straight ahead. Whatever software Noam is using, it's impressive. It's managed to pick the girl out via her profile. She sits by the window on the bus, and someone is sitting next to her. It's hard to make out what they look like. Within the confines of the bus, they're nothing more than a dark shadow. They might not even know the girl, but at the same time, they could be an accomplice.

The footage starts running across the screen again. James sees the bus moving in reverse now.

"Noam is running back through the footage," Shira says. "Tracing it back to its source. Back to where the girl got on."

James nods then steps back again. He wants to leave the room, but he can't look away.

He's a cop. He's supposed to uphold the law. And yet, here they are, breaking it. He tells himself, tries to persuade himself, that the ends will justify the means. They're doing this to help. They're not looking to make any kind of personal gain. They're just trying to find who is responsible and bring them to justice.

Noam searches through the footage for a while. He keeps Shira updated on what he's doing, and she, in turn, relays this to James. Occasionally Noam loses track of the girl, usually in a dark spot where there are briefly no cameras, and he has to hunt her out again.

James steps away, beginning to pace. He feels antsy, and this feeling only grows the longer the process takes. He runs the fingers of his right hand back through his hair, then strokes at his cast. It's getting itchier. He doesn't know if this is a good thing or if perhaps it's just his nerves.

"*Hmm*," Shira says. "We've got something interesting."

James goes to her and watches the screen. It's paused on a bus stop.

"This is the earliest footage Noam can find," Shira says. She puts her phone down while she explains to him. She points at the screen. "He's still looking, but he thinks this is it. The first time she gets close to a camera he's able to access. Do you see the woman next to her?" Her finger points out the woman standing to the girl's left. There are a handful of people at the bus stop. It's hard to tell if these two are together. "Watch."

Shira is back in control of the laptop. She plays the footage. The woman and the girl don't talk, but they stand close. They're silent, waiting for the bus to arrive. They don't look at each other. In fact, it's hard to tell if the girl is looking at anything. Her eyes are empty. There's something disconcerting about it. Her face is impassive, with a thousand-yard stare. It doesn't look natural. It makes James's skin crawl for reasons he doesn't fully understand. He doesn't think he's ever seen anyone with eyes like that, especially not on a teenage girl.

The woman looks to be in her early forties. Her eyes are not empty. She looks to be in her early forties, with an attractive face and dark hair tied back in a ponytail. Her jaw is strong, and her cheekbones are well-defined. It's hard to make out what kind of build she has with the turtleneck and raincoat she's wearing, but from these facial features, James would guess that she keeps in shape. Yoga, perhaps, running or swimming, maybe even weights. She looks taller than average.

The bus pulls into view and comes down the road. The woman turns her head to watch its approach. The girl does not. She continues to stare straight ahead. The bus pulls to a stop alongside them. The people waiting to begin to file onboard.

"Watch," Shira says. "It's coming up."

The woman reaches out and takes the girl by the arm. She turns her. The girl's face does not change. The woman leads her onto the bus.

"They were together?" James says.

"It looks that way," Shira says.

"The girl looked like a zombie. Do you think she was on something?"

Shira shrugs. "Who can say?"

"Do we know who the woman is?"

"Noam is working on it. Let me check." She picks up her

phone and speaks into it. After a couple of seconds, she looks at James and mouths, "*Not yet.*"

James reaches over to the laptop and replays the footage. Watches again as the woman turns, looks at the girl, then takes her by the arm. Guides her onto the bus. James thinks back to the dark shadow he saw sitting beside the girl on the bus. Was it the same woman?

"Does he know if the woman gets off the bus before her?" he says.

"He's checking that, too," Shira says. "We should know that before we know her name."

James nods, then backs away, giving Shira some space in case she needs to do anything. Minutes pass. Shira keeps the phone by her ear, but she's silent. He can't hear much through the phone from Noam's end. Occasional words, more like he's muttering to himself while he works.

James pulls up a stool next to Shira while he waits, angled toward the laptop. His leg bounces. He chews on a thumbnail. He checks his watch. A couple more minutes pass, and then the footage is playing on the screen. Noam is in control of the laptop again.

"This is when the girl reaches the city," Shira says.

They see her at the bus station. She gets off. The woman is still with her, still by her side, as they step down off the bus. She's holding the girl by the inside of her arm. They get clear of the bus, walk deeper into the station, and then the woman lets go of the girl's arm and just walks away. James frowns. The girl keeps walking. Neither of them falters. They go their separate ways without a word or a glance.

"What the hell was that all about?" James says.

"Noam is going to see if he can find where the woman goes," Shira says. "He's got enough footage of her face. He can run the facial recognition software on her this time."

"Does he have a name yet?"

Shira speaks into the phone. "Still working on it," she says to James.

The footage on the screen begins speeding by again, searching, this time for the mysterious woman.

James waits. It's hard, but he's learning to be patient with the process.

"We've got her name," Shira says suddenly.

James looks at her expectantly.

"Noam is sending through the details."

A file appears on the screen, and Shira clicks to open it. They both quickly read it through.

The woman's name is Heather Morrow. She's forty-two. It has her address. She lives in a suburb outside the city. She's married—her husband is called Derek Morrow. He's forty-five. They both work from home as stockbrokers. They don't have any children.

"No kids," James says. "So, who's the girl? Cousin? Niece?"

"Noam still isn't getting any hits on the girl," Shira says. "Even with the knowledge of who the woman is. He can't find any connection to her."

"We have her address," James says.

Shira nods, understanding, likely having the same thought. They can go to her home and ask her themselves.

More minutes pass by. Shira speaks into her phone. James looks at her. She's frowning.

"There's no sign of the woman," she says. "Noam can't find her from the station. He says it's like she just disappears."

She speaks back into her phone again. Her features have softened now. It sounds like she's saying goodbye. She hangs up and puts her phone down. The images on the laptop have ceased. Noam is no longer in it.

"He's going to keep looking," she says. "For Heather. Where

she went. And he's going to keep trying to find out who the girl is. But it's getting late. We all need to rest."

"We should probably eat," James says, staring at the screen. He isn't hungry. He's seen too much and has too much on his mind now to be hungry.

"We'll order pizza or something," Shira says. "I'm not in the mood to cook—are you?"

James shakes his head.

"We've got a lot to think about," Shira says.

"The woman," James says, nodding toward the laptop, "she couldn't have just disappeared. She had to have gone somewhere. It's a city. There are cameras everywhere."

"Noam will find her," Shira says. "He found her already. He found the girl. Some things just take a little longer, is all."

James folds his arms. "And you trust him, right?" he asks, not for the first time.

"*Yes*," Shira says, reaching out and stroking his unbroken arm. She squeezes his wrist. "I trust him unquestionably. I've known Noam for a long time. We worked together. We've stayed in touch since I came to America. He's not just a former co-worker—he's a friend."

James nods along.

"You've been tense since we first talked about this," Shira says. "I know it's hard, but you need to try and calm down. Let go of the tension. We'll eat, we'll go to bed, and tomorrow morning we'll go to Heather Morrow's house. We'll continue our search for the people responsible. You might not be comfortable with this," she motions to the laptop, "but it all serves the greater good."

"The end justifies the means," James says.

Shira nods once.

She's right. James knows she's right. It's all hands on deck. Matt may believe that the best thing for James is to sit back and rest and leave it to the rest of them, but sometimes everyone else can be so fixated on what's in front of them they miss what's happening outside of the box. If James and Shira—and Noam—can help to find the ARO, to capture them, then they have to do that.

"All right," he says, standing. "I'll take your advice. Now, let's order pizza."

26

Georgia has been driving since she left Minnow. She's still in Alaska. She still has a couple of days' drive ahead of her before she gets out of the state. She's not sure yet where she's heading. A part of her knows that there's only one place she can go, potentially one person who can help her. She's not sure if she wants to see them or speak to them, but she might not have an option.

What she *does* know is that she's been tracked down, and she can't go back. She needs to get out of Alaska. Lose them completely. Make it harder for them to track her again.

She watches her mirrors as she goes. She's been watching them all day. She's stopped only twice. Once for fuel, to grab some food, and to use the bathroom. The second time was at a store to get some more clothes. She was wearing her trousers and blouse for the library. They still had some blood on them from this morning. She's changed them out for jeans and a black t-shirt. She swapped her pumps for some hiking boots.

No one is following her. She's been careful.

It's getting late now. She's getting tired. As much as she'd like to keep going, she needs to get off the road, to rest. She doesn't;

all she's going to do is crash—figuratively and literally. She spots a sign for another gas station ten miles down the road. Beneath the sign for it, there are also advertisements for a twenty-four-hour diner and a motel. She'll pull in there and make sure she pulls her truck around the back and keeps it out of view of the passing road.

She'll get herself a room, and from there, she'll consider her next move. Right now, she thinks she should head for Washington, DC, but her instincts tell her this is probably wrong. Washington could be the worst place for her to go, despite the fact this is where Kayla Morrow is. She knows she needs to go to her, to find her, to help her, but Kayla seems to be evading all the people that are hunting for her so far. If she's smart, she'll get out of the city. Keep moving. This is where Georgia will find her—on the road.

Of course, that's if she finds her at all. There's a chance Kayla could get caught. There's a chance she could get killed. She's new to this. She doesn't know what she's capable of yet.

Georgia has kept the radio on, tuned to the news. This is how she knows Kayla is still at large. She keeps waiting for a breaking news bulletin announcing her capture, but it hasn't come yet.

The gas station comes into view. It's getting dark, but the area is all lit up. She can see the neon glowing signs of the diner and the motel just behind it. As she gets closer, she sees that the forecourt is filled with long-haul trucks parked up for the night. She pulls in and goes straight to the motel, parking down the side of it, in the shadows, out of reach of all the lights in the area, and out of view of the road. She goes and books herself a room. She requests the one on the end, nearest to her truck. Luckily, it's unoccupied. She checks it out before she goes for food. If necessary, she has a clear route out of her back window to get to her truck.

Before she leaves, she watches out the window. Makes sure the way is clear. Makes sure that no one has followed her in, and that there aren't any suspicious vehicles in the parking lot that look like they might be waiting, watching. There aren't, so far as she can see. Most of the vehicles in view are empty. The parking lot is clear of people. Way off in the distance, she sees a thickset man with a long beard climbing into the cab of his truck. She watches him start it up and pull away.

She leaves her room and goes to the diner. She pauses and looks through the window before she goes in. At a guess, she'd say it's about half full. Georgia goes inside. She takes a seat in a booth near the window. She can look out over the diner and see through the window. After a couple of minutes, the waitress comes over and takes her order. She asks for salad and a glass of water. Keeps it light. She doesn't want anything heavy. At any point, she might need to get on the move again. She doesn't want a stomach cramp to slow her down.

The other occupants of the diner are mostly men. The majority of them look like truckers—thickset, bearded men with checkered shirts and caps. She spots a couple of other women sitting in booths with their boyfriends or their husbands. Georgia is the only woman on her own.

A group of truckers at the counter notice this fact. They keep glancing back at her, then talking amongst themselves. The one in the middle—the biggest of the three and seemingly the ringleader —winks at her.

The waitress brings her food, then hangs around. "You here alone?"

Georgia nods.

The waitress glances back at the three truckers at the bar. "Can I give you some advice?"

"Sure."

The waitress is middle-aged. Looks like she could have worked here since the place first opened. "Guys like that, they're spending a lot of time on the road. Away from their wives, from their girlfriends. From their *homes*. You get my meaning? A pretty young thing like you, all on your own, they're probably gonna try and talk to you. If you're into that kind of thing, then fine, good for you. But if you're not, well, they can be persistent. They're the kind of guys where one '*no*' ain't enough. You get me?"

Even as the waitress tells her what the men are like, they're still looking her way, peering around the waitress. The leader blows Georgia a kiss. His two henchmen start to giggle.

"I've seen them watching you," the waitress says, "checking you out. And I know you've seen them too, and I don't think you're interested. So all I'm suggesting is, if you don't want them to come talk to you, maybe eat your meal fast and then leave, or don't feel too bad about asking me to take this back and wrapping it up to go."

Georgia has already run because of a group of men once today, and they were a lot more fearsome than the three at the counter. "I appreciate your concern," she says to the waitress. "But I'm going to eat right here."

"Suit yourself," the waitress says. "Just watch yourself, okay?"

The waitress leaves, and Georgia starts eating. She ignores the three men at the counter, though she can feel how they stare. She sees out of the corner of her eye when they turn to look at her.

Part of her thinks she should have taken the waitress's advice and gotten her food to go. Taken it back to her motel room and ate it there in peace. She doesn't want to draw attention to herself. She's trying to keep a low profile. At the same time, she's not going to be forced into doing anything simply because some creeps like the look of her.

She eats her salad and minds her business. She refuses to react to their stares and the way they try to goad her.

It's when she's almost finished that the leader of the group comes over to her. He rests an arm on top of the booth and leans in close. "Evening, darlin'," he says. "You here all alone?"

Georgia runs her tongue around the inside of her mouth, wiping her teeth clean. She looks up at him and says nothing. She takes a sip of her water.

The leader grins. "Looks to me like you are. You like some company?"

"No," Georgia says.

"Hey, hey, don't be so abrupt. Maybe hear me out, huh?"

"Not interested."

The leader's grin doesn't slip. He's persistent. He glances back over his shoulder toward his buddies, who giggle like schoolgirls. "That waitress that served you, she sure hung around, didn't she?" he says, turning back around. "She try and tell you something about us, that it?"

"She didn't say anything about you," Georgia says. "What makes you think you're so important?"

He raises an eyebrow at this. There are only so many times Georgia can rebuff him, she knows, before his friendly exterior begins to fade and his true self comes through. It's not yet, though. "Good for her," he says. "Just making conversation, was she? Being real friendly, thinking about the tip, I'm sure. You staying near here, darlin'? At the motel, maybe?"

"I'm just passing through," Georgia says.

"That right?" He slips into the booth and sits closer to her than is necessary. He glances at her plate. He sees some leftover lettuce and turns his nose up at it. She's sure that if it had been a fry, he would have helped himself. "So, you're gonna leave here right after you've finished your meal? Where you going?"

"I don't see why that's any concern of yours."

"Just worried about you is all, darlin'. Just being a gentleman, as is my duty." His tongue flickers out and runs over his lips. "Pretty young thing like you, all alone out on the road

—*and* it's getting late. You aren't concerned about creeps?" He inches a little closer to her. Too close. Their shoulders are touching.

"I've never had trouble in the past," Georgia says. She's trying to stay calm. To defuse this situation. To not rile this man up. To not draw attention to herself.

"Good for you," he says. "But times change, don't they?" He's leering at her. He's showing his teeth. He's trying to crowd her into the corner of the booth.

Georgia doesn't appreciate him being so close to her. Doesn't appreciate his attempts at intimidation. She certainly doesn't appreciate his body odor or his hot breath on her cheek, which smells of meat from the steak he's eaten. She grits her teeth and looks him in the eye.

"You want to be a gentleman?" she says. "Get out of the booth. Go back to your idiot friends, and forget all about me, or I'm going to break your nose."

He frowns at this, caught off guard. Of all the reactions he might have been expecting, this was not one of them. He manages to recover himself with a smirk. "You ain't gotta be like that, darlin'?"

"I'm not your *darlin'*," Georgia says. "Now, leave. Don't make me tell you again."

"I don't think you're in a position to tell me *anything*—"

His right hand is lying flat on the table as he leans in closer. Georgia grabs her fork and drives it through the back of his hand into the fleshy gaps between his bones. The tines sink in deep, though not deep enough to reach the wood on the other side. The man gasps, more in shock than pain, and before he can make any noise, Georgia slams the back of her elbow into the bridge of his nose, breaking it.

He raises his hands to his face, the fork still sticking out of it. Georgia pulls the bloodied fork out, then jabs it into his neck, right into his carotid. She tweaks his broken nose, making sure she has his full attention.

"Empty your pockets," she says. "Pull out some cash. You wanna be a gentleman? You can pay for my meal. Make sure you leave a good tip, too."

He scrabbles in his pockets, pulling out crumpled notes and dumping them on the table.

Georgia lets go of his nose. "Now do like I told you in the first place, and fuck off."

The trucker hurries away, head lowered, holding at his wounded face and hand. His two buddies aren't giggling anymore. They look shocked and concerned.

Georgia's adrenaline is high. Her hands are trembling a little. She finishes her water, then hurries out of the diner.

27

Georgia thinks on how what she did was satisfying, but she still regrets doing it.

She's gone to the window in her room about half a dozen times since she got back to it, looking out, looking back to the diner to see if the three men have regrouped and come looking for her. They may have even called in some friends, too, telling them what she did and how they needed to take some revenge on her. She can imagine what kind of revenge they might have in mind—the kind that ensures a woman like her doesn't try anything like that ever again. Making sure she knows her place.

She hadn't seen any sign of them, though, not since they left the diner, the leader propped between his two friends as they went back across the parking lot toward their trucks. They each went to their own vehicle, though none of them had left yet. They're probably staying in them overnight, saving money by not checking into the motel.

She can't settle. Even if she hadn't had the altercation in the diner, she was not sure she'd be able to settle. It feels like she's still living through the last few nights back in Minnow, knowing there were men out there watching her. Hanging around her home.

She lies on the bed, but she doesn't relax. She doesn't have the television or the lights on. She's in darkness, listening, staying alert.

She should sleep. She knows she should. But she can't. Another reason to be annoyed at the truckers. Her adrenaline isn't coming down. She stays on edge, more so than knowing she is already being pursued.

Checking the window again, she sees that the parking lot remains clear. She runs her hands down her face. Stopping was a mistake. She should have kept going. She's too wired to rest.

The truckers from the diner remain in their trucks. She doesn't believe they're going to hassle her any further, not anymore. She sighs, goes through to the bathroom, and runs the shower. She runs it hot. Steam fills the room. She needs to loosen up. To relax. She wants to sleep.

Before she strips off and gets in the shower, she takes one more look out the window. The way is clear. She doesn't feel comfortable getting into the shower unguarded. She takes a bulb from one of the bedside lamps and drops it to the ground outside her door. She shatters it with her boot heel, then spreads the shards across the ground. She puts the lock back on the door, then drags the chair from the corner and wedges it against it.

Now she showers. She stays on edge, listening, but it is a soft-ened edge. The hot water does her good. It calms her nerves and relaxes her body. The last of the adrenaline still coursing through her veins from earlier in the diner is finally draining away. She turns her face to the water and closes her eyes, and thinks how she only left Minnow this morning. It feels like it's already been so much longer.

She thinks of Camilla, too. Poor Camilla. Georgia has never had to grieve for anyone before. She's not sure if she was close enough to Camilla to grieve. She knows she feels... *something*. Some sadness, deep within herself, knowing that she'll never see this older woman again. Never see her smile, or hear her gossip. She feels a similar kind of sadness for the town of Minnow itself. She had built a life there. A private existence away from her past, from everything she had run away from and left behind.

And now she's on the run again.

Minnow is far behind her. It's unlikely she'll ever see it again, too. The small town came to mean so much to her without her even realizing it.

She gets out of the shower and dries herself. Wrapped in the towel, she goes to the window. It has become second nature to her this night. She goes to it to look out.

As she crosses the room, she hears the crunch of glass outside her door. She freezes, her eyes whipping toward it. She doesn't stay frozen long. She doesn't go any further forward. She backs up, grabbing her underwear and jeans from the floor. Her eyes never leave the door as she pulls them on. It could be the truckers, but she's not sure how they would have found her room.

She hears the glass crunch again. She doesn't hear any voices. Whoever is out there, they have to have realized what they've stepped in. They need to know that it didn't get there by itself.

Georgia begins to think it isn't the truckers. Her blood runs cold. It could be the people looking for her. Not necessarily the four from this morning, but others like them. If so, there'll be a team of them, and they'll be moving to surround her.

Moving fast, she upends the bed and pushes it up against the main window. She goes into the bathroom as they start trying to get inside. She hears their attempt to kick the door open. The chair stops them. Georgia tears down the metal bar at the top of the shower railing, letting the rings of the curtain run off it and dumping it into the bathtub. She waits in the doorway of the bathroom, the shower pole held in both hands. It's her only weapon. There's little else in the room she could use.

The lights remain off. There are gunshots and shattering glass.

The men are trying to get inside through the door and the window. The chair and the mattress hold them back, slow them down. To her right, the rear window is smashed. She's left this one uncovered. A man clad all in black, wearing body armor and a balaclava, starts climbing through. He carries an HK416 assault rifle, the stock of which he used to smash the window. Georgia jabs the pole down into him. She impales him through the flesh between his neck and his collarbone. He gives out a choked, strangled cry as she forces it in deep. Blood sprays. His body slumps, half in and half out of the broken window.

Behind her, the man at the window gets the mattress out of his way. He's dressed the same as the man Georgia has just killed and carries the same kind of weapon. They'll all look the same, undoubtedly—an extraction unit. Georgia reaches for the dead man's rifle, but the straps are tangled under him. She moves fast around the edge of the dark room before the other man can see her. She grabs the television and slams it down onto the top of his head. He lurches to the side, his neck snapping with the impact. Georgia is able to get his HK416 with more ease. With it, she races to the rear window, leaving the man at the door who is still trying to get in. She pushes the dead body out, the pole still sticking out of him.

There's another man here, rounding the corner. Georgia drops and rolls and comes up firing, strafing him across the chest. She moves on, weapon raised, pausing by her truck and waiting for others to come at the sound of the gunfire.

Another appears at the opposite corner. She mows him down, then pushes on, and checks the front of the building. Four down. In the parking lot, she spots a black van, its side doors open. The driver remains inside. He sees her. The engine roars into life. He drives for her. Georgia stands her ground and fires into the windshield. Her bullets break through, hit the driver. He slumps to the side and the van veers, coming to a stop as it crashes into the side of a parked car.

The area is clear. Others have no doubt heard the gunshots, but no one is coming to investigate. No one is stupid enough to poke their heads out.

Georgia throws the gun aside and gets into her truck. She knew she shouldn't have stopped. She should have kept going, no matter how tired or hungry she may have been. Somehow, they've tracked her again. As she spins her truck around, she wonders how they could have done it—facial recognition software? She hasn't passed too many cameras. She's kept an eye on them. Even here, she's kept her face lowered, turned away from the security cameras outside of the diner and the motel. How else? Satellite? If that were the case, they would have found her sooner. They would have run her off the road.

The only thing she knows for sure is, that they don't have a tracker on her.

She stops the truck, slamming her foot on the brake. The *truck*. Once she was out of Minnow, she should have stopped, pulled over, and checked the truck over. There's probably a tracker on it.

"*Shit*!" She slams her hands on the steering wheel. She doesn't have time to check it over now.

Opposite her, across the parking lot, she sees one of the long-haul truckers turning, preparing to leave. The truck doesn't belong to any of the assholes from the diner.

Georgia gets out and starts running. She wonders if he heard the gunshots. Perhaps he's fleeing from them, though he doesn't seem in too much of a rush. At this distance, he might not have noticed. His running engine may have drowned out all sounds.

She reaches the truck as it halts at the junction, preparing to pull out. She jumps up onto the step and pulls the door open.

The driver inside gives a start. "Jesus Christ!" He has music on, turned up loud. Black Sabbath. He turns it down as he turns to her. "The hell are you doing?"

"Where are you going?" Georgia says. "North or south?"

"What?" He's a younger guy. He's not as thickset as the others she's seen, and his beard isn't as long. He's not wearing a cap. Instead, his hair is slicked back. She notices steam coming from the thermos in his coffee holder.

"Where are you going?" she repeats, louder this time.

"Uh, south," he says.

Georgia climbs inside, slamming the door shut after her. "I'm coming with you," she says, strapping herself in.

The driver looks at her, eyes narrowed, startled and confused.

Georgia waves her hands at the steering wheel. "Let's go!"

The driver gets to it. He pulls out of the parking lot. Georgia looks out the window as they pass by on the road. She can see people at the motel and diner stepping outside, tentatively coming to investigate now that the shooting has stopped for a while. The driver doesn't seem to notice. She doesn't see them for long. The truck gets past and puts the buildings behind them. She looks back in the mirror, but there's nothing to see. Soon, there's only darkness. Everything else is left behind.

"Has it been raining or something?" the driver says.

Georgia turns to face him.

"Just, uh, your hair. I mean, it's wet."

"I just got out of the shower."

"Oh. Okay."

Georgia narrows her eyes. "Let me make one thing clear," she says. "You seem like an all right guy, but looks can be deceiving. I'm not gonna put out for you just to get this ride. I'm not gonna suck your dick or jerk you off. That clear?"

The driver's mouth opens and shuts a few times, unsure how to respond. Finally, he coughs and says, "Yeah, yeah, of course. Of course not. I, uh, I'll just be grateful for the company."

Georgia takes a deep breath and relaxes a little. "I'm sorry if that was harsh," she says, turning and looking out the window, into the darkness, the seemingly endless void ahead. "I've just had a very long day, is all."

"Do you, uh, want me to turn the music down or anything?"

Georgia settles back into the corner, folding her arms and making herself comfortable. "Play it as loud as you like," she says, then closes her eyes.

28

D om returns to his apartment late, but he brings food. He carries a stack of pizzas in his arms.

"I figured y'all were probably hungry," he says, setting the boxes down on a table, "so I got a lot. And I didn't know what anyone likes or dietary requirements... *Shit*, I sure hope none of y'all are lactose or gluten intolerant. Damn it. I knew I forgot something."

Keith stands by the window with Charlie. Charlie has been watching the road, far down below, remaining vigilant. There's nothing much to see. It's quieter than it would ordinarily be, though. Not as much traffic, nor as many people. The city is still reeling from the bomb and from every revelation that has come since. People are scared. They're wary and worried.

Keith leaves the window. The pizza smells good, and he realizes just how hungry he is. His mind has been distracted up to his point. He hasn't had a chance to think about food. "Any luck out there?"

"Not yet," Dom says, shaking his head apologetically. "But I'll figure something out; just bear with me. For now, the city's still locked down, and the girl's face is everywhere. The two of you, too."

"Grand," Charlie says from the window, still looking down. "I mean, who among us hasn't wanted our face plastered all over the newspapers and the telly?"

Dom's eyes narrow. To Keith, he says, "Is he being sarcastic? I can't tell."

"I think so," Keith says. "I'll go get Kayla. I'll be right back."

"I'll grab some plates," Dom says. "Charlie, you wanna give me a hand?"

Keith leaves them to it and goes to the room where Kayla has locked herself away. It's not a huge apartment. Away from the kitchen and living room, there is a bathroom and two bedrooms. Kayla is in the spare. Keith has stayed over a few times after watching a football or basketball game or a boxing match. He knows there's not much in the room—a single bed and a weight bench takes up most of the floorspace.

He raps his knuckles softly against the door. "Kayla?" he says. "It all right if I come in?"

A moment passes, and he thinks she might be asleep, but then she responds. "Sure."

Keith opens the door a crack and peers inside. Kayla sits atop the bed, her knees drawn up to her chest, her back against the wall. "How you doing, kid?" he asks, stepping inside and closing the door behind him.

Kayla looks like she doesn't know how to respond, so she just shakes her head.

Keith doesn't join her on the bed. He remains standing. "Dom just got back," he says. "He's brought pizza."

Kayla grunts.

"You hungry?"

"Not…not particularly."

"You should try and eat something. With everything going on, you're gonna need to keep your strength up. All of us are."

Kayla doesn't say anything. She doesn't look at him. She stares down at her thighs, her arms wrapped around them.

"You don't have to join us," Keith says. "But I'd like it if you did. You might not feel hungry now, but you probably will soon. I mean, especially once the smell of that pizza starts wafting through here. You're gonna get hungry then, I'm sure of it."

Kayla smiles a little. Keith hasn't seen her smile since her face first came up on the news back in the diner. She's no doubt had a lot to think about since then.

"Maybe I'll even come along with a box and place it right outside this door," Keith says. "Put a fan at the back of it, waft the smell inside. You'll be like in them old *Tom and Jerry* cartoons, where the smell carries him along by the nose."

Kayla laughs.

"Come on, you gotta have some pizza," Keith says, holding out a hand. "Dom has bought a *lot*. I don't know how many of us he thinks we might've smuggled in while he's been out or how much he thinks we're all gonna eat. It's gonna take all the mouths we got."

Kayla stares at his hand, considering. "How many pizzas has he gotten?"

Keith snorts. "About six. Maybe seven."

Kayla laughs again. She takes Keith's offered hand, and he pulls her from the bed. They leave the bedroom and go through to the living room. Dom and Charlie have opened and laid out the pizzas on the table in the kitchen area. Dom is filling a jug of water.

"Hey, girl," he says, seeing Kayla. "Sure hope you're hungry."

"Dom here looks like he's trying to feed a small army,"

Charlie says. "I know I told you to tell him we were hungry, Keith, but I didn't mean *this* hungry."

They sit around the table and eat. Keith and Dom talk about the diner. They tell stories that make everyone but Kayla laugh, though she does smile. She doesn't say anything. She doesn't eat much, either. A couple of slices of pepperoni, and then she seems content. She stays at the table with them, though. Doesn't retreat back through to the spare bedroom. She sits with her legs drawn up to her chest and her arms wrapped around them. Every so often, Charlie gets up and, goes to the window, looks down to the street. He always comes back. Never raises the alarm.

"Dark out there," he says, eventually. "Not much to see. Hasn't been for a while now."

When they finish eating, there's still a lot of pizza left over. "It'll keep. It'll do for breakfast." Dom laughs. "Reheated or cold, take your pick!"

"I'm just gonna go wash my hands," Keith says, standing from the table and going through to the bathroom. He's glad to see that Kayla looks as if she's going to stay put rather than retreat back to the bedroom.

When he leaves the bathroom, Dom is waiting for him in the hall. His face is serious. He tilts his head to the left, toward his bedroom, wanting Keith to follow. "Let me talk to you real quick," he says.

Keith follows. Dom closes the door after them. He moves away from the door and speaks with his voice lowered. "Listen, man, your business is your business, and you're gonna do what you're gonna do, and you know I'll back you on that. I'll help you any way I can."

"I appreciate that."

"Uh-huh. But I gotta ask, *why* are you getting yourself so involved in this? It don't have anything to do with you. You can just walk away, any time, go to a police station and resolve this straight away."

"You really believe the cops would be interested in hearing my side of the story?"

"I mean, maybe not," Dom concedes. "But someone out there's gotta, right?"

Keith looks to the ground. "Y'know, I've wondered that myself. Not a lot, but the thought is always there, in the back of my head, asking why I'm so involved." He looks back up. "Mostly, I think it's because of the girl. Because she's not got anyone else who *will* help her."

"Charlie's there."

"Charlie's gonna get out of the country the first chance he can get. I mean, he followed through when the agent was gunning us down, but if the opportunity comes up, he's gonna take it. But I look at her, and I see she's lost, and she's confused, and she's scared. I can't just abandon her."

"And what if she *did it*, man?"

"Does she look like a bomber to you?"

"Both of us know that looks can be deceiving. I've seen child soldiers, man, and I know you have too. This wouldn't be any different."

Keith nods at this. He knows Dom is right in this regard. He thinks of Kayla's house, of what he and Charlie found in the basement. He doesn't tell Dom about it, though. He doesn't know how he could get him to understand through words just how unnerving the whole thing had been. Only someone who had been present could understand.

"It's more than just Kayla, though," Keith says. "This whole thing, it just feels *off*. Something ain't right about it. We got people shooting at us, they're calling me and Charlie accomplices, and that agent killing two cops—there's just a lot going on here that don't add up." Again, Keith thinks of the wooden hut in the basement.

Dom takes a deep breath through his nose. "Like I said, man, I'll help you out any way that I can. If you're gonna do this, then I'm with you. You need me to find you a way out of the city. I'll find you one. What you do beyond that, though, that's on all of you."

Keith nods. "Thank you, Dom."

"Yeah, you're gonna really owe me after this." Dom laughs, lightening up a little. "How you holding up, anyway? How's the anxiety? None of this is gonna be any good for it."

"It's been touch or go a few times, I'm not gonna lie," Keith says, remembering last night on the roof.

"I know it's hard, but you try and take it easy, man. In between getting shot at, of course."

It sounds like he's making a joke, but Dom's face looks serious. "You know I'll do my best," Keith says.

"Remember your breathing. Slow and controlled. Nice and deep. Fill up those lungs. Breathe it out just as slow. Be measured. That's the important thing. Focus on your breathing, and everything else will calm."

"That's what I'll do," Keith says, though it's hard for him to concentrate on measuring his breaths when he's being chased or attacked. "By the way, has anyone been by the diner? Looking for me, I mean."

"Cops have been by, yeah, but no one's told them anything. No one has anything to tell them. And besides, even if they did, they'd know better than to speak to cops. You're one of us, man. We look out for our own."

"Well, when I get outta here, you let them all know I appreciate it."

They bump fists and then leave the bedroom. In the living room, they find Charlie and Kayla sitting in front of the television. They're watching professional wrestling. Charlie looks up, and Keith and Dom return. "I couldn't find anything else," he says. "And Kayla doesn't have a favorite show. She liked the look of this."

"It's bright, and it's colorful," she says without looking up. There are two women wrestling in the ring. "And I felt like I needed something bright and colorful."

Keith takes a seat with them. "Sounds good to me."

"I'm gonna go clean up," Dom says. He waits a moment. "Don't any of y'all rush to help."

"Thanks, mate," Charlie says. "You know how to treat your guests, *eh*? I've heard about this American hospitality." He winks at him.

Dom shakes his head, but he's laughing. He continues alone to the kitchen area.

29

Lloyd Nivens has been busy.

His first job after Kayla Morrow's breakout was to deal with the footage in the police station. Wipe the fact that he had her transported into the cell in the first place, and then loop the footage to hide that he was the one that transported her out of it, along with the two inept cops he had been supplied with. His tracks covered; he needed to get down to what really mattered—tracking Kayla back down and dealing with the two assholes helping her.

Speaking of assholes, another thing he has to keep dealing with is Ben Clark. A few years younger than Lloyd at thirty-eight, but still his superior in the field. He's been on the phone constantly, checking in, and looking for updates. He's looking for Kayla, too, though he's not having as much luck as Lloyd is.

Back at the station, after the getaway first happened, Lloyd had to report to him directly and explain what had happened. He'd sent his two cop associates to keep Ben busy while he dealt with the footage that incriminated him. When Ben tried checking the cameras himself, it was easy enough for Lloyd to play dumb, and pretend like he had no clue why so much was missing, or why it seemed to be looping back on itself. Luckily, there was nothing of what actually happened in the cells. He'd already dealt with that before he sent Kayla in.

"The ARO could be nearby," he said to Ben, "if they know we've got their girl. They could have hackers in the system. It was likely them that got her out."

Ben frowned at this. "And the Brit—Charlie? He and the Black guy, they could be part of the ARO?"

"I mean, how much do we really know about the ARO? And these two men, they both have military backgrounds. It would make sense, right? The ARO are coming and going as they please, planting bombs—it makes sense that they have people working with them that have some kind of military background."

Ben had spoken to some of the other men in the cells after the fight, but the Nazis—as useless as they were at fulfilling what Lloyd had enrolled them to do—had at least served a purpose in swearing everyone else to tell the version of the story they wanted to be told. The Brit and the Black guy went wild, started attacking everyone, got keys from the guards, and broke free.

Lloyd was the only one who had spoken to Kayla at the station. It was easy enough to keep her name from everyone else —he just claimed she hadn't shared it. Almost like she'd refused. He checked for ID, but she didn't have any. Her name will remain a mystery—unless he's told otherwise. He's yet to have received that call.

Ben is good at his job. He's dogged. Lloyd knows that this could be a problem. Right now, he's managing to keep him off the scent. As far as he's aware, Lloyd is out working the streets, doing all he can to track down the girl and her two accomplices. So long as this is what Ben continues to believe, they shouldn't have any problems.

"Have we heard anything about the two cops that disappeared at the same time?" Ben asked.

Lloyd thought of the looks on their faces as he shot them. Killed them. He'd had to. Couldn't take a risk on Charlie talking to them. Who knew what they might have told him? He'd called a team in to clean up their bodies and to speak to the occupants of the building, who had no doubt heard the gunshots. To present themselves to the occupants as government agents and reassure them that things were under control.

"No, nothing," he said. "Nobody's seen or heard from them. Although judging from the timing, we need to entertain the possibility that perhaps…" He left the suggestion hanging, waiting for Ben to seize upon it.

He saw the look on Ben's face. The way his head twisted to the side a little, his eyebrows narrowed. "*What?*"

"That maybe they were the ones that let them—the girl and her two helpers—out of their cells. Why else have they disappeared? Why else can't anyone get in touch with them?"

Ben's frown deepened. "Are you saying they could be ARO?"

"It's an avenue worth keeping in mind. I think we need to keep all these possibilities in mind, no matter how much we might dislike them."

Ben considered this. A finger curled around his chin as he stared into the distance, his face troubled. "We'll have to find them," he said. "All of them. It's the only way we're going to get any damn answers."

Lloyd isn't making it completely difficult for everyone else to find the girl. He's just trying to throw them off the trail when he can. They weren't even supposed to know about her. But now they do, and it's just better for him and his organization—his *true* organization—if he finds her first. Or, if not him, any of the other number of operatives working in this area. He has a lead on it, though. It all goes through him.

Right now, the edict is that the girl has to die. Something has gone wrong, and they need to cover up the mess. They need to take her out of the equation before she can cause any more problems.

The Nazis were supposed to do that. It was all going to be nice and simple. Put her in with them, and they kill her. Lloyd feigns ignorance as to what she was even doing in the station in the first place. The blame falls upon the cops, on the station. There'd be a brief uproar, but it would be mild in comparison to the death of the vice-president. People would have more pressing concerns on their minds. Then, life would go on. Plans would continue as intended.

Instead, those two assholes decided to get involved, and all hell broke loose. And, to make it worse, some cop—who was supposed to be on leave—went and found the footage with her face in it, implicating her in the bombing. And now *everyone* is looking for her.

Lloyd runs his hands on his face. He's sitting in his car, pulled over to the side of the road, the city looming around him. It's late, it's dark, and his body is getting stiff. He sips from a steaming cup of coffee he nipped out and bought ten minutes ago. He's expecting a phone call. Any minute now.

He holds the coffee cup in both hands, feeling its warmth spread into his palms. He takes another long drink. He hasn't slept much these last few days. He hasn't had the chance. He's running on caffeine and stress.

His phone begins to ring. The number is private, but he knows who it is. "Nivens here," he says.

The voice on the other end is smooth and cultured. Lloyd knows it well. "How are things going?"

"Not as well as I'd like, but they're coming along."

"Do you know where the girl is?"

Lloyd looks at the apartment building at the bottom of the block. The one he's got a clear view of the entrance of. The one he's been watching this whole time. "I know where she is," he says.

She is hiding out in an apartment belonging to someone named Dominic Freeman. He assumes this is a friend of Keith Wright's. They both work in the same diner. Even without this knowledge, he can't imagine Charlie, a foreigner, has too many contacts in the city.

"And she's nearby, I trust?"

"I'm not letting her out of my sight," Lloyd says.

"Good. I received your request for a team. Do you think that's really necessary?"

"I've seen what the two men with her can do," Lloyd says. "They're trained. I don't want to take any chances."

"*Mm*. Have you figured out yet what, if anything, their connection to the girl is?"

"I wish I knew. Seems like just a pair of Good Samaritans."

He hears the other man laugh, though it's more of a derisive snort. "Who knew such things still existed?"

"Caught me off guard, too."

"I've arranged a team for you, but they're otherwise engaged at the moment. They won't make it to you until late tomorrow morning—perhaps even as late as midday."

Lloyd sucks his teeth. "That *is* late."

"It's the best I could do. You wanted reliable men, yes? So I've sent for reliable men. Unfortunately, when you're good at what you do, you find yourself getting pulled in many different directions, with many different responsibilities to take care of, which is what they're currently preoccupied with. But they're very aware of the importance of what you're doing. I've been assured that they'll get to you as fast as they can."

"Then I guess that's the best I can hope for."

"If they make a move before then, I put faith in your discretion."

"I'm not going to lose her," Lloyd says. "I can't. I know exactly where she is at all times—sometimes, it just takes a little catching up, is all. If they go on the move, I'll be sure to inform the team you're sending me. I assume you're going to send me their details?"

"Of course. I'll do that as soon as we're off this call. In the meantime, make yourself comfortable, Nivens. I can't imagine it's going to be the most relaxing night for you, crammed in your car like that."

Lloyd frowns. "I haven't told you where I am."

The voice chuckles and then hangs up.

Not the first time, Lloyd finds himself wondering if his employers have cameras on him. If they've planted a tracker on him, perhaps. It's not the first time they've alluded to the fact that they know exactly where he is and exactly what he's doing at all times.

A message comes through on his phone—a contact number for the team that is coming to join him tomorrow morning. Tomorrow morning feels a long way off. Lloyd yawns at the thought of the long night ahead of him. He settles himself in his chair, lowers himself until he's as comfortable as he can get, and then drains the last of his coffee.

30

James and Shira wake up early and make their way to Heather Morrow's home.

Noam got in touch through the night, sending an email to Shira to let her know he wasn't having much luck, but he'd continue trying the next day. He told her to temper her expectations, though. *At this point*, he wrote, *if I haven't found anything obvious yet, it's unlikely that I will.*

Shira drives. James looks out the window as they go, stroking his cast. "How does it feel?" she says.

"Itchy," James says. "Always so damn itchy."

"That's good, though. It means it's healing."

"I guess so. I just wish it didn't have to do it in such an aggravating way. I have a hell of a time getting to sleep with it."

Shira laughs. "Have you ever broken a bone before?"

"A finger," James says. "And my right foot, in high school, playing football. Both at the same time. It was a bad tackle."

"On you?"

"*By* me." James laughs, remembering. "I landed badly. Anyway, I don't remember either of them itching so bad."

"You were a lot younger then. Everything heals faster when

we're younger. I was told once, when you're in your twenties, your body looks after you. Once you reach your thirties, you must look after your body."

James grunts and then looks at the satnav. They're getting close to the house. It's still early morning. The sun is rising, its beams cutting through the trees that line the road. Heather and her husband should both be home. They work from home. James and Shira don't have to worry about missing them as they head out for their commute. James wonders if they'll be home, though. He thinks of how Heather disappeared from the security footage. It just evaporated as she left the bus station. A person capable of doing that would stay hidden if they didn't want to be found. If they don't want to be found, the last place they're going to come back to is their home.

"We're getting close," James says. He looks down the road. It's a pleasant neighborhood. The kind of place he could see himself and Shira moving to when they were ready. When the time comes that they're ready for marriage and kids, this would be the ideal kind of place to live, to raise a family, to comfortably retire in.

James grins to himself at the thought. All of that is still a long way off.

Shira slows the car as she gets close. "This is the one," she says.

The house is nondescript. It slots in among the rest; nothing extraordinary about it. Its lawn is plain, lacking the decoration and styling of a lot of the other lawns here. Shira pulls to a stop in front of it.

"It doesn't look like anyone's home," she says, turning her head to look the house over.

James grunts. He'd noticed this too. "Let's go take a look," he says.

They get out of the car and walk up to the front door. They

knock and ring the doorbell, but there's no answer. James isn't surprised. He's been expecting this. He thinks about Heather Morrow in the footage they saw with the girl. Thinks about her disappearing act. There was no sign of Derek Morrow. James wonders what role he might play in all of this—if he plays any part at all.

"Let's look round the back," he says, tilting his head.

They go around and look in the back windows. There's nothing to see. The kitchen is empty. In frustration, James attempts the handle. It's locked.

"Did you try that at the front?" Shira says.

James shakes his head, and they head back around, but he's not hopeful. The door, however, is unlocked. He and Shira look at each other. James goes in first. Shira follows him.

"Hello?" he calls. "Heather Morrow? Derek Morrow? Is anyone home?"

There's no answer, but that doesn't necessarily mean anything. James has entered plenty of properties where the occupants are lying low, staying quiet, not wanting to be found. "My name is James Trevor, and I'm with the police. The door was unlocked."

Still nothing. The house is silent.

"We should take a look around," Shira says.

James nods. "I'll go upstairs. You check down here."

James heads upstairs. He takes his time, wary in case anyone should jump out at him. No one does. The house is empty. Upstairs is just as quiet as down, save for the sound of Shira going room to room. James checks the bedrooms. They don't look to him like the rooms of people who have fled in a hurry. He's seen plenty of rooms like that before in the past, too. These wardrobes, however, are still full. He looks at a picture of Heather and Derek together. He recognizes Heather from the footage.

With nothing left to see, he leaves the room and explores the rest of the top floor. There's another bedroom. He frowns. It clearly belongs to a girl, maybe a teenager. Things are not as neat as elsewhere. Clothes are missing from the wardrobe. He steps closer, turning as he looks around the room. There's something hanging on the back of the door. A green woodcut in the shape of a rainbow. It says '*Kayla's room.*' Kayla? Could this be the name of the girl from the footage? The name of the bomber? If so, why does she have a room here, in the home of this childless couple?

As he ponders this, Shira calls up to him. "James? Come take a look at this."

He goes back down to her, jerking his thumb back toward the bedroom he has just come from, but before he can say anything, Shira is holding up a framed photograph. It's Heather and Derek, younger, but that isn't what catches his eye. It's the small child in between them.

"They didn't have children," Shira says. "Not according to their official records. I suppose this child could be a niece or something. But look closely—doesn't she look like the girl we're looking for?"

James leans in closer. She's younger, a lot younger, but he can see what Shira means. Same nose and mouth. The eyes, though, have more life in them than they do in all the videos he's seen. This child is smiling, and her eyes reflect that. The girl in the footage has blank eyes. Hollow. *Dead.*

James tells Shira about the room upstairs. About the name *Kayla.*

"But Kayla *who*?" Shira says.

"It looks like she lived here," James says. "I don't know if they'd maybe, I dunno, taken her in or something? She could have been a runaway. But there should have been some kind of record of that, something Noam would have found."

Shira nods at this, then says, "I found something else."

He looks at her.

"A basement. That's what I called you down for before I noticed this picture." She puts the framed photograph back down on the table near the door. "I thought it probably best if we go down there together."

James agrees. Shira leads him to the door in the kitchen that leads down into the basement. They pull the light switch and begin their descent. The rest of the house has been a bust, save for finding the potential name of the girl on the run. The basement is the last place to search, though James doesn't have high hopes for it.

He reaches the foot of the stairs and stops in his tracks. Shira almost bumps into the back of him.

"What's up?" she says, but then falls silent when she sees what he does.

A small wooden house takes up most of the space in the basement.

31

J ames and Shira sit in the still parked car, contemplating what they have just seen.

"That was…" James begins, not sure how he's going to finish. "That was…"

"Really fucking *weird*," Shira finishes for him.

James nods in agreement. "I mean, what the hell was *that*?"

He stares up at the house, feeling a cold chill now when he looks at it. They left promptly after they explored the small cabin, closing the door behind them on their way out. They've sat down to give themselves a chance to decompress, but they're not done yet in the neighborhood. James shakes his head.

"We need to talk to the neighbors," he says. "Find out if they know anything about the girl—or about that building in the basement."

"They're not going to know about that," Shira says. "If they did, they would have called the police. They were clearly holding someone captive down there."

James agrees. It certainly looked that way. He takes a deep breath, bracing himself. "All right," he says. "Let's go."

He gets back out of the car, unable to tear his eyes away from the house. He feels a little sick, his stomach roiling.

They go to the house on the left. An old lady answered. James introduces himself and shows her his police ID. The old lady frowns a little, but she's smiling. She doesn't ask who Shira is.

"We're just trying to get in touch with either Heather or Derek Morrow," James says. "Do you have any idea where they could be?"

The old lady seems surprised. "Oh, they're not home?" She leans a little further out of her house and looks toward theirs. "They're usually home. They work from home."

"They're not in," James says. "We're pretty sure of that."

"I'm sure they'll be back soon," she says. "They've probably just gone out for groceries."

"Hopefully so. Do you know the Morrows well?"

"Not really. They keep to themselves. Why do you need to talk to them?"

"We just need their assistance with something. You said you don't see much of them?"

"Not really, no."

"Have you ever noticed a young girl living with them?"

"Of course," the old lady says. "Kayla."

James glances at Shira. "And who's Kayla?"

"Their daughter."

James tries not to look too surprised. "Do you know how old Kayla is?"

The old lady has to think about this. "I'm not sure. Sixteen—seventeen, maybe?"

"And do you see much of her?"

"Not really. She's in the house a lot, though. She's home-schooled. She doesn't go out much—not that I see, at least. I've always thought maybe she has some kind of, you know, *mental issues*." She says this like they're dirty words. "Bobby—that's my husband. He thinks she might be agoraphobic. I mean, I don't know if she's as bad as that. I see her go out sometimes, usually with Heather. I don't know where they go or anything. It might not be very far. But I definitely see her outside the house, and I don't think agoraphobics do that too much."

James thinks about the cabin in the basement. "Do they ever have many other people around? Other kids, perhaps?"

The old lady screws up her face. "Not that I can think of."

"You lived next door to them a long time?"

"As long as they've lived here."

James doesn't have any more questions to ask. Other than the name of the girl they're looking for—Kayla Morrow—she hasn't got anything else worth telling them. No answers to the myriad of questions that being inside the house have raised. "Thank you for your help," James says.

"When the Morrows get home, should I let them know you were here?" she says.

James doesn't believe they're going to come back. "Sure," he says. "You have my name."

He and Shira turn and go back to the car. "We have her name, at least," Shira says over the roof, standing with the driver's side door open.

"For all the good it does us," James says. "It's not exactly worth contacting Matt with. Having her name isn't going to help us find her."

"So maybe we stop focusing on trying to find her."

James raises an eyebrow. "What do you mean?"

"I mean the two men she's with. The Brit and the Black guy. Why don't we try and find *them*?"

James considers this. He gets into the car, and Shira does the same. "They're probably with her," he says. "And we're already struggling."

"Maybe they are," Shira says. "But maybe we'll be able to

find more information about them. Something that could prove useful. Something that could lead us to them *and* Kayla."

James nods along, understanding what she's proposing. "The Brit probably isn't the best bet," he says. "Anything we could find out about him isn't exactly going to be useful. It'll have to be the other guy—Keith."

"I'll call Noam," Shira says. "Put him to work. Get him to find us some leads. By the time we get back to the city, he should have something for us."

James straps himself in, and Shira pulls out her phone. The visit to the house hasn't been a complete bust, but it hasn't proven as fruitful as he would have liked. Despite knowing heading in that it was unlikely Heather or Derek would be here—or Kayla, for that matter—he'd held out some hope that they might be able to find something that could prove useful. Instead, what his mind goes to, over and over, is the smell wooden cabin in the basement and the uncomfortable questions it raises.

The day isn't over yet. It's only just beginning. Shira speaks Hebrew into her phone, finding them some new leads. Off the phone, she starts the engine and turns them around, pointing them back the way they came. If they can find Keith, they can possibly find Kayla. They can possibly find the rest of the ARO if he is indeed involved with them. These are lofty hopes, he knows. At the very least, if they can find Keith, they might be able to find some answers or direction. If they find Keith, it's a start in the right direction toward finding everything else.

32

Lloyd is wired. He hasn't slept and drank too much coffee in an effort to stay awake. When he blinks, his eyelids feel like sandpaper. He rubs at his face, slapping some life into his cheeks. Stifles a yawn.

His body is stiff from sitting in the car all night. The only time he's had a chance to stretch his legs is the brief walk down to the twenty-four-seven coffee shop down the block. He saw the questionable dregs of society lingering in there after midnight. Homeless people slept in the corner. The two men working there—who looked like stoners in their own right—didn't seem to mind their presence. They were too busy talking with their own stoner friends who were hanging around, listening to music. They barely noticed how often Lloyd was coming back for a top-up. They didn't blink an eye at the man in the suit topping up every couple of hours.

No one has left the building. No one Lloyd is interested in, anyway.

A couple of times, Lloyd has almost felt himself nodding off. He's had to slap himself to stay alert.

It's getting close to midday, and he's hungry now. As he's

thinking about going back down to the coffeehouse to get a muffin or some kind of pastry and hoping that it has a better level of clientele and staff at this time of day, his phone begins to ring. He's expecting it could be Ben or someone else in the NSA, but instead, it's an unrecognized number. Lloyd is hopeful—it could be the men he's waiting for.

"Nivens," he says, answering.

"I know who you are," the man says, a slow, humored drawl. "I'm looking right at you."

"Where are you?" Lloyd says, looking around.

"Behind you," the voice says. "End of the block, at the corner. Down the alleyway. You got a track on the girl?"

"Yeah."

"Thencome down and say hello."

Lloyd hangs up the phone and slips it into his pocket. He heads down the block, eyes scanning the area. He reaches the end, the corner. Looks down the alleyway. There's a van parked at the end and a man leaning against the front of it, cross-armed. He's grinning.

"Nivens," he says, nodding.

Lloyd gets closer. "I wasn't given your name."

The man holds out his hand to shake. "Adam Neville."

Lloyd knows the kind of man he is, as he accepts his proffered hand. They shake. Adam isn't part of the cause. He's a mercenary.

He's dressed casually right now. Jeans and a loose shirt. No doubt his equipment—body armor, weapons, etc.—is loaded into the back of the van. The rest of his team, too, probably.

"How many men have you brought?" Lloyd says.

"Six," Adam says.

"They in the van?"

"No—they're getting food."

Lloyd cocks his head.

Adam chuckles. "We've been busy, man. We didn't stop until we got here. They're hungry."

Lloyd doesn't bother telling him that *he's* hungry, too, yet he's still doing his job. "All right," he says through his teeth. "Are they nearby, at least?"

"Don't worry where they are," Adam says. "We're here now. Where's the girl? Down the block?"

"She's in an apartment, yes."

"And she's got the two soldiers with her?"

"One of them was Navy."

Adam waves his hands. "Whatever. Anything else I should know? What about the guy whose apartment it is?"

"Dominic Freeman," Lloyd says. "It looks like he's out most of the time, so he might not factor in to anything when you make your move. He was in the Army, but not anymore. He works with Keith in a diner."

Adam raises an eyebrow at this. "You've brought us in to deal with a couple of short order cooks?"

"That might be what they do now, but it isn't what they've *always* done," Lloyd says, annoyed. "If that was all they were, I could have dealt with them myself a long time ago—and let's not forget about the Brit. Records on him are cagey, but all signs point toward him being SAS."

"Current or former?"

"Former, it would seem."

Adam snorts. He's not impressed. "They've left the forces, and they've gotten soft. I don't sweat them."

Lloyd doesn't like his attitude. "Maybe you *should* 'sweat' them. There's a lot riding on this, and you're being paid well."

"And I'll keep it professional, don't worry about it," Adam says. "My whole team will. It's what we do. That's why your boss keeps coming back to us." He winks.

His laconic drawl is grating on Lloyd's nerves. "Are you clear on what we want done here?"

Adam uncrosses his arms and stretches. He yawns while he does so. "We go in and, if we can, we extract the girl. If we can't," he shrugs, his arms folded again, "no biggie. Kill on sight. Which goes for her two buddies."

"No extraction for them," Lloyd says, to be clear. "They have no worth. Kill them."

"That's what I said," Adam says, scratching his chest. "And likewise for Freeman, if he's there." Adam makes a gun shape with his fingers and points it at Lloyd's head, then mimics shooting. He winks again.

Lloyd grunts, unimpressed. "When are you doing this? Soon? Once your men are back?"

"Oh, shit, no," Adam says. "Hell, once I'm done here with you, I'm gonna go find something to eat, and I ain't going in there with a full belly. No, we'll wait until tonight. When it's dark."

"*Tonight*?" Lloyd says. "What if they leave? What if they go back on the move?"

"Then you can follow them and keep me updated. Try not to worry so much, Nivens. This time tomorrow, you won't have any worries left." He pushes himself off the front of the van and claps Lloyd on the shoulder as he passes.

Lloyd glowers as he watches him go. He glances back at the empty van, then turns and leaves the alley, returning to his car. As annoyed at Adam's laidback style as he feels, the walk and the fresh air have done him good. He feels rejuvenated as he gets back behind the steering wheel and looks toward the apartment building once again. He checks the tracker on his phone. Kayla is still in there. She hasn't moved. He takes a deep breath. It's midday now. There's still a long time to go before it gets dark.

His brief rejuvenation begins to ebb away at the thought of this.

The tiredness he feels at running on so little sleep creeps back into his bones. He runs a hand back through his hair. He wants a nap. A shower, too. In an hour, he'll call Adam. Get either him or one of his men to watch the building and keep an eye on the tracker. While they do that, Lloyd will finally get some sleep in the back of his car.

33

James and Shira make it to the diner where Keith works, but no one knows where he is. James senses that the workers aren't being as helpful as they perhaps could be. They all answer distractedly, continuing to work while they talk, whether they're busy or not. They're guarded. James isn't sure whether they really do know where Keith is or not, but he gets the feeling that even if they did, they wouldn't tell him.

He and Shira head outside to regroup. "They weren't happy about talking to a cop," he says, leaning against their car.

"They weren't happy talking about their *friend*," Shira says. "It's admirable, in a way."

James grunts. "Admirable or not, it doesn't give us the answers we need."

"Then we move on," Shira says.

"What's there left to move on *to*?"

"His home."

"It'll have been searched already. They'll have someone standing watch."

"Someone you more than likely know," Shira says. "Just like

at the bomb site. Are they going to have a problem if you want to come in and take a look around?"

"His place will have been tossed," James says. "What can we hope to find?"

"Something that was missed," Shira says. "It's worth looking."

James agrees that it's worth taking a look if only to fully satisfy their attempts at finding him and the girl. They go to his apartment, and sure enough, a cop is standing guard outside the door. James knows him. They make friendly small talk, and then the guard lets him go inside.

"What're you hoping to find?" the cop says.

"I dunno," James says, shrugging. "Just anything that might help out. That's all I wanna do, y'know? Sitting at home while all of *this* is going on, it's torturous."

The cop nods knowingly. "I get that, man." He leaves them to it.

James and Shira look around the small apartment. As James suspected, it has been well-searched. In the bedroom, he sees a framed photograph of Keith in his Navy uniform. There's another picture of him with his arm around the shoulders of an older, white-haired woman, presumably his mother. James finds himself staring at the picture. He looks up and out of the bedroom window. The neighborhood is low-income. The apartment is cramped. Keith doesn't look to have much in the way of possessions. It could be that he prefers to live that way, but there's also the possibility that he can't afford anything else.

"What do you think this means?" Shira says. She's calling from the kitchen.

James goes to her. She's standing in front of the refrigerator. She points at a note stuck to it with a magnet. James reads the message: *Meeting at 9 am*. The time is underlined as if this isn't the usual time for the meeting.

"What kind of meeting?" Shira says, voicing what James is thinking.

"I'm not sure," James says, looking around the rest of the kitchen for any kind of clue that might reveal the answer. He wonders if perhaps Keith is an alcoholic or a recovering drug user. It's not uncommon for ex-military to end up with such problems. The meeting could pertain to that.

"Call Noam," he says. "Get him to check Keith's medical records. Maybe even his Navy record, too. It might give us some kind of idea of what this meeting was. It might even prove useful."

Shira nods and pulls out her phone. She relays the request to Noam, and then they wait. Shira goes through into the living room and sits on the arm of the sofa with the phone pressed to her ear. James continues to look around the kitchen.

When Shira starts speaking again, her tone sounds first surprised and then morose. She talks with Noam for a while longer. Not for the first time, James wishes he understood the language. Eventually, she hangs up and comes into the kitchen. "Keith was discharged with PTSD."

"Oh really?" James says, his mind racing at this revelation. A disgruntled, PTSD-suffering vet would certainly fit the profile of a domestic terrorist. He wonders that if they were to look into Charlie's background and records, would they find something similar?

"No history of drug or alcohol abuse," Shira says. "So I posited to Noam that perhaps he was attending a PTSD support group. Perhaps that's what meeting his note was referring to. Noam searched for support groups in the area. He found one of interest. They'd meet in a building near the site of the explosion. It was actually badly damaged in the blast."

"What was interesting about it?"

"It's run by a man named Dominic Freeman. He's ex-Army."

"Should I know who that is?"

"No," Shira shakes her head. "*But*, he works at the same diner Keith does. Noam sent me a picture of him—he wasn't there today. He wasn't any of the people we spoke to."

"All right," James says, "that *is* interesting. Do we have an address for Dominic Freeman?"

Shira grins. "Of course we do."

"Then let's go talk to him."

34

It's late. They've kept the lights off in the apartment, and the only illumination comes from the television. The volume is turned down low. Keith can feel himself beginning to drift off on the sofa.

Behind him, maintaining his vigil by the window, Charlie watches the dark road below. Kayla is back in the spare room, possibly sleeping. Dom has gone back out. He's been gone for hours now. Most of the day. They haven't heard from him yet. Keith doesn't think this is a particularly hopeful sign for them.

As he slips into unconsciousness, a phone starts ringing. He wakes with a start and looks around the room. It's not the burner. He looks back at Charlie, who is looking into the kitchen area. Keith turns. The landline on the wall is where the ringing is coming from. He looks back at Charlie.

"Don't answer it," Charlie says.

"I wasn't going to," Keith says.

"Dom has the burner. He's not going to ring the landline. Whoever it is, it's not for us, and not at this time of night."

Keith nods and turns back to the phone. They both watch it,

almost like they expect something to happen. The phone finally stops.

Almost instantly, it starts up again.

"They're persistent," Charlie says, "whoever they are."

The phone rings out again, then immediately starts back up.

Keith stares at the phone, a bad feeling rising within him. He swallows. His stomach feels knotted up.

For a third time, the phone stops ringing. For a fourth, it promptly starts back up again.

Kayla has come through to the living room, drawn by the sound. She doesn't say anything. She just looks at the phone, her face betraying the same mixed-up emotions Keith is feeling. Keith stands.

"Don't answer it," Charlie says. "Nowt good can come of it."

Keith hesitates. He steps toward the phone, unsure what he's going to do when he reaches it. "They're not giving up," he says to Charlie over his shoulder.

"Doesn't mean anything," Charlie says. "Let it ring until Dom gets back, and then let him deal with it."

Keith is close enough to the phone to reach out and pick it up. Still, he hesitates.

The phone stops ringing. The silence stretches and feels almost as deafening as the shrill ringing that preceded it.

Kayla clears her throat. "It sounds like they've given up," she says.

As if it hears her, it starts ringing again. Keith grits his teeth. The sound runs through him and sets him on edge. "I'm answering it," he says.

Charlie tries to protest, but Keith is already picking up the phone.

He puts the receiver to his ear. He waits a beat before he says, "Hello?"

"I was beginning to think you weren't going to answer." It's a man's voice. Keith doesn't know it, and yet, at the same time, there's something familiar about it. He frowns, racking his brains, trying to think where he knows it from.

"You've kept the girl safe," it says, and then Keith remembers. The voice from the police station, cutting through on the staticky line while he attempted to make his one phone call.

"Who is this?" he says.

"You don't need to know that, not yet," the voice says. "Is Kayla there?"

"How did you get this number?" Keith says.

"I have my ways."

"Stop being so vague. Do you know where we are?"

"Of course I know where you are. You think I'd call without checking first?"

"And how do you know *that*?"

"Because I know where Kayla is," the voice says. "Think about that, Mr. Wright. I know where she is. Do you think I'm the only one?"

Keith feels his blood run cold. "What do you want?"

"I want to talk to Kayla."

Keith glances across the room. Kayla and Charlie are both watching him, but neither of them has moved from where they are. He presses the phone tighter to his ear, though he doesn't think they can hear. "That's not going to happen," he says, turning back around.

The voice sighs. "Suit yourself. I'm only trying to help you, Mr. Wright. I'm only trying to help you all."

"Then maybe you should cut the shit and stop being so vague."

"Would that I could. You can never be sure who's listening. Now, Mr. Wright—may I call you Keith? Keith, listen to me. Are you listening? *West. Clementine. Buds. Harvest. Red. Run. Ghost.* Did you get that? Don't say them out loud, not yet. *West. Clementine. Buds. Harvest. Red. Run. Ghost. West. Clementine. Buds. Harvest. Red. Run. Ghost.* It's just seven words. I'm sure you can remember them. *West. Clementine. Buds. Harvest. Red. Run. Ghost.*"

Keith doesn't understand. "What are you saying?"

"It's very clear: *West. Clementine. Buds. Harvest. Red. Run. Ghost.* Do you hear them? Remember them. They're important. *West. Clementine. Buds. Harvest. Red. Run. Ghost.* Use them only if you need them. Use them if the girl is in danger. And then again, in reverse, when she's not. Is that clear? *Ghost. Run. Red. Harvest. Buds. Clementine. West.* Forward if she needs them, backward if she doesn't."

Keith's head is starting to hurt. None of this makes any sense. "What are you saying—?"

"Once more for luck—*west. Clementine. Buds. Harvest. Red. Run. Ghost.*"

"If you don't stop talking in riddles, I'm going to hang up."

"If you don't like riddles, you're really not going to like what I say next." The voice starts reciting a series of numbers and letters. Keith realizes what they are. Coordinates.

"Wait, wait, hold up," Keith says, holding the phone between his ear and shoulder while he rummages through Dom's drawers, looking for a pen and paper. He manages to find a pen next to the cutlery, and then he spots a notepad on the refrigerator door. He tears a sheet of paper off. "Tell me again."

"36.5323° north, by 116.9325° west."

Keith writes them down. "Where is that? Just save me some damn time and tell me."

"You shouldn't stay in one place for so long. They'll be coming for you. They're probably coming for you right now."

"What's that mean? Do you know that for a fact?"

"Keep the girl safe," the voice says. "*Run.*" The line goes dead.

"Hello? You there?" Keith shakes his head and puts the phone back, his head swimming. He stares down at the coordinates. They'll be simple enough to look up.

"Who was it?" Charlie says.

Keith looks at Kayla. The seven words run through his mind. *West. Clementine. Buds. Harvest. Red. Run. Ghost.* He doesn't know what they mean. What their significance is. He bites his bottom lip.

"Keith," Charlie says. "What's going on, mate?"

"I'm not…I'm not sure," Keith says. He holds up the slip of paper with the coordinates written on. "It was the same guy that spoke to me back in the station. He gave me these."

"What are they?" Kayla says.

"Look like coordinates," Charlie says.

Keith nods. "That's exactly what they are. I'm gonna—" He stops talking when he sees how Charlie is acting.

Charlie has glanced down to the road. He's stiffened, leaning closer to the glass.

"What is it?" Keith says.

"There's a van," Charlie says without turning. His eyes are narrowed. "Seven guys have gotten out. I don't like the look of it. It's hard to tell from up here, but I think they're wearing body armor. They've pulled on long coats, covering it up."

Keith joins him at the window and looks down. The men are inside the building now. It's dark. There are streetlights, and they illuminate the area enough, but he can't see them. He sees their van, though.

"I haven't seen anyone like them come in or out," Charlie says. He glances back at Kayla. "I think they're here for us. They've tracked us again."

"Shit," Keith says. "Then we need to get out."

"Aye," Charlie says. He pulls out the Glock from his waist-band. "Call Dom. Tell him to get back here as quickly as he can. We need to find out way down and out, and when we get there, I wanna make sure he's waiting for us."

35

James and Shira reach the building where Dominic Freeman lives. Shira pulls to a halt down the road. James looks to the entrance. There's a van parked out front, and they count seven men heading inside. They're wearing long coats, but James catches flashes of body armor.

"They have weapons," Shira says. "Do you see the bulges under their coats? They're heavily armed."

"How could you tell?" James says. It's dark.

"The streetlamps are light enough if you know what you're looking for."

James looks around. He can't see anyone else in the area, and the men didn't look to have any agency logo printed on their armor. "Who were they?" he says.

Shira grits her teeth. "I can't help feeling that they're looking for the same people we are. Why else would they be armed like that?"

James feels his leg beginning to bounce. He chews his bottom lip, feeling antsy. "We can't just leave them," he says. "We don't even know who they are—who they work for."

"Do you have your gun?" Shira says.

"Yeah, why do you—"

"I have mine. We should go in."

James isn't so sure. There are only two of them, and his arm is broken. They don't even know who the guys are or what they're here for. "Let me call Matt first," he says.

"There might not be any time."

"There's only two of us, Shira," he says and waves his cast at her to illustrate his point. "I'm calling him and telling him what's going on."

He pulls on his cell phone and calls Matt's number. It rings three times, nice and clear, but then it begins to break up. The ringing stops. James frowns and looks at his screen. He doesn't have any signal. "I had full bars a second ago."

"There could be a scrambler running," Shira says. "They might have just activated it. They could still have someone outside—maybe in the back of that van or anywhere in this area."

"*Shit.*" James grits his teeth.

He looks around, trying to find anything of use—a payphone, perhaps. There isn't one. They have no other option. He twists uncomfortably to get at his handgun—a Glock. Shira pulls out hers, too. She has a Beretta.

James pushes his door open, taking a deep breath and bracing himself. "All right. All right. Follow me."

"No," Shira says, looking down at his broken arm. "Follow *me*."

36

Charlie checks the Glock. He's a couple of bullets shy of a full magazine.

He leads the way down the corridor, gun raised. Kayla is behind him. Keith covers the rear. They only have one gun between the three of them.

Charlie has nixed the elevator, and Keith agrees. Too much risk of it being covered in the lobby. They take the stairwell. Charlie looks down. He can hear footsteps pounding up, distant still but coming for them. Coming for all of them now, not just Kayla.

Charlie signals for his group to stop. They huddle up and press themselves against the wall. When he speaks, he keeps his voice low.

"They're coming," he says. "There's another door one floor down. We go through that, wait it out until they pass by."

Kayla and Keith both nod that they understand.

Charlie continues on down. They remain close to the wall. The pounding footsteps below are coming up faster and faster. Charlie is cautious, holding the Glock in both hands. They get down the next flight of stairs and move around toward the door.

"Up top!" the voice shouts up from down below. From the men coming for them. "Drop down, *now!*"

Charlie drops to a knee, pressed against the wall, out of view of the men below. They're so close to the door, but now they've been spotted. Even if they get through it, it won't make a difference. They'll know where they've gone—they follow. Even if the men below aren't sure they're the three they're looking for, they'll follow to be sure. Charlie knows they will. It's what he would do.

Kayla is lying flat. Keith covers her. He looks at Charlie. Charlie signals to him to grab Kayla and take her to the door. The men below aren't storming up the stairs now, but that doesn't mean they aren't still coming. They could just be quieter now that they have a target in sight. Charlie waves them on. He'll cover them.

The men below spot movement as Kayla and Keith make their move. They don't call again. They don't issue any warnings. They start shooting. Their automatic fire tears chunks out of the wall above. Concrete rains down on Kayla and Keith as they move, Keith taking the bulk of it, his body covering Kayla's.

Charlie gets close to the railing and sticks the point of the Glock through. The man at point down below, firing at them, is carrying a Kalashnikov. The other men in the group are moving past him, continuing up the stairwell. They carry different assault rifles. He spots a couple of AR-15s.

Charlie takes careful aim. He has a limited amount of bullets. The Glock is nowhere near as powerful as the variety of assault rifles the group is carrying. The shooter hasn't seen him. He's still firing at the last place he spotted Keith and Kayla, keeping them pinned so his buddies can get to them. Charlie fires. His first bullet catches the shooter through the cheek, snapping his head to the side and throwing him back into the wall. Charlie shoots him again to be sure he's down, this bullet planted into his chest.

Another man in the group has spotted where the shots came

from and is opening up, but Charlie has already thrown himself back. The powerful bullets cut through empty air. They rattle against the railing and embed into the wall behind and above him. Charlie knows better than to stay in one place too long, especially after firing from it. He stays flat and starts crawling. Keith and Kayla are moving again. Charlie follows them. They reach the door, and Keith cautiously reaches up to the handle and throws the door open. Charlie wonders how he's holding up and how his anxiety is.

The men spot the door open. Charlie hears them calling to each other about it. He takes a risk of getting closer to the edge, peering down. The men are gaining on them. They're getting closer. The one at the rear has his AR-15 raised and is covering the area. He spots Charlie and brings his weapon to bear. Before he can fire, Charlie is faster. He shoots three times. It's more than he'd like to fire, but panic gets the better of him. Two of his shots find their mark, though. They hit the torso of the man, hit him low, and he doubles over and stumbles toward the railing. Charlie fires again, and the man falls over the railing, screaming as he plummets down the center of the stairwell toward the ground far below.

Charlie scrambles up and starts running toward the door. Keith is watching for him, is holding the door open a crack. As Charlie gets close, he pushes it wide. Charlie dives through.

"Let's go, let's go!" he says, pushing himself up to his feet. He got two of them. That means there're five left—that they know about. There could be any number still outside, or at the van, or waiting in the lobby.

Kayla is pressed up against the wall, breathing hard. Charlie looks at Keith closely. He has a hand pressed to his chest, but he looks all right. He's breathing deeply through his nose. "Do you hear that?" he asks.

"Hear what?" Charlie says, but then he does.

Behind the door Keith has slammed shut, out in the stairwell —it sounds like a firefight has broken out. He hears some doors opening on the floor. People are peering out. They can hear the gunfire.

"Get back inside," Keith calls to them, waving his arm. "Get into cover—stay safe!"

Charlie frowns, not understanding what could be happening out in the stairwell, but then he shakes his head. "We don't have time to worry about that."

Keith nods at this. "Where do we go?"

"Fire escape," Charlie says.

"They're probably waiting for us at the bottom."

"Then we don't go to the bottom," Charlie says. He turns and starts running toward the end of the hall, toward the exit onto the fire escape.

"What does he mean?" he hears Kayla saying behind him. "Then where do we go?"

37

J ames and Shira get into the lobby. Shira is leading the way. They scan the area. It's clear. Shira goes to the elevator. It's not running. "They must have taken the stairs," she says.

They go to the stairwell and look up. Gunfire opens up. James grabs Shira around the waist with his good arm and pulls her back. They soon realize it's not aimed at them. It's many floors above them.

"Jesus Christ," James says.

Debris scatters near them, falling from above—emptied shells and chunks of concrete.

Then a scream, and someone hits the ground barely eight feet away from them. Blood splashes out from under them. It hits the walls and spreads across the ground. James feels some of it splash onto his face and get into his hair.

Shira bolts from their cover and starts making her way up the stairs. Stunned, James stares at the corpse. He can see the weaponry strapped to it, though most have been crushed and damaged in the landing. The man wears cargo pants and a dark shirt, most of which is obscured by his long coat. James's mind races. Who is this man? He's not from any agency. He's clearly not here in any official capacity—not with that weaponry, and not without a barricade outside, without a police presence, without attempting to evacuate the rest of the building first. Who is he—a mercenary? It's the word that keeps repeating in James's mind.

He snaps back to reality and sees Shira racing up the stairwell. He wants to call out to her to get her to stop before she places himself in danger, but he doesn't want to draw attention to her. He follows, cursing his broken arm as it knocks against the wall in his haste. He assures himself that Shira knows what she is doing. She's well-trained—she's better trained than he is. All he concentrates on doing is catching her up. He tries not to think too hard about what comes next. If he does that, all he'll want to do is turn around and run back the other way.

The shooting above has stopped, but he can still hear footsteps heading up. He's getting closer to Shira. She's paused. James looks up. He can see five men ascending the staircase opposite and above.

Shira raises her Beretta, clasped in two hands. "Stop right there!"

James catches up to her, holding up his Glock one-handed, cursing his broken arm again. "Police!" he says. "Freeze!"

At the sound of their voices, the men twist and, without hesitation, they open fire.

Shira's reflexes are quicker than James's. She leaps and grabs him and covers him as they tumble down the stairs, a flight down and into cover. The space where they were a moment before is filled with high-impact rounds that almost tear through the wall and the ground.

Tumbling down the steps, James feels a shooting pain run through his broken arm. He cries out, and then they're flat at the bottom. He isn't able to get up as fast as he'd like. The shooting pain reverberates from his wrist up to his shoulder. Shira, however, once again, is faster. She's up on a knee, and she's returning fire. James rolls toward the wall and presses his weight against it, using it to help himself get up. He raises his own gun and lets off a couple of shots in the direction of the men.

The men stop firing, but they're probably still there. A couple of them, at least. Waiting for an opportunity. Waiting for him or Shira to show themselves.

Shira turns to him. "Cover me."

Before James can respond, she's already on the move, heading back up the steps, Beretta raised. She rolls through and comes up on a knee, and immediately begins firing. James braces, frozen, fearing that Shira is about to be torn apart in a hail of assault fire. Instead, he hears the throaty grunt of one of the men, then the thud of his body as it hits the ground. Shira lets off two more rounds, then rolls back before the men above open fire.

"Go, *go*!" she says. "They're coming!"

James glances back before he turns and sprints after her. Two men are in pursuit, armed with AR-15s. They take potshots, but none of them land anywhere near. James fires off a couple of shots in return to back them up. On the next floor down, Shira is waiting, gun raised. She fires as he passes, keeping their pursuers at bay. James understands, and at the next floor, he does the same as Shira passes.

The two men don't relent. They maintain their chase, storming down the stairs after them, held up by their gunfire. Occasionally they attempt to fire back, but James and Shira keep moving, keeping them out of range. They're determined, though. They don't break off their chase. Now that James and Shira have gotten involved, they're going to kill them. Getting rid of witnesses, James thinks.

"We're nearly at the bottom," Shira says as James passes her.

James tries not to think about it. He just keeps moving—that's all that matters—getting down the stairs and getting out of the building.

38

Charlie climbs out the window first, handing the Glock to Keith to keep them covered. Keith tries not to focus too hard on what is expected of him. He breathes deep and slow through his nose. Long, calming breaths. No matter what is happening, he has to keep himself calm. He's useless to them otherwise. He's a dead man, otherwise. They're all dead.

He points the Glock at the door and prays it doesn't open. He's certain he heard shooting outside it. He doubts the men have turned on each other, so he wonders what the cause could be. Perhaps the police have arrived, drawn by the gunfire and the heavily armed men. He's not sure about that, though. He hasn't heard any police sirens for a start. However, if it *is* the police, they're not exactly the saviors that he, Kayla, and Charlie could hope for—it would be a case of jumping out of the frying pan and into the fire.

At the window, they're not as close to the fire escape as they'd like. They'd need to be inside one of the apartments, at their window, in order to get out onto a platform. Instead, Charlie has reached out for the nearest step in the metal frame. Keith glances back over his shoulder to see what he's doing. Keith swallows hard, knowing that soon he'll have to climb out there, too. He's not a fan of heights. He doesn't suffer vertigo or a crippling phobia. He *does*, however, have a fear of falling. Of dropping all that way to the hard ground far below.

Charlie gets onto the frame and hooks his legs over, getting himself into a more secure position. There's another apartment building next to them. Through the dark, Keith can see faces at some of the windows, watching them, horrified. Charlie reaches back for Kayla.

She steps closer to the window and looks down. "I can't do that!"

"Come on, pet!" Charlie calls, shaking his arm. "We don't have time!"

Gunfire erupts outside the door again, but now it sounds as though it's diminishing, as if it's moving further away, down the stairwell. The door opens a crack. Wherever the other men have gone, some of them are still nearby. Keith fires once, just to scare them off. The door slams shut as the bullet crashes into its frame. Keith spins and takes hold of Kayla by the waist.

"I'm going to lift you out," he says. He can feel how she trembles. She shakes her head.

"Trust me," he says. "I'm not going to drop you, and Charlie is going to be right there on the other side."

He starts edging her toward the window, aware that at any moment, the door could open again, and a bullet could find his broad back. He grits his teeth. Kayla is still shaking, but she starts to nod now.

"Okay, okay," she says, steeling herself. "Don't drop me— don't drop me."

She raises a leg and presses her foot into the frame, then draws her other leg up in the same way. Keith holds her steady. Charlie stretches his arm as far as he can. Kayla reaches for him, but she glances down to the street below, and she falters.

"Don't look down," Keith says.

She leans forward and grabs Charlie's arm in both hands. Keith raises her and lifts her out. He has to let go, and for a moment, she dangles, but then with a grunt, Charlie is hauling her up and onto the fire escape.

"Howay then, big lad," Charlie says. "You next."

Keith looks back at the door. It remains closed. He tucks the Glock down the back of his jeans and climbs into the window. He takes his own advice and doesn't look down, keeping his head resolutely raised. He reaches for the metal railing, which is just out of reach. Charlie's arm remains thrust out, ready to grasp him or steady him once he gets close. Keith needs to lean forward. His left hand holding tight to the frame. He stretches his right arm as far as he can.

Behind him, the door opens.

He hears it flung open, smacking against the wall. He hears gunfire. Without thinking, he jumps.

In the split second before he reaches the steps and railings of the fire escape, he sees the look on Charlie's face. Charlie thinks he's been shot. But then Keith slams into the structure and scrabbles for purchase, and Charlie realizes what he's done. He grabs for him, hooking an arm under Keith's. With a roar, Charlie hauls him up. Keith scrambles to get his legs over, his heart hammering.

Keith pushes himself up, trying not to think about what he's just done. All that matters is that he's on something solid. He's not tumbling through the air, the end of his life getting closer and closer.

Although that latter remains to be seen.

Charlie pulls the Glock out of Keith's waistband and fires at the window they've all just climbed through. Keith hasn't noticed the men reach it, but he trusts that Charlie saw something. "Go up, mate," Charlie says. "Follow Kayla."

Keith looks up and sees Kayla climbing the stairs above and

wonders where Charlie has told her to go. To the roof? There's not much they can accomplish up there. They'll be trapped.

Keith follows, and Charlie comes up behind him, moving backward, Glock still pointed down at the window.

Kayla has stopped two levels up. "Are you okay?" Keith says. "What's happened?"

"This is as far as he said," Kayla says.

Keith frowns. He doesn't understand what Charlie is planning.

Charlie spins now and faces them. He checks the magazine of the Glock. "Three bullets," he says, shaking his head. He looks down, and Keith does the same. The pair of men following them climb out the window. While they do this, they can't fire.

"What's the plan?" Keith says.

Charlie is looking down at the road. "Do you think that's Dom's car?" he says, pointing to a vehicle pulled to the side of the road, its headlights on.

"What? I don't know—we're too high to tell. *Charlie*—what are we doing here?"

Charlie looks to the building opposite. It's not so far. All of a sudden, Keith understands. He feels his stomach drop. "Are you insane?"

"Let's fucking hope not," Charlie says. He points with the gun. "That window there. That's what we're aiming for."

"Aiming for?" Kayla says. Her eyes are wide. "What are you talking about? Are we going to *jump*?"

"Aye," Charlie says, grinning. "It's not that far. We jump from here, throw ourselves towards it, hit that corridor, and get out of the building." He starts shooting, firing the Glock's last three bullets. They crack the window but don't break it.

"Right," he says, starting to pull himself onto the railing. "Wish me luck. This doesn't work—well. I guess you'll be on your own, so you'll have to figure it out."

Keith realizes he's breathing hard. But it's normal. Despite everything, he's *only* breathing hard. He's not having a panic attack. His chest isn't tight. His vision isn't bleary. He places a hand on Charlie's shoulder and holds him back.

"I'll do it," he says.

Charlie looks back at him. "Can't expect the two of you to do something I'm not prepared to do myself, mate."

"I get that," Keith says. "But I'm bigger than you—I'm heavier—I've got a better chance of breaking through that glass."

Charlie considers this briefly. He doesn't have long to think about it. He knows that Keith is right. "Okay," he says, stepping back. "Good luck."

Keith looks down. Sees that the first man out the window is still clambering back up onto the escape, the other man covering him with his assault rifle. He can't get a clear shot up through all the grating.

"If this doesn't work," Keith says, bracing himself, "keep Kayla safe. All right? You'll help her, won't you?"

Charlie doesn't say anything. He just nods, once.

Keith nods back, then climbs up onto the railing. He takes deep breaths. His chest feels loose. He can breathe easy. He almost starts to laugh.

Instead, as he jumps, pushing himself off the railing with his powerful legs, he shouts, "*Fuck*!"

He flies through the air, and before he knows it, the bullet-cracked window is coming up on him. Keith raises his arms to cover his face and head and lifts his boots to lead the way. The soles make contact, and for a split second, he fears they're not going to break through. The glass is too strong. But then it begins to crack, and it shatters, and the glass rains down around him as he lands in the corridor and rolls through.

There are bleeding cuts on his arms and hands, on his face and head from the vicious shards of glass, but he doesn't care. He made it. He lies flat on his back, surrounded by the broken window, the cold air from outside blowing in around him. As much as he'd like to, he can't stay lying and thinking about what he's just done. He needs to get back up, to keep pushing. He goes back to the broken window and waves to Charlie and Kayla.

He watches as Kayla gets into position with Charlie's aid. Charlie is speaking to her, talking her through it, instructing her. As she leaps, Keith prepares himself to step back to clear the way as she gets closer. He doesn't want to watch. He's terrified in case she doesn't make it. In case she plummets. He stays, though, feeling his limbs turn to jelly in much the same way hers must be. She's getting closer and closer. Keith is ready to grab her if she starts to fall short. She's almost at him. He can see the terror on her face. Keith spreads his arms. She lands hard against his chest, and they fall back together.

Kayla is gasping, almost hyperventilating. "*Holy shit, holy shit, holy shit—*"

Keith holds her tight, arms wrapped around her. "You're all right," he says, as much to himself as to her. He pats her back, both of them breathing heavy with relief. "You made it. You did it."

As they pull themselves up, they see that Charlie has already jumped. They hurry to get out of his way. He crunches through the glass as he lands and rolls through with a cry. "*Shit!*" he says, staying down, not hurrying back up to his feet as Keith expected he would. He grabs at his left ankle. "*Fuck*!"

"What have you done?" Keith says, kneeling by him.

"Think I've twisted it, mate," Charlie says, grimacing.

"Can you—can you walk?" Kayla says. She looks back out the window across to the other building.

Keith does the same. The two men have seen what they did. They've decided against following in such a way. They're dragging themselves back through the window. Keith reaches down and hauls Charlie up. "Keep your weight off it," he says, slinging one of Charlie's arms around his shoulders and wrapping one of his own around Charlie's waist.

"I'm gonna slow you down, mate," Charlie says, steadying himself on the other side with a hand against the wall.

Kayla notices how he struggles and ducks under his arm, taking his weight on that side.

"No, you're not," Keith says as they start walking. "Because we're here now. And we're gonna use this elevator at the end of the hall, and then you know what? We're gonna be outside, and Dom's gonna be waiting for us." This latter he says as much to himself as to the others.

He needs to believe Dom has reached them, that he's out there waiting with the engine running. When Keith called him earlier, he made sure to tell him not to come inside. To wait for them by the road.

He reaches for the phone now, hoping it hasn't shattered in the jump. It's still intact. He calls Dom, but it doesn't ring. There's no signal.

"Could be a jammer," Charlie says as they reach the elevator. They all slump against the sides as Keith jabs the button for the ground floor. He stares at the phone, but it doesn't gain any signal. He puts it away, shaking his head.

"Could be," he says.

He stares at the door, holding his breath. He feels a familiar tightness in his chest but swallows it down. He does his best to ignore it. Not now. He needs to be alert. They're nearly at the bottom. He can't be struggling to breathe when they reach it. He needs to be ready for whatever comes next. Someone could be waiting for them. Any number of people could be waiting for them.

They reach the bottom. The door opens with a ding. A robotic voice tells them it's the ground floor. Keith braces, the tightness in his chest increasing.

There's no one there. The way is clear.

He and Kayla carry and stumble with Charlie across the lobby and to the door. They don't go straight out. Keith checks the way. He can see the van parked outside Dom's building, not far down the road. Jumping distance, he thinks to himself. The thought of what they've just done makes his legs begin to shake.

He shakes his head. Beyond the van, a car careens around the corner, skidding. Its headlights block out the shape and model of the car. Keith can't tell if it's Dom. It could be reinforcements for the men after them. The car comes to a halt in front of Dom's building, close to the van. No one gets out.

"That's got to be him," Charlie says. He shifts his weight and winces.

Keith isn't sure.

"We can't wait here forever," Charlie says.

Keith thinks about the jump between the buildings. He wasn't sure he was going to make it. He'd had to try, though. Because the alternative was certain death. It was a leap of faith.

He grits his teeth and pushes open the door, and waves at the car. After a moment, it spots him and lurches back into life. As it gets nearer to them, Keith sees that it's Dom.

"Come on," he says, and they haul Charlie out and onto the sidewalk.

Dom's car screeches to a halt in front of them. Charlie and Kayla tumble into the backseat. Keith dives into the front. "*Go!*"

Dom doesn't ask any questions. He does as he's told, slamming his foot to the pedal and speeding away from the area. Keith looks back toward the van. It stays where it is. It doesn't follow. He sits back in the seat, pressing his head into the headrest. His heart is hammering in his chest. He rubs at his ribcage with his hands, closes his eyes, and concentrates hard on keeping the panic attack at bay.

39

J ames and Shira get outside and clear the apartment building, crossing the road and taking cover behind the first car they reach, weapons raised and aimed at the entrance. In the distance, James can hear police sirens approaching. He's surprised it's taken them this long—if indeed they're coming *here*.

The men that were chasing them down the stairwell don't immediately emerge. Time passes. James wonders what could be happening inside the building.

"They're taking their time," he says.

"We're already out," Shira says. "They'll be regrouping. Anyone else who was in there with them, they could be waiting for them, giving them a chance to catch up."

James doesn't like the sound of that. He thinks of their weaponry. If another gunfight breaks out here, he's not sure how much of a barrage his car could take. Silently, he wills the cop cars he can hear to hurry up. The sirens are getting louder, but they're not loud enough, not yet.

A figure emerges from the entrance, his assault rifle raised, scanning the area.

"That's a TAR-21," Shira says, referring to the weapon. "It's Israeli."

The man spots them and their raised weapons. Shira fires first. The man keeps his cool. He stands his ground and returns fire. James hears his bullets crumpling the side of the vehicle. He ducks down, covering himself behind the wheel arch, covering his head with his cast as the shattering windows sprinkle down around him. He sees Shira lying flat, trying to take aim from under the car.

He peers out as the shooting stops and sees three other men rush out of the building and dive into the waiting van. The fourth man, the one who has fired upon them, keeps them covered, watching the car. He sees James looking and fires again. James throws himself on top of Shira, keeping her covered. She fires a couple of times under the car, but James doesn't think any of them make contact. He doesn't hear any pained screams. The man's shooting doesn't suddenly stop. It stops only before the van screeches away.

James uses a door handle to pull himself up and sees the van speeding off down the road. A moment later, a police car speeds by in pursuit. There are other sirens still approaching.

"Come on," Shira says, stepping out from behind the shot-up car.

"What? Where to?"

"The apartment. Before the cops get here." Shira is already crossing the road. James hurries to catch up.

Back inside the building, they take the elevator up. They look at each other as they ascend. They look like hell. They look exactly like they've just been in a gunfight and running for their lives. James swallows, but his mouth and throat are dry. When they reach the floor of Dominic Freeman's apartment, they're both surprised to see how undamaged it is. It doesn't look like anything has happened here. Despite all the gunfire they've heard and been a part of, there is no damage. No holes in the wall, no chunks torn from the ceiling. The door to Dominic Freeman's apartment is still on its hinges. It doesn't look like anyone has attempted to break it down.

James looks it over. "I feel like I should knock."

Shira nods, and he does. There's no answer. "Is it locked?" she asks.

James tries the handle. It is. "It's unlikely, but we have to consider the possibility that those men we've just had the run-in with have nothing to do with the people we're looking for."

Shira's face is firm, her jaw jutting a little. "It's a possibility," she says, "but it's a slim one. It's too much of a coincidence. We come here looking for Dominic Freeman, a friend of Keith Wright, and who should get here right before us but a group of armed men? Like I said, it's *too much* of a coincidence."

James nods at this. He knows she's right.

Shira steps forward. "I'm going to pick the lock," she says, pulling a hairpin out of her hair from near her braid.

James frowns as she kneels down in front of the handle and gets to work. "I didn't know you knew how to do that," he says.

She winks at him over her shoulder. "There's still a lot about me you don't know." She returns her focus to the lock.

"Outside," James says, thinking about when they were pinned behind the car, "you said the gun he was using was Israeli?"

"Yes," Shira says.

"Do you think that's important?"

A moment passes before Shira answers. "It's hard to tell. They had a mix of weaponry; I'm sure you noticed. I assume they were mercenaries."

"Mercenaries?"

Shira nods without turning. "If that's the case, their weaponry has more than likely come from all over. It doesn't necessarily mean that it has been supplied to them or that the man using it was from Israel."

"Jesus," James says. "This whole thing…it just gets more and more messed up. Who could have hired them?"

"I assume that's a rhetorical question," Shira says, moving her body as they both hear a click and the door unlocks. She gets to her feet. "And that you're just wondering out loud because you know I don't have an answer to that."

They go inside the apartment. There isn't much to see. James notices a pile of pizza boxes on one of the counters in the kitchen as if Dominic has recently hosted a party.

Shira moves deeper into the apartment, and James follows, scanning everything as he goes. He looks into the main bedroom and then the spare. "It looks like someone's been staying in the spare," he says.

"Could have been Keith," Shira says.

They hear someone enter the apartment, and they spin, weapons raised. A stranger in the suit freezes in the doorway, arms raised. "Don't shoot!" he says. "NSA!"

James cautiously lowers his weapon, though Shira keeps it trained on the new arrival. "Police," James says. "Show us your ID."

The man reaches slowly into his inside pocket, pulling it out. He flips it open, and James gets close enough to read the details. The ID shows that he is, indeed, NSA. His name is Lloyd Nivens. James waves for Shira to lower her weapon. James pulls out his own ID and shows it to Nivens.

"What are you doing here?" Lloyd says.

"Could ask you the same thing," James says. "There other agents here with you?"

"Just me," Lloyd says. "For now. I was closest. But that doesn't answer my question."

"We were nearby," James says warily. "We heard the gunshots and came to investigate."

Lloyd looks at James's broken arm. "Looks like you shouldn't be investigating anything," he says. "Looks like you should be on leave."

"Sure. Looks like."

He and Lloyd stare at each other for a moment longer, then Lloyd steps past him, deeper into the apartment.

"What are you doing in *here*?" Shira says. She's lowered her Beretta, but she hasn't put it away.

Lloyd looks at her. "And you are…?"

"She's with me," James says.

"Still doesn't answer my question."

"And you haven't answered *mine*," Shira says, her gaze steely.

"I followed *you*," Lloyd says. "I saw you come inside with your guns, and I saw which level you came to in the elevator. This was the only door open. So why don't *you* tell me what's so interesting about this apartment?"

James and Shira exchange glances. James clears his throat. "We have reason to believe this may be where the suspects in the DC bombing have been hiding out."

Lloyd turns back to him, eyebrows raised. "That so? And what gives you that idea?"

"The apartment belongs to Dominic Freeman, a friend and co-worker of Keith Wright. I'm sure you know *that* name. We came here to talk to Dominic Freeman, and then we witnessed the armed men come inside the building. We pursued them, and they opened fire upon us."

"And you're sure they were here for Dominic Freeman or Keith Wright?"

"Not certain, no." James looks at Shira. "But it's a hell of a coincidence."

Lloyd grunts. "*Mm*. Did you see if Keith was accompanied by the other two—Charlie Carter and the girl?"

James notices he doesn't use Kayla's name. Chances are he doesn't know it. "We didn't see them at all."

Lloyd runs his tongue around the inside of his mouth. His lips bulge for a moment as he sucks on his front teeth. "So, no idea if they're still alive?"

"We haven't seen any bodies, either—other than those of the men who came in here armed."

"Dead?"

"Yes."

"How many?"

"Two, that we saw. Could be more."

Lloyd nods. "Did you see them escape?"

"Four of them, jumping in that van and driving off. That doesn't account for anyone who might have already been inside the van, but we didn't see anyone."

Lloyd nods at this and strokes his chin, looking around the room. He sees the pile of pizza boxes, and his eyes narrow.

"Do you know Agent Matt Bunker?" James says. "He's a friend of mind."

Lloyd's face lights up, and he looks upon James and then Shira with a sudden recognition. "Are you that off-duty cop that found the footage of the girl?"

James nods.

Lloyd turns to Shira. His eyes are narrowed. "And if you're the girlfriend—you're ex-Mossad, isn't that right? I thought I detected an accent." He turns back to James. "Do you think it's the wisest idea, dragging along a former secret service agent from a foreign power on your little private investigation?"

James ignores this. "Is Matt coming here?"

"I don't know," Lloyd says, his tone cold. Outside, there is a cacophony of police sirens. Their blue lights illuminate the night and the surrounding buildings and can be seen through the windows even up here. "I'm sure you can imagine—and I'm sure he's told you—we're all very busy right now. In fact, as I recall, didn't he tell *you* to take your leave? To stop running around and looking into things and leave it to the rest of us?"

"Sounds like you and he talk a lot."

"We're acquainted."

All three stand in silence, James and Shira eyeing Lloyd, and he eyeing them right back.

Lloyd is the first to break the silence. "Perhaps we should all go downstairs," he says. "And let the on-duty police officers do their jobs."

James feels a tension running through his body, and he can see from Shira's face, her stance, that she feels it too. He gets a bad vibe from Lloyd Nivens, though not something exact that he can put his finger on. He's curious as to how he was able to get to the building so fast and is seemingly the only NSA agent here. It could be a different story downstairs, though. The area could be flooded now with agents from all different departments.

It's the story of following them up to this apartment that James isn't comfortable with. They weren't being followed; he's sure of that. After the gunfight, their senses were heightened. They were alert and aware of everything. And, even if he had somehow missed someone following them, he's certain that Shira wouldn't have.

"Yeah," he says. "That's probably the best idea. Let's go downstairs."

40

C harlie winces and rubs at his twisted ankle. Kayla watches
him with wide eyes. "Is it broken?" she asks.

Charlie shakes his head. "Just landed bad," he says.

Probing with a finger under the cuff of his jeans, he can feel
the skin at the top of his boot is swollen. Nothing broke when he
landed; he's sure of that. He felt it roll as he landed and then its
instant refusal to let him put any weight on it. "Just needs some
ice. Maybe a dressing to keep it tight."

Dom is driving them around the city. He manages to keep
them under the limit, but it's clear that he's frantic. Under his
breath, Charlie can hear him constantly muttering, "*Shit, shit,
shit,*" while his eyes dart between all three of his mirrors.

"Is there any way out of the city?" Keith says.

"No, nothing," Dom says, raising his voice now. "That's why
I keep circling, man. All the blockades are still in place. Man,
how'd they even find y'all?"

"I don't know," Keith says. "Seems like no matter where we
go, they keep finding us."

Charlie looks at Kayla. She's looking into the front of the car now, between Keith and Dom as they speak. He thinks about how they keep finding them. Out near the diner and now at Dom's apartment. They've been careful every time. They've kept their heads down, secreted themselves away. And yet still, they come.

He thinks about the little wooden cabin in the basement of Kayla's house. About the shackles on the floor and the television that played static.

"A tracker," he says.

Keith and Dom fall silent in the front. Keith turns a little. "What was that?"

"They keep finding us," Charlie says, "because they have a tracker on one of us. Maybe *in* one of us." He looks at Kayla.

"In *me*?" she says.

"I think so. Back when you ran out of the diner after your face had flashed up on the news when they came after us then they found you and Keith. They didn't come for me, and I was right there in the diner, all alone. And it's your face they have. Seems like it's you they've got a vested interest in. I think they've planted a tracker on you, pet."

"But when? Back at the police station? I didn't see them do anything."

Charlie can feel Keith watching him, and Charlie gives him a look. "Might've been earlier than that," he says.

Keith's face darkens. He understands. He's thinking about that little cabin in the basement, too. "It makes sense," he says. "I'm not saying for certain that the tracker is on Kayla, but it surely seems like no matter where we go, they keep finding us."

"Which means we should keep moving," Charlie says to Dom. "So keep circling, and watch out for those guys that came looking for us at your building because chances are they know exactly where we are right now, and they're coming for us."

Dom resumes his earlier mantra. "*Shit, shit, shit.*"

"We can't drive all night," Keith says. "And I'm not comfortable with dragging Dom deeper into this."

"Man, I told you, I'm here for you, and I ain't going anywhere," Dom says.

"I'm still not comfortable with it. There are limits to what I can expect from anyone."

"Who are they anyway?" Dom says. "Guys coming after you. Guys that came to my damn *house*."

"I'm not sure," Keith says.

"Mercenaries," Charlie says.

Keith raises an eyebrow. "You sure?"

"I'm sure, mate. I've had some experience. When I left the SAS, I did some brief work as a mercenary in South America as a favor to a mate. A regrettable favor, at that."

"Then I guess the question is who hired them."

"Probably the same bloke that killed two cops right in front of us."

"Did you see him back there?"

"I wasn't looking," Charlie says, trying to ignore the pain in his ankle. It's reduced from a shooting pain down to a dull throb. "Chances are he was probably near—probably the one who was manning the jammer."

"A jammer?" Dom says. "That explains a lot. I was trying to ring you over and over when I was getting closer, and it just wouldn't get through."

"We need to figure a way out of the city," Charlie says. "They're coming for us, and we're unarmed. We need to put some space between them and us so we can find which of us has the tracker and get fucking rid of it."

"What are they doing at the blockades?" Keith asks. "Are they checking every car?"

"Thoroughly," Dom says. "In them, under them. In the trunks. They're checking ID. The works, man."

Keith curses and shakes his head. He looks out the window as they reach a traffic signal. None of them are comfortable being stopped. They look around, keeping an eye out for the van.

"Wait…" Keith trails off, thinking. He's staring at something through the window. Charlie tries to see what it is. All he can see is a storm drain.

"We can't go *through* the blockades," he says. His brow knits together. "But we can go *under*."

"Are you thinking the sewers?" Dom says.

"That's exactly what I'm thinking. Do you have a torch?"

"In the trunk, yeah."

Keith nods. "Get us as close to one of the blockades as you can without them seeing us. We're gonna go under. We'll come out the other side on foot, and then we'll work something out from there. You should find somewhere safe to stay. Maybe take a few days away from your apartment."

"No, naw, screw that," Dom says. The traffic signal has turned green, and he starts driving again. "You go *under* the blockade, and I'll meet you out the other side. Y'all are gonna need some wheels, especially if Charlie's bust his ankle."

"If the mercs were looking for your apartment," Charlie says, "and if Nivens sent them, then he might've given your details out. You might get pulled at the blockade as a person of interest."

Dom considers this. "I'm gonna take my chances," he says. "You get through the other side, and when you come up top, you call me. I answer, great. I'll come pick y'all up. I don't—*well.* Then you'll know the blockade didn't go so well for me."

"You sure?" Keith says.

"I got you," Dom says. "And y'all are the ones about the go wading through some shitty tunnels—I got the easy job."

"Thank you, man," Keith says. "Listen—you got a pen and paper?"

"Should be in the glove compartment."

Keith reaches inside and pulls out a pen and a notepad. He pulls the piece of paper from his pocket that he was writing on back at the apartment when he was on the phone call. Charlie peers over his shoulder. He jots down the coordinates, then puts the slip of paper back into his pocket. He tears the page out of the notepad. "If—*when*—you get to the other side, look up these coordinates. Wherever they are, I figure that's where we've gotta go."

Dom takes the paper and puts it into his own pocket. "Got it."

He drives them west and takes them to the furthest edge of the city before a blockade. They turn down a quiet street near a storm drain. Keith gets out and goes to the trunk, and retrieves the torch.

"It ain't gonna be comfortable for you," he says to Charlie.

"I'll manage," Charlie says, winking. "I've been through worse."

Charlie takes his hand when he opens the door and uses it to pull himself out. Kayla comes around from the other side and joins them. Keith gives her the torch and takes one of Charlie's arms over his shoulder. He leans down into the window to speak to Dom.

"I don't know how long this is gonna take us," he says. "But we're gonna come as quick as we can."

Dom needs. "See y'all on the other side." He reaches out a fist for Keith and Charlie to bump. They do. Dom calls to Kayla. "Come on, girl, you too! Don't leave me hanging here!"

Kayla grins and takes the bump. They walk away from the car and go to the storm drain. Dom doesn't leave straight away. He waits and watches them go inside. Kayla climbs down first. As the smallest of them, she has the easiest time. Charlie goes down next. Landing is hard, and he grunts as his left foot makes contact with the ground. Keith is the biggest of the three, but he's able to squeeze through.

Kayla turns on the torch. A nearby rat scatters. They look

down the length of the tunnel into the darkness, impossible to see how long it is or how far it goes.

"Keep out of the water," Keith says. "Let's go."

41

James and Shira remain outside the building, which has now been blocked out and surrounded by police cruisers. James, as usual, knows most of the people present, and they don't object to him being on the other side of the barricade.

James thinks how there isn't much of a crowd gathering, drawn by the blue lights and the sign that something has clearly happened. Usually, something like this would bring a large crowd gathering around, all eager to find out what's happening. Instead, he counts half a dozen people, and they watch only half-interested. He thinks it has something to do with the bombing. People are staying inside, out of the way. They possibly worry that this could be another bomb situation, and they don't want to get caught up in the blast.

Shira keeps an eye on Nivens. "There's something off about him," she says. "I don't like it."

James nods. "Me neither," he says.

If Nivens feels her watching, he doesn't acknowledge it. He stays to one side, staring down at his phone.

James spots a familiar car pull up, and Matt gets out. He spots James and Shira, but he doesn't look pleased to see them. He walks straight by them with a hand raised as if telling them to stay where they are and that he'll get to them soon. He continues straight on toward Nivens, and the two of them talk for a while. James and Shira watch. Matt listens while Nivens explains, nodding occasionally. Neither of them glances toward James and Shira.

Finally, Matt speaks to Nivens and then walks away, coming toward them. "I told you to leave it alone," he says, jabbing a finger. "The two of you are going to get yourself killed—hell, you came *real* close tonight."

"We *got* real close to tracking the bomber down," James says. "But a bunch of armed men got in our way. Doesn't that concern you? Because it sure as hell concerns us."

"*Nothing* about this should concern you," Matt says.

James bristles at Matt's level of dismissiveness. He bites his tongue, annoyed. "Have you had any IDs on the dead men, at least?"

Matt sighs. "Jesus Christ, James, leave it alone. First of all, I've just got here, so if anything's known about them, I haven't been told yet. I've had my hands busy with the two of *you*. Second of all—*please*, I'm begging you, leave this alone before you get yourselves hurt. Hell, before you get yourselves *killed*. You came very close tonight. Don't push your luck any more than you already have."

James doesn't respond. Shira folds her arms and looks off to the side. James believes she's watching Nivens. "How well do you know Agent Lloyd Nivens?" James says.

"We're done here," Matt says, shaking his head. "It's time for the two of you—"

"He got here *real* fast, Matt," James says. "He got here before anyone else did."

Matt's eyes are hard. "What are you getting at?"

"Do you trust him?"

Matt raises an eyebrow. "I'm going to pretend I didn't hear that. The two of you," he points a finger between them, "get out of here. I'm not gonna tell you again. You continue hanging around; I'll make sure everyone knows to treat you as intruders. That clear? So help me, James. I'll have you both arrested if that's what it takes to protect you from yourself. I don't know what it is you're trying to accomplish, but enough is enough." He stands firm and stares them both down, waiting for them to leave.

James reaches out and takes Shira by the arm. "Let's go," he says. To Matt, in parting, he says, "Just be careful, okay? Watch your back, man. Stay safe."

Matt sighs, but it's not so exasperated this time. "I'm doing exactly that, James. Now I want the two of you to do the same." He smiles, so they're not parting on such bad terms, but it's a tired, weary smile.

James and Shira return to their car, passing the one they took shelter behind while they were fired upon. The car slumps on one side where the wheels have been blown out. Its doors and wings are dented and holed from the bullets. They get into their car, Shira behind the wheel, but she doesn't start it yet.

"You think we should do as Matt wants?" James says.

"We've come too far," Shira says. "And we've come close. We're not walking away now."

"Good," James says. "Just checking."

He looks toward the front of the building. Matt is talking to Nivens again. They nod at each other, then Matt separates from him and goes into the building, out of sight. Nivens remains outside. He looks around and then looks down at his phone. It must be ringing. He looks around again and then steps to the side to answer it.

"I don't suppose one of those hidden talents you've been keeping from me is lip-reading, by any chance?"

"I'm afraid not," Shira says.

Nivens gets off his phone and looks around again. He walks away from the building. His stride is purposeful. James and Shira duck low in their seats as he nears them. He passes them by and goes down the road. They watch him in the mirrors. He goes to his own car, starts it up, and drives past them. Shira waits a beat, then starts the engine and follows. James looks at the apartment building as they pass it. Matt remains inside. There's no sign of him. It's for the best.

42

The driver's name is Ian. He doesn't bother Georgia. He doesn't hassle her with questions or seem determined to make small talk just to pass the time. Georgia has been grateful for all of these things. He just watches the road, and he drives. Does his job.

It's late now, and he's pulled over for the night. They've stopped a few times during the day—once for gas and the rest of the time for bathroom and snack breaks.

"I've gotta rest every so often," Ian told her. "I'm on a schedule. It's the law. If I don't rest up properly, I can get in a lot of trouble. I could lose my job."

Georgia didn't hurry him. By that point, she was convinced no one was following them. The men who had come looking for her, they'd lost her. They might have known the details of her truck, but they don't know Ian's.

"I'm gonna sleep in the cab," Ian tells her. "It ain't big. There's a motel there, you see it?"

Georgia spotted it as they pulled in. The area is similar to where she was last night when she first ran into Ian's can after being attacked in her room.

"You can go check into a room there if you want," Ian says. "You're welcome to try and squeeze in here, but that's up to you, and it ain't gonna be too comfortable if you do."

"I'll take the motel," Georgia says.

"That's probably best," Ian says. "I won't leave without you in the morning, don't you worry none. I enjoy our long silent journey too much." He winks, and Georgia laughs at this.

She gets out of the truck and stretches her back out before she crosses the lot toward the glowing neon sign of the motel. The night is cold, and she pulls her jacket tight around herself. She's grown accustomed to the warmth of Ian's truck. She pays for a room and goes instantly to it. On her way, she spots a payphone at the side of the building. She bites her lip as she unlocks the door to her room.

She doesn't go straight to the payphone. Instead, she checks the room over first, then sits on the end of the bed. Her lower back is aching from sitting all day.

The payphone plays on her mind. She considers her next move. She has no destination in mind, not yet. One phone call could change that. That phone call could give her an idea of what to do next—the only problem is that one phone call could drag her back into a life she's been trying to escape for a long time.

Sighing, she pulls out some loose change and goes outside. She slots her coins into the payphone and dials a number from memory, and hopes that the person she's calling is still at the other end.

He answers on the sixth ring. Has to clear his voice before he speaks. "Hello?" His voice is gruff, not accustomed to use. Just the way she remembers it.

"It's me," she says.

"Hello, me," the voice says. "What can I do for you?"

"Don't get smart."

There's a moment of silence, and then he says, "Hello, Georgia. Or have you changed your name again? I was wondering if I was gonna hear from you soon."

"It's still Georgia. It's always going to be Georgia. And if you've been expecting me, then I'm sure you know why I'm calling."

"I have an idea. I don't know if I'm right. Been a long time since we last spoke. Where you at?"

"You know I'm not going to tell you that."

He chuckles. "Yet I'm sure you're going to ask where I am, right?"

Georgia is silent for a moment. "Maybe. We'll see if it comes to that. I've been attacked. Twice now."

He grunts as if this doesn't surprise him. "How'd they find you?"

"I don't know. I've been careful."

"I'm sure you have. But they were never going to give up."

"No. My guess is they exhausted every other option. It's been a long time. Long enough for them to track me down, I suppose. I got too comfortable. I should've kept moving."

"That's what I told you, but you never did like taking my advice."

It feels like a tease, but Georgia doesn't rise to it. "What's happening?"

"So far as I can tell, with what happened in DC, they're making their move. They'll be coming for everybody now. Chances are they've known where you've been for a while, and they were ready to move in when the right time came."

"You worried they might already know where you are?"

"It's a concern. It's always been a concern. But I'm being careful. Nothing's changed yet, so far as I can see."

"What are they trying to do?"

"You know the answer to that. And in the coming days, or weeks, or months, it's all going to become a lot clearer. To the likes of you and me, at least. Joe Public isn't gonna be any the wiser. What's your plan?"

"The immediate plan is to stay alive and to keep moving. Beyond that, I don't know."

"What are you like for weaponry?"

"Nothing right now."

He laughs. "Then good luck to you."

"This isn't funny."

"I know it isn't, but I'm sitting on a goddamn armory here. They come for me, I'm taking a lot of them down with me."

"You aren't gonna keep moving?"

"I'm too tired for that. And I knew this day was always gonna come. Deep down, I've always known that. Truth be told, all this time, I think I've been waiting for it. They ain't gonna catch me unaware. You should come see me while you still can, for old times' sake. Let's not pretend that isn't why you've rung. You need help, and right now, I'm probably the only person that can give it to you."

Georgia doesn't acknowledge this. Not yet. She doesn't want to, not if she can help it. She needs to know that all other options are exhausted first. "What do you know about the girl?"

"The girl with your name?" He chuckles again. "Sorry, your old name. Probably about as much as you do."

"*Mm.*" Georgia stares off into the distance, across the parking lot and the dark road with its scant lighting. Off into the darkness, which stretches as far as her eyes can see.

"You still there?"

She takes a deep breath and closes her eyes. "Where are you?"

She can almost hear him smile at this, knowing he was right, knowing there's nowhere else she can go. "I'm in Washington."

"DC?"

"No, state."

That isn't far from where Georgia is now. Another day's driving at most, and they'll be crossing the state line. "Where?"

"I'm not gonna tell you right now, not over the phone. You get to Washington, call me again, and I'll tell you where I am."

"It's not gonna take me long."

"Good. Then I'll look forward to seeing you. I'll be sure to have the coffee ready. Goodbye, Georgia. Stay safe." He hangs up.

Georgia puts the receiver down. She doesn't go straight back to her room. She stands out in the cold and looks around, watching the road. It's silent here. There's nothing to see or hear. Everything is still.

43

I t takes Lloyd a little while to catch up to Adam and his men.
"We had to shake the cops first," Adam says, "before we
could call you."

Lloyd finds them hiding out in a factory, closed for the night.
They've broken in through the back door. Lloyd sees a security
guard lying unconscious and tied up in the corner of his office.
"You checked for cameras?" he asks.

"We've deleted the footage and cut the feed," Adam says. "So
don't worry none. Is the scrambler running?"

"Put it on before I went inside," Lloyd says.

The signal jammer is in the inside pocket of his jacket. He
flashes it to show them. He was cautious on his way here, wary of
being followed. It's quiet here, and Lloyd can see why the mercs
have chosen this area to hide out in. Adam's van was parked in
the shadows, and Lloyd parked his own car beside it. He checked
the area before he went inside the factory. It was clear. The
sounds of the sirens that are looking for Adam and his team were
distant, and their lights were nowhere to be seen.

"Do you know where the girl is?"

Adam leans back against a counter and folds his arms. The air of the factory holds the smell of oil and grease and heavy machinery is everywhere, though Lloyd is not familiar enough with engineering to guess at their purpose.

"Before we get into that," Adam says, "maybe you should tell me about what the hell went on back there. We were expecting two washed-up ex-military types, and instead, we're getting ambushed by some chick and a guy with his arm in a sling? What was that all about? Who were they?"

"They were unexpected," Lloyd says. "Believe me, I'm as mad as you are about them turning up like that, but I've dealt with them. There's always gonna be complications, and you've gotta be prepared for them. That's your job, right?"

"Those complications cost me three men," Adam says. "Three *good* men." He doesn't look happy. He stares at Lloyd. "I assume we'll be compensated for their loss?"

"That's already three cuts you'll get to split between the four of you," Lloyd says. "Look at it that way."

Adam straightens up, bristling, his arms unfolded, and his fists balled. His three men, gathered to one side while they talk, a couple of them smoking, perk up at this. They stare at Lloyd, too, and he feels a nervousness rising. Perhaps that wasn't the best thing to say.

"You trying to be funny?" Adam says.

Lloyd holds up his hands in a placatory gesture. "I'll talk to him," Lloyd says. "Tell him about your loss and all your hard work. I'm sure he'll pay you more."

"You see that he does," Adam says, settling back down.

Lloyd nods, lowering his hands. "Now, *where's* the girl?"

"Do you see her?" Adam says.

"If I could see her, I wouldn't be asking."

"Then that's answered your question."

"It doesn't answer shit. For all I know, she could be lying dead in a gutter with a bullet in the back of her head."

"That would be preferable," Adam says. "But she got away. They all did."

Lloyd grits his teeth. "I told you not to underestimate the men with her. Hell, you shouldn't underestimate *her*, for that matter."

"Yeah, well, they pulled some crazy shit, and they were able to get away."

Lloyd takes a deep breath. "Look," he says, trying to stay calm. "You need to stop being so fucking vague. We're wasting valuable time here. You don't have the girl—she isn't dead—we've covered this. *Where* is she? Do you know that much, at least?"

Adam nods. "With the cops on our tail, we couldn't exactly scour the area," he says. "But we've got her on the tracker. We got here and took a look on it. Took us a while to figure out what was happening, where they were going."

"How do you mean?"

"I mean, they were moving *slow*. Whatever car they got away in, they must've ditched it or something. They were travelling on foot, and they were walking right towards a blockade."

Lloyd raises an eyebrow. "Have they been detained?"

"No. They walked right through. Not even a pause. Which is what got us thinking—how'd they manage that?"

"And?"

"We worked out, they didn't go *through*—they went *under*. They've taken the sewers."

"Shit—they're out of the city?"

"Almost. They're not gonna get far. We've just been waiting for you to catch us up, and then we're gonna go after them."

"I'm coming with," Lloyd says.

"Damn right you are," Adam says. "We're three short. You're gonna make up the numbers."

"I've already said I'm coming," Lloyd says. "Now let's stop standing around discussing it, and get fucking down there."

44

J ames and Shira kept their distance from Lloyd Nivens. A point came as they made their way down quiet streets and toward a more industrial area where Shira killed the headlights. They crept around corners Lloyd turned down, peering before they followed. Eventually, they saw him pull down an alleyway down the side of a factory.

"Stop here," James said. "I know this area. There's nothing down there. Parking for the factory, that's all."

Shira did as he said. She reversed the car back around the corner, out of view, and parked it up. "Do you know how to get us in close, so we can see better?"

James nodded. "Follow me."

He took her down alleyways between the buildings until they reached an area opposite where Lloyd pulled down. They stared into the darkness at the end and finally made out the shape of his car, parked next to the van from outside the apartment building.

Ten minutes have passed. They've stood and watched in silence. Finally, they see movement. They're leaving the warehouse out the back door, moving through the shadows. There are five of them. It's hard to make out who's who. A group of lookalike figures. They don't go to their vehicles, though. They move together off to one side. James notices how the man at the rear scans the area with his assault rifle raised. He feels himself instinctively pull back further behind the cover of the building.

The men at the front duck down. Then, one by one, they disappear into the ground until only the man remaining at the rear remains. He scans the area one more time and then follows the others down.

"Where'd they go?" Shira says.

"The storm drains," James says, straightening. "They've gone down into the sewers. And I think Nivens was with them. His car's still there." He pulls out his phone. "He's not gonna be happy about this, but fuck it, I'm calling Matt." He curses when he notices there is no reception.

"They must still have their jammer running," Shira says. "We must follow them."

"I'm gonna text him," James says, starting to type. "And I'm gonna leave my phone here. I'll explain what's happening, where we're going, and what Nivens is doing—that he's crooked and working with these guys, these mercenaries or whatever they are. Hopefully they have the jammer on them, and the further away they get, the more likely this message will actually send." He sends the message and then places his phone in the corner of the alleyway. "I've told him to contact you if he needs to, but it's unlikely the call will come through."

"I doubt he's going to get it in time," Shira says. "And he won't get here fast enough to make a difference. It's up to us. We'll have to stop them, and we saw back at the building that they won't give themselves up. Do you understand that we're going into another firefight?"

James nods solemnly. He takes a quick, sharp breath. "I get it."

He looks at Shira and feels almost like he's seeing her for the first time. This version of her, certainly. The coolness, the grim determination. He sees the Mossad agent she used to be. It's never left her.

"There's no one else I'd rather be heading into a firefight with," he says. He cups the side of her face with his good hand and kisses her.

She presses her forehead to his. "Stick close to me," she says. She straightens and turns, then hesitates and looks back at him. "I love you," she says.

"I love you, too." It feels like they're heading to their deaths within the confines of the sewer system. "If we wait too much longer, they're going to get away from us."

Shira nods. She turns and crosses the road, into the darkness, toward the storm drain. James follows, his stomach sinking with every step.

45

It feels like they've been walking a long time through the dark confines of the sewers, the torch cutting a narrow beam through the blackness ahead of them.

Keith has been trying to measure the distance in klicks, but it's hard to do while trying to support Charlie's weight, unable to complete a full stride.

Kayla leads the way with the torch. Keith holds Charlie upright. Charlie hops, keeping the weight off his left ankle. "Do you need to take a rest?" Keith asks.

"No, mate," Charlie says, through gritted teeth. "I'm fine. Let's keep going. We don't know where they might be. Could be coming right up behind us."

Keith glances back. Nothing but encroaching darkness behind them. He wishes he knew where they were. It's all guesswork. The sewers, save for some twists and turns, are unchanging. He thinks they must be past the blockade by now. He checks his watch. They've been walking for forty-five minutes. He'd like to give it at least fifteen more minutes, over an hour, before they attempt to surface.

"Is it going to be much further?" Kayla says.

"Not too far now," Keith says. "Just be careful. Watch where you step."

Rats scurry in the darkness, fleeing before them, keeping out from under their feet, and away from the shine of the torch.

"Soon, we'll start looking for a way up and out," Keith says. "You'll have to start pointing that torch up."

"Just tell me when," Kayla says.

They walk on. After a while, Keith hears something. He looks back. Still nothing. He stares into it, willing his eyes to focus.

"What is it?" Charlie asks, keeping his voice low.

"I thought I heard something," Keith says. They both whisper. Their steps have slowed as Keith looks back.

"What?"

"A footstep." He turns back around. "Just the one. I don't hear anything now."

"You think you imagined it?"

"No. But if there *is* anyone back there behind us, there isn't much we can do about it. So we just keep walking and hope we can get out before they make a move. Kayla—don't turn around. Just keep walking. When I tell you, turn off the torch. Brush your shoulder if you hear me."

She brushes her shoulder.

"All right. Let's keep going. Everyone stay aware. When we get the chance, we're gonna have to move fast and—"

Behind them, someone whistles.

They all hear it. Kayla starts to turn, frowning at the sound.

The whistle comes again. "Just hold up there, friends," a voice says. "That's as far as you go."

They all freeze.

"That's good," the voice says. "That's real good. Stay just like that. Now, any weapons you have on you, throw them over."

"We don't have any weapons?" Keith says. He starts to turn, to see them better. There aren't any lights on them. The men behind them remain in darkness. He wonders if they're wearing night-vision goggles.

"Don't turn around," the voice says. "And I can see you've got a gun. I can see it down the back of the British guy's jeans."

"It's empty," Keith says.

"I'm sure it is. Throw it over anyway so we can take a look at it."

Keith grits his teeth. His eyes dart, trying to find a way out. Kayla is still half-turned toward them. He looks at the torch. If the men behind them *are* wearing night vision, the torch could help. "All right," he calls back. "I'm gonna throw them over. I'm gonna move nice and slow, so don't freak out."

The speaker chuckles. "Sure thing. Nice and slow."

To Kayla, he whispers, "Pass me the torch."

"What're you doing with the light there?" the voice says, seeing it being handed over.

Keith doesn't answer. He takes the torch. He braces himself. He needs to move fast. If this doesn't work—if he's wrong—they're all dead. Hell, even if he's right, they're probably all going to end up dead. He has to try something. They can't give up. That isn't an option.

Letting go of Charlie, he spins with the torch, shining at what he assumes to be head level. When the light of the torch comes into contact with their goggles, their night vision will bloom out, temporarily blinding them. He hears them cursing as the torch illuminates them.

He recognizes their clothing and weapons as the men from back at Dom's building. "*Run!*"

Charlie has been propping himself against the wall since he was dropped. Keith grabs him and throws him over his shoulder. Kayla is already running blindly into the tunnel. Keith shines the torch past her. Behind them, he hears the men giving chase. They fire. Bullets whizz around them. He hears them make contact with the tunnel around and above them, blowing out chunks from the concrete.

"Just drop me, mate!" Charlie says. "I'm slowing you down! Just drop me. I'll trip a few of the fuckers up!"

Keith ignores him. He shines the torch up, looking for a way out. He spots a ladder built into the tunnel a little further down. Wherever it leads, that's where they're going to have to go. "Kayla! Up there!" He shines the torch onto the ladder.

Gunfire erupts behind them and rattles against the ladder, aimed at the beam of the torch. Instinctively, Keith throws himself forward onto Kayla, covering her with his body and Charlie's. Charlie hits the ground with a thud and grunts, the air driven out of him.

They're close. The men are close. There's no getting up.

Beside him, he thinks Charlie throws the empty Glock at their pursuers and says, "Fucking wankers."

Keith is sure it doesn't have much effect.

He takes a deep breath. They're about to die. About to be torn apart in a hail of automatic fire, down here in a stinking sewer, escape so close at hand. He finds, in the moment, that he's not scared. He's not panicking. Again, his chest is not tight. His breathing is calm and clear. If anything, he feels disappointment. He feels sadness for Kayla, caught up in this all—potentially the unwitting cause of this all. So young and yet just as close to death as he and Charlie.

But then he hears another voice, further back down the tunnel, and not the same as the one from earlier, the one that whistled at them.

In fact, he thinks this new voice is telling the group chasing them to freeze.

46

"We've got you covered!" James says, gun raised, with Shira beside him. "You try anything, we'll fucking mow you down, you got that?"

The men slowly turn. Behind them, James can see three dark shapes sprawled on the ground.

Following them has been difficult. The men moved confidently, and James and Shira had to rely mostly on sound to follow their direction. They didn't make much noise, though. They moved almost silently, like professionals. Their eyes adjusted to the dark as much as they were able, and eventually, they could make out their outlines. It helped when the chase began—when the torch came into view, and the shooting and the stomping boots. They became a lot easier to follow at that point.

"You think we're concerned about your peashooters?" one of the men says. "Put them down now, and press yourselves up against the wall, and we don't have to have any trouble here. Whoever you are, this ain't none of your concern. Just back it up and keep out of it. Hell, we might even conveniently forget the fact you killed some of our buddies back at the apartment building there. *Might*."

"Where's Nivens?" Shira says. "We know you're there, Lloyd."

"The two of you should've listened to your buddy Matt." It's Lloyd's voice. James can just make him out on the edge of the group. "And kept your noses out of this. Are you determined to get yourselves killed?"

"We're determined to find out what is going on here," James says.

"I came here to do a job," one of the other men says, "and I'm getting real tired of all this fucking talk."

"Adam, wait!" Lloyd says. "Let me deal with these two—"

Adam isn't interested. James sees him raise his weapon. Shira sees it too. They both start firing, backing up as they do so, rounding a corner a little to give themselves some cover.

The men with Lloyd—the mercenaries—fire back. Everything turns to chaos. Flashes of light in the dark. The sound of a bullet flying through the air, too close for comfort. The feeling of concrete dust raining down around them as a shot lands near. James hears pained cries, but he can't see what's happening, how many of the mercenaries remain. The flashing affects his eyes, dulls how they have become accustomed to the dark. He tries to aim, but it's a next-to-impossible task. He fires and hopes for the best.

47

They don't know who the new arrivals are who have instigated the gunfight, but they seize the opportunity to escape.

Charlie rolls to the wall and uses it to get up, pressing his back against it. Keith ushers Kayla toward the ladders. "*Go!*"

Charlie looks toward the gunfight. He sees someone coming toward them. They haven't been completely forgotten in the confusion.

"Keith!" He dives as he shouts, throwing himself at the no doubt unfriendly figure. He feels the cold steel of his weapon pressed between them as Charlie drags him to the ground.

Keith comes running. The mercenary struggles beneath Charlie. He forces him up, the rifle across his chest, but with the new distance between them, Keith is able to make a move. He kicks the merc in the side of the head. He kicks him *hard*. Charlie hears the merc's neck break. He's close enough to see his head snap to the side. Charlie collapses on top of him. Then, he's hauled back up, Keith's hands under his arms. Charlie grabs the rifle as he rises. Keith drags him to the ladder and pushes him up ahead. With his two arms and his one leg, Charlie is able to climb out.

Kayla has climbed out through a manhole cover. Charlie pushes the rifle out ahead of him. Kayla grabs it and then his hand.

Charlie looks around. It's nighttime, but it's not so dark up here. The sky is clear and filled with stars. They're on a quiet road next to a field. When he looks back, he can see the city. He sees Kayla reaching back down into the hole, grabbing for Keith, and he rolls back over and helps drag him up.

"Ring Dom," he says, but Keith is already pulling the phone out of his pocket.

"Keep moving," he says, holding the phone to his ear and reaching for Charlie's hand to drag him up. "Down the road, away from here!"

48

Lloyd let off a couple of shots as the gunfight began but then promptly threw himself to the ground and covered his head. Too many bullets were flying by too close. He's not prepared to die in this tunnel. He has a mission and getting caught in a battle with a broken-armed cop who doesn't know when to quit, and his ex-Mossad agent girlfriend/muscle, doesn't figure into it.

He crawls to the side of the tunnel, away from Adam and his men, where the worst of the gunfire is concentrated. The air is thick with gunfire, the smell of it overwhelming even the stench of shit down here. He feels a rat run over his leg, and he kicks at it, but it's already gone.

Something digs into his chest, and he shifts his weight to pull it out, to stop it from stabbing at him. It's the jammer, destroyed upon impact as he threw himself down.

Looking up, he sees the outline of a scuffle. One of Adam's men grappling with, he thinks, Charlie on the ground. He sees a smaller figure climbing up the ladder, escaping the sewer. Then, the biggest of the three—Keith—strides into view and kicks the mercenary in the side of the head. The scuffle ends, and Lloyd thinks the mercenary is dead. He ducks his head down, covering it with his arms in case Charlie and Keith happen to look his way. He plays dead, though he's unsure whether they'd even be able to see him in the dark or not. Their eyes could be better adjusted than his. A flash of gunfire could illuminate the area at the exact moment they look, and they could see his eyes watching him. He's noticed they've taken the dead merc's AR-15, and Lloyd doesn't want to be on the wrong end of it.

All three of them leave the sewer, and Lloyd waits a moment. He looks back, but the gunfight is still ongoing, neither side gaining any traction. They're at a stalemate. As James and Shira move into cover, Adam and his remaining men go after them, deeper into the sewer. Lloyd sucks his teeth. He can't let Kayla and the others get away, but he doesn't want to go after them alone, especially not when he knows they're armed.

He starts to push himself up, but an errant bullet crashes into the wall just above his head. He dives back down, and sewer water splashes up into his face. Another rat runs over him, over his head, its little feet getting tangled in his hair and scratching at his scalp. Panicked, Lloyd grabs its hot, wet little body and throws it to the side. He scurries on all fours to the opposite side of the sewer, almost tripping over the body of the dead merc as he goes. He presses himself up against the wall. The bullets can't reach him here. He breathes and runs a hand down his face. Down the tunnel, he hears someone cry out, injured. He thinks it's one of Adam's men.

"Jesus Christ, wrap it up already," he mutters, wondering if Adam has just lost another one. He hears less gunfire than he did before.

He stares at the ladder opposite, leading up and out of the sewer. He can see better here. The round cover at the top of them has been pushed aside, and the dim light from the outside world is pouring in. Dim as it is, it's like daylight down here.

He has to follow. He *has* to. If he waits too long, there's a chance they'll get away. He has the tracker, sure, but he could end it right here, right now. No more running after them, no more chasing, no more fucking gunfights. It'll be over. When they first came upon them in the sewer, he should have insisted to Adam that they immediately open fire. Adam was cautious, though. He saw the gun down the back of Charlie's pants. He wanted to be sure they weren't packing anything else—for all the good it's done.

Fucking James and Shira. Whatever Matt said to them earlier, it obviously wasn't enough.

He goes to the foot of the ladder and pulls out his gun. He checks the magazine. With one last glance down the sewer, checking that the gunfight hasn't suddenly ended, he starts to climb the ladder, gun in hand.

49

Dom isn't far away. He was down the road when Keith called. He managed to get through the blockade all right. The cops looked him over, checked his ID and his vehicle, and asked him about where he was going. They seemed satisfied enough with his lie of going to visit his mother in Takoma Park, then sent him on his way.

Keith can see his headlights racing down the road, coming for them. He takes the rifle from Charlie and straps it to his back, then takes Charlie's weight. They continue on down the road to meet up with Dom. He starts turning the car around in the middle of the road, then reverses back to meet up with them. Kayla reaches him first. She holds open the back door for Charlie. Keith puts him in as Kayla hurries around to the other door. Keith gets into the front, putting the rifle into the footwell.

"Holy shit," Dom says, eyes wide. "They find you?"

"Just get us out of here, man," Keith says. "I don't know what the hell was going on down there, but it's keeping them busy."

The glass in the rear window shatters. Kayla screams. Keith doesn't hear the first gunshot. He hears the second.

"Fucking go!" he says. "*Go!*"

Dom doesn't go. He doesn't do anything. Keith looks at him. His eyes are closed. Blood is running from his lips, dribbling down his chin and to his neck and chest. There's another gunshot behind. It bounces off the roof of the car, but they all wince and duck under it. Except for Dom. Keith reaches for him and gently checks the back of his head. His fingers come away bloody. The bullet has penetrated the back of his skull, but it has not exited. It has rattled around inside his skull. Keith feels his eyes burn. His chest goes tight, but not with panic this time, with grief.

Dom is dead.

The gunshots continue from behind. Keith gathers up the AR-15 and pushes his door open.

"Where are you going?" Kayla says, sheltering as broken glass rains down on her and Charlie. "Keith!"

Keith doesn't hear. He stands from the car and turns upon the shooter. He expects the men from down in the sewers, though their gunfire is not as powerful as it was back there. Instead, it's one man. It's Nivens. NSA Agent Lloyd Nivens. The constant thorn, tracking them, chasing them. How close his bullets have come to killing them. And now Dom is dead.

Lloyd sees Keith, and he sees the assault rifle. He panics and fires upon him, but in his panic, his shots go wild. They fly through the air above and around Keith. They hit the ground in front of him.

Keith gains on the agent with a burning hatred like nothing he's ever felt before. He fires the AR-15. A short blast and he aims it low. The bullets cut through Lloyd's legs, through the knees, almost severing his legs. He goes down screaming, blood squirting from his near-stumps. His gun has fallen away from him. He tries to reach it, but it's clear he's already too weak to scrabble across the ground and get it. Keith advances on him. He's deaf and blind to the world, to everything except what's directly in front of him. Everything except for Lloyd, lying on the ground, too weak to crawl.

Lloyd raises a hand in surrender as Keith gets close. "Please!" he says. "Please, no!"

Keith hears him. He ignores him. He squeezes the trigger and empties the magazine into him. It was half full, but it did more than enough damage. Lloyd is dead. Lloyd isn't Lloyd anymore. He's a bloodied pulp. It's impossible to tell whom he used to be.

Keith stares down at the dead man. It doesn't feel like enough. His friend is dead, and this doesn't feel like enough.

"Keith."

It's a small voice behind him. It's Kayla.

He turns. Her eyes are turned up to him, avoiding looking at the corpse of Lloyd Nivens. She holds her hand out. "We need to go."

Keith stares down at her hand. He looks at his own. He's still carrying the AR-15. It's empty now. Useless. He drops it. He studies his empty hands. There is blood upon the tips of his fingers—Dom's blood. And now, he has more blood to add to them. Another dead body to add to the dozens already there.

Kayla's hand is so much smaller than his own. So pale and fragile-looking. There is blood on her hands, too, whether she knows it or not.

He looks into her eyes. The words run through his mind. *West. Clementine. Buds. Harvest. Red. Run. Ghost.*

He takes her hand, and she leads him back to the car.

Charlie is at the driver's door. On one leg, he's trying to remove Dom's body. Keith takes over from him, carrying the body out of the seat, cradling his friend's head as he lowers him to the ground at the side of the road.

"I'll drive, mate," Charlie says, placing a hand on his shoulder. "It's an automatic. I can manage it."

Keith doesn't say a word. He doesn't look at either of them.

He goes around to the passenger seat and gets in. Kayla is in the back again. She brushes the shards of glass from the seat before she gets inside.

Charlie starts driving, getting them away from the city and from the sewer where they crawled out. Keith can feel Charlie glancing toward him.

"I'm sorry about your friend," he says, finally. "Dom was—he was a good lad. I didn't know him well, but I liked him."

Cool air fills the car through the broken back window. Keith doesn't feel it. He stares straight ahead. He rolls Dom's sticky blood between his fingers, then feels his eyes drawn down to it. He stares at the blood.

"I found this," Charlie says, holding out a small piece of folded paper. "It was in the center console. He must've looked it up before he came to go us."

Keith takes the paper and opens it up. He gets Dom's blood on the corners of the sheet. It's the coordinates Keith wrote down for him earlier. And, beneath that, it says where they lead. It tells them where they're going next.

Death Valley.

50

S hira covers James as he reloads, which is next to impossible one-armed in the middle of a gunfight. He covers his head, wincing. "I'm running low!"

Shira steps into cover beside him. She checks her magazine. "Shit," she says. She doesn't need to say anything else.

James gets the magazine in. "How many are left?"

"I think three, but one of them is wounded. It's impossible to get a decent aim on them."

The gunfight has only been a couple of minutes, but it feels like a lifetime. James grits his teeth.

"We can do this," he says.

He has to shout to be heard. It sounds like the gunmen are moving in on them, advancing, getting closer. They're pinned. They're going to have to fire back soon, or else they're just sitting ducks.

"We just have to be careful. The only way out of this is through them. We try and run, and they're just gonna gun us down."

He thinks Shira nods. He sees a solemn tilt of her head

through the shadows. She reaches out to him, to his shoulder, and squeezes.

They prepare to stand, guns ready.

A light shines from behind them. James feels it in his face, and then it moves to Shira's. A torch. It's not powerful, but it's enough to blind down here. James blinks against the spots it has caused in his eyes. It moves away from them, toward the shooters.

A voice calls out, shouting as loud as it can to be heard above the gunfire. "Agent Matt Bunker, NSA! We've got you outnumbered! Put down your weapons and surrender!"

The shooting stops, but the gunmen don't surrender. James thinks he hears them considering their options. Then he hears footsteps, loud and fast, retreating, running down the sewer in the opposite direction.

James feels a sense of relief wash over him. A breath he didn't realize he was holding explodes. His tense chest deflates. Matt reaches them and kneels beside them, Glock raised.

"Either of you hurt?" he asks.

"No—no, I don't think so," James says. "We're both fine."

Shira looks beyond Matt, back down the tunnel. "Where are your men?" she says.

"It's just me," Matt says. "I got your message, came as fast as I could."

"You said you had them outnumbered," Shira says.

"Good thing they didn't hang around the check," Matt says. He helps James to his feet. Shira stands of her own accord.

"We need to go after them," she says.

James expects Matt to disagree, but instead he's surprised when he says, "You're right. You both up to it?"

"Let's go," James says. They start moving down the tunnel, Matt's torch lighting the way. "Did you see what I said about Nivens?"

"I saw it," Matt says, his jaw set. There's one dead body in the tunnel. Matt stops and shines the torch into its face. It's no one they know. They notice his neck has been snapped. There isn't a bullet wound on him. "The hell happened to him?"

"The others were here," Shira says. "Kayla, Keith, Charlie. That's who they were chasing. They must have done this."

Matt shines the torch around. There is blood on the ground and the walls.

"I think I winged one of them," Shira says.

Matt's torch lands on the nearby ladders and the open manhole cover above. "Only one way it looks like they could've gone."

They climb, James at the back and struggling one-armed. He reaches the surface, gulping lungfuls of clean air. He looks around. Shira is in the middle of the road, gun raised, looking around. Matt stands to the side, looking down at a dead body. James gets closer. He feels his stomach do a small flip at the sight. The body is a mess. It would be impossible to tell who it is. Did James not already know that it's Nivens? He's been annihilated.

"Jesus," he says.

"There's another dead body over there," Shira says, indicating with her gun.

James looks. "Is it Keith?"

Shira shakes her head. "No, I think it's Dominic Freeman. It's hard to tell, but it looks like the picture we saw of him."

"Can you see the shooters anywhere?" James says. "They can't have got far."

"I don't see them," Shira says. "But they'll be near. In the grass. Be careful."

James turns back to Matt. He's still staring at the dead body of Lloyd Nivens. "Are you all right?" he says.

Matt's face is blank. Whatever he's feeling, his expression doesn't give it away. He looks up. "I'm fine," he says.

"I get he might have been a friend of yours," James says, motioning to the corpse, "but whatever's going on here, he was complicit in it."

Matt grunts. "Yes," he says. He turns and looks out across the neighboring field. To Shira, he says, "You think they're out there somewhere?"

Shira nods.

"Leave this to me," Matt says. He turns to the field. "Adam!"

James frowns. He looks at Shira. She's confused, too.

"Adam! You and your men, stand up! Show me where you are!"

"What's going on here?" James says. "Who's Adam?"

The men stand, revealing themselves as hidden behind a far-off bush. One of them has his left arm crudely bandaged and already soaked through with blood.

"Matt," James says. "What's going on—"

Matt turns, gun raised and pointed at James's head, and he pulls the trigger.

51

M att turns his gun toward Shira, but she's already moving. She's fast. She swings her Beretta in his direction, and Matt doesn't take any chances. He throws himself to the ground as she squeezes the trigger.

From across the grass, he sees Adam and his two remaining men come running, already firing. Matt balls up. "Jesus Christ, I'm right here! Be fucking careful!" He can't be sure if they can even hear him.

He sees Shira running. She dives into the road, back into the sewers, through the open manhole cover.

Adam is at his side, helping him back to his feet. He's sending his two men after her. Matt doubts they'll catch her. He's already seen how fast she is. And with her training, there's a chance she could take them out in the tunnels.

"Wasn't sure what you wanted us to do back in the tunnel," Adam says. "Figured the best thing we could do was run and work it out after."

Matt nods. "You made the right call. I needed a little separation to figure out what was going on."

"Who the fuck were they?" Adam says, nodding toward James's dead body.

Matt looks at him, lying flat on the tarmac, arms splayed. Blood pools under his skull. Matt's bullet caught him under the right eye. It looks like one shot was enough.

Matt sucks his teeth. "He was a friend," he says. "An old friend who couldn't take my damn advice."

"And the woman?"

"His girlfriend. She was Mossad, once upon a time."

"That figures," Adam says. "She certainly knew her way around a gun."

"She did. And that's why she's going to get the blame for *this*." Matt points to the three dead bodies on and by the road.

Adam grins. "You worried about what her government might say?"

"I don't give a shit about her government. She should have kept her nose out of things. Both of them should have." He takes a deep breath. He's annoyed—annoyed at what they've made him do. Annoyed at what they've caused.

He didn't want this. He didn't want to have to kill James. He didn't want to have to hunt down Shira. And, furthermore, if it weren't for them, they'd have Kayla right now—either dead or alive, it doesn't matter, but the problem would be resolved.

He sighs. "I'll figure out the fine details of the story. Likely she had something to do with the ARO. Left Mossad to come to the states and join their organization. Something like that."

Adam nods along. "Sounds like it'll fly. Add an element of foreign menace to the domestic one."

Matt grunts. "You should get out of here. Follow your men. If you get Shira, let me know. You know how to get in touch. In the meantime, I need to call all of this in."

Adam returns to the sewer, and Matt watches him go. He

stands alone for a moment, surrounded by death. He goes to James's body and looks down. He shakes his head.

"Why couldn't you just listen?" he says. "I would've taken care of you. I would've made sure you were well looked after. You would have had a position you could be proud of."

He sighs hard, then pulls out his phone.

52

President Frank Stewart hasn't been sleeping well since the bombing. Since Jake O'Connelly was killed. The days have felt long, and the lack of progress has eaten at him.

It's early morning. He sits in the Oval Office, his elbows on the table as he rubs at his bleary eyes. The ARO claimed responsibility, and Frank had thought this would make it easy enough to bring them to justice. This hasn't been the case. No one knows who they are or where they are. Anyone who might have any information doesn't seem interested in coming forward with it. He's never experienced anything like it, and neither have his advisers. Director Henry Carver, head of the NSA, has told him that there's nearly always someone who will give the group away. A member who begins to doubt what their objectives are, or a suspicious partner who's beginning to fear the worst. There's always someone who becomes willing to talk.

But not with the ARO. They're like ghosts. They come and go as they please, and their members are extremely loyal.

"The one thing I would say to this," Henry added, "is that they haven't been on the scene for very long. There's still a chance that we may get a breakthrough in this regard."

Frank isn't going to hold his breath. The American people are expecting retaliation for what the ARO has done, and so is he. He's not prepared to wait for however long someone deciding to talk to them might take.

It's hard for him to believe that it's only been a few days since the explosion. They haven't even had Jake's funeral yet. He's barely seen Louise since. He knows she needs his comfort as much as he needs hers. The hospital had been a passion project for her and a way to honor the memory of their daughter, Mary. Louise has been in a depression since. He needs to calm the country, resolve these problems with the ARO, and *then* he can finally tend to his wife.

Frank's greatest support through all of this has been Zeke Turner. The Speaker of the House of Representatives and a fellow Democrat. Zeke has stepped up and become his right hand in Jake's absence. He's provided moral and physical support.

"You're looking tired, Frank," he says, sitting on the opposite side of the Resolute desk. Zeke is a younger man than Frank is, at fifty-five, but he looks about ten years younger than that. He sits up straight in his chair. Frank doesn't think he's ever seen him slouch.

"I'm feeling it," Frank says. "And I feel like you spend most of the time telling me I look it."

"That," Zeke says, "and stressed."

"Uh-huh. I would appreciate it if you withheld from making such comments about my appearance while others are in the room."

Zeke nods. "Noted."

Frank checks the time. "Robert will be here soon."

Zeke nods. "We can always hope for good news."

Frank laughs, but it's humorless. "I've given up on good news at this point."

As if on cue, there's a knock at the door. Robert Fielding,

White House Chief of Staff, enters with the daily briefing. "Mr. President," he says. "Mr. Speaker." He hands them each a copy of the daily briefing.

"Spare me the misery," Frank says. "Sum it up. Has anyone been caught?"

Robert shakes his head. "No, Mr. President, I'm afraid not." He clears his throat and takes a seat. "One of Henry's boys came close this morning." Director Henry Carver, head of the NSA. "But I'm afraid it didn't end well."

Frank grunts. He gives a look to Zeke as if to say, *As I suspected.*

"Agent Lloyd Nivens was able to track down the girl and her companions, but it seems they had some help with them. He'd managed to locate them at an apartment belonging to a Dominic Freeman, and a shootout ensued. Our three fugitives appear to have hired a team of mercenaries."

Frank sits up at this. "Mercenaries? How can we be sure they weren't ARO?"

"They could well have been, but some of them were killed at the scene, and we were able to identify the bodies as known mercenaries. Unless they've suddenly changed their ways, it seems they were motivated to fire upon a government agent by financial gain, as opposed to any philosophical belief."

Frank shifts in his seat, leaning forward. "So what happened?"

"The girl and her two associates were able to escape, but Agent Lloyd Nivens received notification of their whereabouts and followed, at this point joined by Agent Matt Bunker. They pursued through sewers leading out of the city, at which point they were able to kill at least one more mercenary, as well as Dominic Freeman, who was aiding the escape. Unfortunately, in the gunfight, Agent Lloyd Nivens was killed. Um, quite brutally from what I'm told."

Frank sits back, shaking his head and clicking his teeth. "These bastards."

"Uh, I'm afraid there's a little more, sir."

Frank looks at him.

"Upon joining Agent Lloyd Nivens in pursuit of the fugitives, Agent Matt Bunker was shocked to discover they were being aided by a friend of his."

"What?" Frank says. He notices Zeke leans forward at this, too, brows narrowed. "A fellow agent?"

Robert shakes his head. "No, sir. A police officer, accompanied by his girlfriend. The policeman in question was called James Trevor, and Matt managed to return fire and kill him, but the girlfriend escaped, and the girlfriend is of particular interest."

"How so?"

"Her name is Shira Mizrahi, an Israeli national, and she's ex-Mossad."

"*What*?"

Robert nods. "We've been in touch with her government, but they state they've had no contact with her ever since she left Mossad and their country."

"Where is she now?"

"We don't know," Robert says. "She got away. Agent Matt Bunker gave chase, but he was unable to capture her."

Frank runs his hands down his face. "What I'm hearing are a lot more *new* problems and, once again, a lack of solutions." He sighs hard. "So, what are you telling me here? That the ARO are potentially international?"

"We don't know," Robert says. "The biggest issue pertaining to the ARO is that we just don't know all that much about them."

Frank slams a hand down on the desk. Everyone flinches. "I know that! If there's *one* thing I know about the ARO, it's that we don't know a damn thing!"

"Frank," Zeke says softly. He makes a softening motion with his hand. Quietly, he says, "Think of your blood pressure."

Frank appreciates him at least lowering his tone, though Robert is close enough that he obviously heard what was said. Frank takes a deep breath. "I apologize, Robert," he says. "I'm shooting the messenger."

"It's all right, sir," Robert says. "I understand. This is a stressful time for all of us, but I assure you everyone is doing all that they can around the clock."

Frank bites his tongue. He already knows this, and he already knows how little effect it's having. The ARO remains anonymous. The girl who planted the bomb, and her two associates, remain in the wind, and no one seems able to catch them.

And furthermore, compounding the already existing issues, the ARO seems to have enough money to hire the aid of mercenaries. Who knows how far their finances may go? And now they can count an ex-Mossad agent amidst the ARO ranks. Who else? The two men with the girl—one ex-SAS and the other ex-Navy Seal. Who else could they have working with and for them?

"They still haven't even told us what they want," Frank says. He raises his head and looks at Robert and then at Zeke. Neither of them has an answer for him.

Robert clears his throat and shifts in his seat. "Maybe…maybe they don't want anything. Maybe what they want is…is what they've caused. Chaos and fear. Dissension. Paranoia. Maybe *those* are their goals."

"But without goals, what is the endgame? Where does this go? How does it end?"

Again, they have nothing to offer him.

Frank motions toward the brief. "Is there anything else?"

"Yes, but nothing more relating to the attacks."

"Okay. You can go, Robert. I'll read it soon."

"Yes, sir, Mr. President." Robert gets to his feet and leaves the Oval Office.

Frank sits back and cracks his fingers. "Thoughts?"

Zeke strokes thoughtfully at his chin, but he doesn't say anything straight away. "It's a lot to take in," he says. "A lot of developments. Like you yourself said, nothing that really helps us out in any way."

"I don't believe I said that exactly."

"I'm paraphrasing." Zeke glances down at his pocket suddenly, then shifts his weight to pull out his phone. He checks the screen and raises his eyebrows. He stands. "I need to take this," he says. "I'll be right back."

"Everything okay?" Frank says, seeing his reaction to the call.

"Just some personal stuff," Zeke says. "Is it all right if I take this in the bathroom?"

"Of course."

Zeke nods gratefully as he stands, then hurries into the adjoining bathroom.

Frank leans back in his chair and smooths an eyebrow while he thinks. When Zeke returns, he'll discuss things with him further, then, soon after, he'll call in his advisors. Decide on their next move. A press conference might be in order. They need to decide how best to present this new information—a crooked cop and an ex-Mossad agent. These are potentially things people need to be made aware of. Shira's face will have to be flashed. Another fugitive to add to the growing list.

Frank stands and turns to the window, feeling a need to stretch his body. He clasps his hands behind his back. He thinks of his wife. Things with the ARO aren't going to resolve as fast as he'd like, and he needs to tend to her sooner rather than later. After he's talked with his advisors, he'll go and see her. Make sure she's all right. Pay her the attention he should have given her these last few days.

What happened to the hospital has hurt him, too. It felt almost like an attack on the memory of their daughter. With that, he carries the weight of what happened to Jake and to everyone else who was present. The bomb was most likely meant for him. Had he not been at the base they attacked, *he* would have been there for the hospital's opening, and *he* would have been caught up in the blast. He was probably their target all along.

He feels a sharp pain in his back, in his ribs on the left side, almost like a bee or a wasp sting. He twists away from it, then turns around to see Zeke stepping back, putting a plastic cover over the end of a needle, and then slipping it into his jacket pocket.

"Zeke?" Frank says. "What're you—"

"You might want to take a seat," Zeke says, making his way around the desk and returning to his chair. "From what I understand, things are about to get very painful for you."

Frank blinks, not understanding what has just happened. He looks toward the bathroom door, which is closed. He never heard Zeke emerge or approach. The stabbing pain, like a sting, persists. He feels it spreading throughout his back and into his chest. It's getting hard to breathe.

Zeke sits up as straight as always. He crosses his legs and makes a show of picking a piece of lint from his trousers. "Are you sweating already?" he says. "Short of breath? Chest feels tight? I've just injected you with a mix of chemicals that are about to give you a heart attack. Frank, trust me, take a seat."

Frank doesn't have any option. He collapses into it, staring at Zeke as he does.

"Believe me, Frank, this isn't what I wanted," Zeke says. "I swear. Truth be told, I like you. I really do. Especially these last few days, since Jake died, when we've spent so much time together, I've really grown fond of you. I've cherished our time. The thing is, a long time ago, I was approached with a vision. A vision of a better, brighter, more beautiful world—for some of us. And I was offered an opportunity to make that vision a reality. I couldn't turn them down. Believe me, if you'd been in my position, you'd understand. But you, Frank, you were never approached, and there was a reason for that. You didn't fit the criteria. You should probably take that as a compliment. Too much belief in your duty. Too firm on the strength of your convictions. Like I say, take it as a compliment."

"What have you—" Frank struggles to breathe, to speak, but he manages to force the words out. He clutches at his chest, his shoulders heaving. "What have you done? *Why*?"

Zeke smiles at him, almost with pity. "As the speaker, I'm third in line for the presidency. Since Jake died, I'm second. In about five or ten minutes, I'm going to *be* the president."

"You're—you're ARO?"

Zeke laughs. Frank doesn't understand, and Zeke doesn't explain. "Try to make yourself comfortable," he says. "You don't have to make this any harder on yourself than it already is. Just close your eyes and slip away. Think of it as a long nap. That's all you're doing here, Frank—that's all you need to do. Just go to sleep."

Frank tries to fight it. He tries to stand, but all the strength has gone out of his legs. He reaches for his phone, his intercom, but they seem miles away. He slumps down onto his desk, the surface of the wood feeling cooling against the side of his face. He looks up at Zeke from where he lies. Zeke watches him, still wearing that pitying smile. Frank's vision darkens around the edges. Zeke glances at his watch, then back at Frank. He says something, but Frank isn't sure what it is. It sounded like, *Not long now*.

Zeke watches him for a couple of minutes, then he stands. He shakes himself loose. He turns and bolts for the office door, screaming for help.

53

Shira is in hiding. She's found a crack hotel and has secreted herself away in a room on the top floor. She's barricaded the door. People have tried to get in a couple of times, but they don't try for very long. They're quick to give up, to move on and find somewhere else they can sprawl and indulge.

Her face hasn't flashed up on the news yet, but she knows it's just a matter of time. She managed to escape from Matt and the others, but they'll still be looking.

She thinks of James. Her eyes burn. She thinks their apartment, their home, and how she can never go back there. She thinks about how she'll never see him again.

They were tricked. Betrayed. She kicks herself. She should have thought about this—if one NSA agent was compromised, it stood to reason that the corruption may have spread to others. She could never have suspected it would stretch to Matt.

She sits with her head in her hands, though she knows she needs to start making moves. She can't stay static for too long. It's hard, though. Her mind keeps returning to James. To what has happened to him. The knowledge that she'll never see him again.

Never.

There are tears waiting to come. She holds them at bay. She buries the heels of her hands into her eyes and rubs until they hurt.

She disposed of her phone on the way here and bought a burner. After she makes this call, she'll have to start moving again. She dials the number from memory. It's an international call back to Israel.

Noam answers fast. "Shira?"

"Yes," she answers in Hebrew. Her voice is quiet, and she has to clear her throat.

"I'm guessing from the fact this is an unknown number that things have not gone well."

"No, they haven't. I need you to come here, Noam. This goes deeper than we thought. I'm going to need help."

Noam doesn't hesitate. "I'll get there as soon as I can."

"Thank you."

She hangs up. She stands, taking a deep breath. She's not sure where she'll go next. All she knows for sure is that it's important to keep moving. Another place like this will do. A place where no one pays her any attention, and if anyone comes looking, the residents here won't remember or care.

She takes a step and feels her knees buckle. She sits. Thinks of James yet again.

The tears come this time. She can't stop them. She doesn't try to. The tears come, and they flow freely. Shira draws her knees up to her chest and wraps her arms around them. She shakes, and she sobs, and she doesn't care. She cries harder than she has in her life. After this, she can't let herself cry again. Not until it's over.

Not until the mission is completed.

54

fter they escaped from the mercenaries, after Keith killed
Lloyd Nivens, they drove through the night, the air
whistling through Dom's car from the broken window. Kayla sat
in the back with Keith, but he was silent. He stared down at his
hands. Kayla noticed there was blood on them, and she thought it
was from Dom. She knew that was whom he was thinking of. She
thought of his too. She placed a hand on Keith's shoulder, trying
to comfort him, feeling tears run down her own cheeks. Whether
Keith felt her or not, it didn't show.

As dawn approached, Charlie decided they needed to ditch the
vehicle. They did so in a ditch near to a bus stop, then they caught
the bus and rode on. They got off at the next motel they saw.

In all this time, Keith hasn't said a word. He went to the store
and bought some tape and an ice pack for Charlie's ankle, and
some other medical supplies. He also bought some beers for
himself. He sits in the corner of the room, working his way
through the bottles. He rubs at his eyes. He occasionally makes
little sounds, like muffled sobs, though he doesn't cry. He just
looks *numb*.

Kayla is tired, but Charlie says she can't rest yet. He straps the ice pack to his left ankle, which is swollen and bruised.

"If there's a tracker on you, we need to find it," he says, finishing up and stretching out his leg, inspecting it. "No point in us trying to rest if they're just gonna track us down here. We need to get the tracker out, and then we need to move again."

She has to strip down to her underwear while Charlie checks her. She asks what he's looking for. "A tiny scar," he says. "And I mean *tiny*. You ever spotted something like that?"

Kayla hasn't.

He checks the back of her neck. He checks her armpits and her inner thighs. Checks everywhere creased and hidden away. From the corner, Keith ignores them. One time, Kayla glances his way, and she sees him staring back. His face is dark. He rolls his eyes away from her. Kayla feels a cold chill run through her. She feels like there was blame in his eyes. She swallows, feeling sick.

Charlie runs a hand down his face. "I can't see anything," he says, blinking. He glances at her underwear and bra. Kayla doesn't feel anything lascivious in his gaze.

"Go in the bathroom and strip yourself off," he says. "Check yourself out. And look *closely*, all right? This is important."

Kayla does as he says, locking herself in the bathroom and inspecting her intimate areas under the harsh light of the bulb overhead. Outside the room, she can hear Charlie talking to Keith. Keith doesn't respond.

She stays in the bathroom for a while, wanting to be sure, but she doesn't see anything. Nothing like Charlie described. She puts her underwear back on and leaves the bathroom. She notices the television is on, playing the news. Charlie is watching it, but he turns as she re-enters the room.

"Any luck?" he says.

Kayla shakes her head. "Can I put my clothes back on?"

Charlie sighs and nods. "Aye." He's already checked her clothes for anything that might have been stitched into the fabric.

"It just doesn't make sense," he says while she dresses. "They keep finding us. But we're being careful. Avoiding cameras. Changing vehicles." He shakes his head.

Kayla leaves her feet bare and sits at the head of the bed. She watches the news with Charlie. She glances in Keith's direction a few times, worried about what she might find there, but he ignores them both. He looks down at his hand sometimes. The blood is still there, but it's dried now.

Charlie turns a little, mouth open, about to say something, but then he stops. He stares at her bare feet, then looks back up at her. "Did I check the bottom of your feet?"

"I don't—I don't remember. I don't think so…"

Charlie nods, then awkwardly lowers himself down off the bottom of the bed, avoiding knocking his ankle. "Raise them up a little," he says. Kayla does, and almost instantly, Charlie zeros in on her left heel.

"Fucking hell," he says. "It's hard to see, but it's bloody there!" He slams a fist down onto the mattress in victory. "Get in, man! All right, right, we know where it is now."

He looks Kayla in the eye. "We're gonna have to cut it out. I'm not gonna lie, pet; it's gonna hurt a bit, but nowhere near as much as getting shot. So, while I'm cutting into you, maybe just remind yourself of that, all right?"

Kayla can feel her eyes go wide. "You're not exactly putting me at ease, Charlie."

He draws his lips back from his teeth. "Well, I've never been complimented on my bedside manner, I'm not gonna lie."

He gets to it, gathering up the other medical supplies Keith bought from the store. Kayla tries not to look at them. Charlie looks back at Keith. "You gonna give me a hand with this?"

Keith raises the bottle to his lips and takes another drink.

Kayla hasn't known him long, but she's never seen him like this. He doesn't seem like the same person. It's hard to see him clearly grieving, in pain.

Charlie looks at the beer. "Then again, maybe you're not up to it."

Keith puts the bottle down and clears his throat. "What do you need?"

"I need you to hold her leg still," Charlie says. "Cos it's gonna hurt, and her kneejerk reaction is gonna be a literal kneejerk reaction, and I don't wanna get kicked in the face."

"I can do that," Keith says, joining them at the bed.

"All right," Charlie says. "And once it's out, once we've got rid of it, we're gonna have to move again—so be ready for that, too. You probably should've held off on your drinking until then."

Keith doesn't respond to this.

Staying on the bed, Kayla rolls onto her front and bunches up the pillow beneath her face. She feels Keith's bit hands brace her left leg, pinning it to the bed. Charlie wipes the area clean and then cuts into her. Kayla bites into the pillow. She never saw the blade and wonders if it's a scalpel. She's not sure they can be bought in stores. Whatever it is, it's sharp, and it hurts. She can feel the blood running down her sole, tickling her. She feels something dig inside her heel, probing. It's cold and metal, probably a pair of tweezers. She bites down harder on the pillow and curses into it.

"Nearly got it," she hears Charlie saying. "Here we go, here we go—just gotta get a grip on it—"

Then she feels it slide free from her heel. Her instant relief is replaced by a dull throbbing.

"Stay there," Charlie says, "I've still gotta clean this up."

He cleans and wraps her heel, and while he does that, Keith returns to his chair in the corner and his half-empty bottle of beer.

After, Charlie forces his ankle into his boot, leaving the laces untied, and heads out with the tracker chip. "I'll not be long," he says. "Pack up and get ready to go while I'm out."

Kayla and Keith are left alone.

The silence stretches, punctuated only by the news playing on the television. It doesn't have anything new to talk about. The same stories it's been telling for the last three days, mostly about them. Kayla is getting tired of seeing her own face up on the screen. She wants to speak to Keith, but she doesn't think he wants to talk. He ignores her. Ignores everything except the beer in his hand.

Keith looks down at her wrapped ankle and probes at the fresh wound. Already, she can see a small drop of blood seeping through. It's not getting any bigger, though. She grits her teeth and looks up.

"I'm sorry about Dominic," she says.

Slowly, Keith turns to her.

"And I'm sorry—I'm sorry that he only got dragged into this because of—because of me. I know it's my fault, and I'm *sorry*."

Keith doesn't say anything for a while. He just looks back at her. Kayla can't stand being under his gaze. Finally, Keith puts down the bottle. "I'm not gonna lie and say I don't blame you," he says. "Because a part of me—a small part—does. I'm hurt, Kayla. I'm grieving. And sometimes, when you grieve, you don't think straight. So yeah, I'm mad at you, but there's another part of me that knows it ain't your fault. There's another part that knows it's *my* fault because *I'm* the one that brought him into this, not you."

He takes a deep breath. "And a part of me—the biggest part of me—is hurting because of what I did to that agent. Nivens. Because of what I did to him." He shakes his head. "There was nothing left of him. And *I* did that." He sighs, hard and loud. "I just need a little time, Kayla. I just need some time. And everything going on, I know it's gonna be hard to get. But I can at least get it up here." He taps the side of his head.

Kayla nods. "I *am* sorry, Keith."

Charlie returns. He's laughing to himself. "I found a stray dog! So I took it with me and bought a sausage, then put the chip in that and the dog ate it." He laughs again, likely imagining the run-around the dog is going to give to the people looking for them. He stops and looks around the room, between the two of them. "You all right?"

They don't speak. Keith nods, and then Kayla nods.

"Okay," Charlie says, looking doubtful. "Well, I see you haven't gotten ready to leave. Do I have to do everything around here?"

Kayla starts edging off the bed, but then she stops as something flashes up on the news. A bulletin. She grabs the remote and turns up the volume. It gets all of their attention.

The president is dead.

He's had a heart attack.

"Shit," Charlie says. "Your country's not having much luck at the minute, like, is it?"

Neither of them answers. The news doesn't give much information beyond the broad strokes. One of them theorizes that the stress of recent events has likely caused this deterioration of his health. They announce that Zeke Turner, the Speaker of the House of Representatives, is to be sworn is as president within the hour.

"Well," Charlie says. The bulletin is still ongoing, but it's not saying anything new. "That's all very sad, but it doesn't affect us, so let's get moving before something that *does* affect us gets here."

Kayla turns off the television. She slips into her sneakers. The dressing on her heel is thick and she has to loosen her laces. Keith stands and goes to the motel door, opening it up and stepping out into it. It's early morning. He stands outside in its light, breathing deeply.

"Keith, mate," Charlie calls, "where you going? You're the only one of us with two working legs. We're gonna need you."

Keith comes back into the room. "There's a bus coming," he says. "If the two of you hurry up, we should be able to catch it."

He looks down at Kayla. He holds out a hand, offering to help her up. She takes it. He places an arm around her waist, helping her to keep the weight off her heel. They leave the room.

"Charming," Charlie says, hopping after them. "Don't worry, I'll see to myself. Tell you what, you go on ahead to the bus, and just tell him to wait for me, all right?"

Keith calls back to him over his shoulder. "I sure hope that ankle heals up soon, man, because you've been a real martyr about it ever since you got hurt."

Kayla can see the bus pulling to a stop in front of the motel, just a little further down from where they are. Behind them, she can hear Charlie laughing. She looks up. She can smell the alcohol on Keith's breath, but he doesn't seem drunk. She looks up into his face and sees him shoot Charlie a wry smile.

They'll make the bus. The driver has already seen them coming. They'll make the bus, and then they'll ride it to the next motel, or maybe the one after that, and they'll rest up for a little. They all need it. And then after that…

After that, they go to Death Valley. They don't have any other options.

55

When they crossed into Washington state, Georgia found another payphone and made a call. He told her she was close. In fact, she could walk it. It would be a long walk, but he knew she had it in her.

She's left Ian behind to continue his route without her. She bought a backpack and filled it with supplies, and got herself a pair of hiking boots. She walked three miles down the road, keeping out of sight of the passing vehicles until she reached the woods he told her about. She stepped inside.

Keep heading southeast, he told her. *I'm not gonna give you any more than that. If you can't find me, well, sucks for you.*

He was being cautious. She understands that. She would do the same.

It gets late, and Georgia sets up a camp. She's a light sleeper, and several times during the night, she wakes to the sound of movement, but further investigation always reveals nothing more than a small animal or a bird.

She starts early again the next morning. Southeast, always southeast, deeper and deeper. Eventually, she picks up a trail. Slight footprints in the dirt. A snagged piece of thread. She follows them, part of her wondering if he left them on purpose, knowing she would find them. She wonders if these are as much of a route as he's willing to provide her.

She finds a cabin. She assumes it's his. It's located deep and hidden by the trees. The cabin itself is old; any paint it might have once had is completely peeled and covered in moss.

Georgia hears a rifle click. "You want me to freeze," she says, "or raise my hands?"

"I want to know that you're all alone," the voice, *his* voice, says.

"I'm all alone," Georgia says. "I reckon you've been watching me long enough now to know that."

A bush rustles next to the cabin, and he stands. He's wearing faded jeans and a denim shirt. His face is gaunt and stubbled, his features craggy. His hair has thinned and is slicked back from his face. His rifle is a Springfield, used for hunting. It's pointing right at her.

He looks beyond her, into the woods, then finally slings the rifle onto his back. "Never be too careful."

"I know that," Georgia says. "That's why I'm not holding the fact you were just pointing a gun at me against you."

He smirks. "You look well, girl. Alaska must've agreed with you."

"You're looking old," Georgia says. "I'm not sure this rugged woodland look is suiting you. You're only fifty, Jack. You look all worn out."

"I'm sure glad you didn't sugarcoat that for me," he says, grinning. He tilts his head back toward the cabin. "You wanna come inside? I know you didn't come all this way just to exchange pleasantries."

"I came because I need help," Georgia says. "And you know it's got to be desperate for me to admit that."

"Things are desperate all over, from what I see and hear," Jack says.

"I'm surprised you're able to see and hear much," Georgia says, looking at the cabin. "It doesn't look like it gets electricity."

"It doesn't," Jack says. "But I've got a generator. Come on." He turns and heads up the small porch steps and to the cabin door. He pauses and calls back to her. "Looks can be deceiving—you know that. Come on, now. I ain't interested in hanging around out here all day." He goes inside.

Georgia stares after him. He's left the door open. She takes a deep breath. She's come this far. She follows Jack inside.

EPILOGUE

M att travels down to Virginia, to the Red Onion State Prison. A supermax.

He's called ahead. They know he's coming. As an NSA agent, it doesn't take him long to get through security. He's escorted through the prison to a room with two chairs and a table in the middle. The man he's here to see isn't present yet. In the middle of the table is a hook that the man will be chained to.

"He's on his way now, Agent Bunker," the CO that escorted him here says.

Matt nods. "When he gets here, I want to talk to him alone."

The CO looks unsure.

"It's already been cleared," Matt says. "Well in advance of my getting here."

The CO nods. "Yes, sir."

Soon after, Harlan Thompson enters the room. He wears an orange jumpsuit, which clings tightly to his muscular frame. He's cuffed and shackled, a chain running from between his wrists down to between his ankles, turning his walk into a shuffle. Despite this, he enters the room defiant. His chain is raised. His head and face are shaved smooth. He wears sunglasses, his eyes sensitive after so long spent in solitary confinement. White supremacist tattoos run up and down his arms and no doubt cover his torso, too. He's led to the table opposite Matt and sits down. The chain is loosened from between his ankles and looped through the hook in the middle of the table.

Matt waits for the COs to leave the room. Once the door is closed, he turns to Harlan. Neither of them says anything for a while. Harlan's face is impassive and unreadable. It's impossible to tell where exactly he's looking, his eyes hidden behind his shades.

Harlan is the first to speak. "Who the fuck are you?"

"My name's Matthew Bunker. I'm a special agent with the NSA."

Harlan smirks. "I've got nothing to say to you."

"We'll see."

Harlan shakes his head. "What, you think because I'm in here for life I'm going to help you out with some cold cases? I'm gonna give you some hints as to where the bodies are buried?" He chuckles. "You've got nothing to offer me. I'm not interested. I appreciate this brief excursion from my cell, but you might as well send me back now."

Matt sits back and watches him. He drums his fingers on the tabletop. He notices how still Harlan sits. His hands are clasped. He doesn't fidget. He reminds Matt of a predator, waiting for its prey to slip up, waiting to *strike*.

"I'm sure there are still plenty of bodies out there that the cops never found, Harlan," Matt says. "It was murder they got you on, right? I checked your file. Two counts of murder and conspiracy to murder against a *judge*, no less." It's Matt's turn to chuckle. "And I'm sure that even from in here, you find ways to strike out at others. Even from in here, you've put people underground. You don't have to admit it or deny it. I don't care, Harlan. I'm here to make you an offer."

Harlan cocks his head at this. He raises an eyebrow from behind his shades.

"Do you get to see much of the news from in here?" Matt says.

"I don't care what's going on in the world," Harlan says.

"Have you heard about the bombing in Washington, DC?"

Harlan grunts. "It was hard to avoid hearing about it, even from in solitary."

"We did that."

Harlan doesn't react at first. Slowly, he starts to frown. "What?"

"I work the NSA, but that's not my true profession. The NSA is a means to an end. There are many of us located in many departments, and it's a means to an end."

"What are you saying? You blew up DC?"

"Not me specifically, no. The organization I'm a part of, yes."

Harlan starts to look around. "Is this some kind of a trap?"

"Hear me out, Harlan," Matt says. "About a week ago, a colleague of mine approached two members of *your* organization to assist him with killing a former member of our organization. Someone who was causing us some problems—and still is, but we'll get to that. They agreed to help us, but they weren't interested in a monetary reward. From the fact that I'm here, talking with you right now, can you hazard a guess as to what it is they *did* want?"

Harlan grins.

"They wanted your freedom. At first, with who you are and what you've done, we weren't sure if we could agree to that. But then we got to thinking—our goals aren't so misaligned, yours and ours. We think we could be of benefit to each other."

"What do you need?"

"Your two men failed in the task we gave them. The girl we needed them to kill, and her two associates, have slipped our grasp. Furthermore, we have a couple of other problems we need help resolving."

"It sounds like there's a lot of you already. What do you need with us?"

"Every army can always do with more soldiers. Don't you agree? Why else are you always recruiting? Your organization is spread all across America—in some ways, it spreads further than ours. Help us, Harlan, and we can help you."

Harlan is silent. He's considering, though. "You want my men," he says, eventually.

Matt pulls out his phone and brings up images. He shows Harlan across the table. Harlan leans a little closer to see. "The girl's name is Kayla Morrow, though this is not widely known. This man is Keith Wright, and this is Charlie Carter. This woman is called Shira Mizrahi—"

"A Jew?" Harlan says.

Matt nods. "And ex-Mossad. And finally, this is Georgia Caruso. They're not all traveling together, but we know where most of them are."

"And you want us to kill them? Or capture them?"

"We're interested in getting back Kayla and Georgia, but as for the rest, do as you please."

Harlan smiles at this. He has a terrifying smile. Again, he reminds Matt of a predator. "I'm interested," Harlan says, "but I have a condition."

"You want to be free," Matt says. "Same as your two men in DC wanted you to be."

"If you want the army, you need the general."

"We can't just free you," Matt says. "You're too high profile a figure. The families of the people you killed and had killed know you're here. They wouldn't respond well to a sudden, unexplained pardon. However, one day ago, a man in North Carolina was found dead of natural causes, and as luck would have it, he had your exact same build. Same age, height, and weight. And would you believe it, he even looks a little like you, too."

Harlan frowns. He doesn't understand.

"Right now, his dead body is being tattooed. He's getting *your* tattoos. And if you agree to help us, his corpse will be transported here, into your cell to take your place, and you will be a free man."

Harlan chuckles. "He really die of natural causes?"

"He's dead," Matt says. "Let's leave it at that."

"Uh-huh. And just how much *does* he look like me, really?"

"We had a surgeon make sure of it."

Harlan sits back, smiling. "Let me get this straight," he says. "You're gonna give me carte blanche to get out of this hellhole and hunt down a little girl, a nigger, a kike, and a couple of others?" He laughs. "You should've led with that." He unclasps his hands and holds one out to shake. "What, you scared? I ain't gonna bite. It ain't a deal until we shake. It's the only kind of guarantee I get in here."

Matt looks down at his hand. Cuffed and manacled, but soon to be free. A weapon for them to point at their enemies and let loose. A general at the head of an army. Extra muscle for their ranks.

Matt takes his hand, and they shake.

The story will continue in Book 2.

THANK YOU FOR READING SLEEPER CELL!

W e hope you enjoyed it as much as we enjoyed bringing it to you. We just wanted to take a moment to encourage you to review the book. Follow this link: **Sleeper Cell** to be directed to the book's Amazon product page to leave your review.

Every review helps further the author's reach and, ultimately, helps them continue writing fantastic books for us all to enjoy.

You can also join our non-spam mailing list by visiting www.subscribepage.com/AethonReadersGroup and never miss out on future releases. You'll also receive three full books completely Free as our thanks to you.

Facebook | Instagram | Twitter | Website

Looking for more great Thrillers?

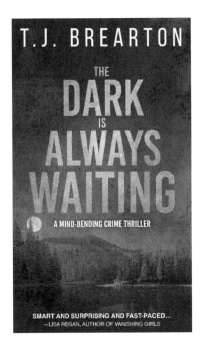

Stopping a tragedy makes him a hero... ...But was any of it real? After surviving a public shooting and saving someone in the process, Alex Baines's life is forever altered... Video of the tragic event spills across social media. Major newspapers are interested. Even movie deals are being offered. This could be a career boost for the neuroscientist and meditation guru. But Alex's marriage hangs on by a thread. His leg is shattered from a bullet wound. Evidence is piling up that the attack was not random. And while police hunt down the gunman, Alex's wife Corrine begins to worry someone is after her and her two children, too. All the while, state Investigator Raquel Roth has never seen a case like this. A criminal who makes major mistakes, yet seems to have a master plan. And is someone pulling his strings? As Roth and her partner race to figure out the madman's motive, signs point to an even more sinister plan in the works. If only they can untangle the mystery and stop the disaster in time...

"Smart and surprising and fast-paced...an excellent book. There were so many small moments in there that I really related to and were just brilliant. (Brearton is) a master at capturing the minutiae of a marriage." —Lisa Regan, *author of* Vanishing Girls *This book was previously published as Breathing Fire, but has been completely revised into this definitive version.

Get The Dark is Always Waiting Now!

Sentenced to life in prison for a crime he didn't commit... Can he be exonerated? After ten years inside a jail cell, Andy Gibbons has abandoned all hope. Resigned himself to the fact that he will spend the rest of his life behind bars. But while Andy may have thrown in the towel, that doesn't mean his wife, Jamie, did. Disillusioned and worn out by the justice system, the Honorable Judge Regan St. Clair is just about to pack in too when a letter from Jamie Gibbons arrives on her desk. A letter that changes everything... Digging deeper, she and a former Special Forces operator named Jake Westley stumble into a frightening underworld of deceit and menace. A world where nothing is as it seems, and no one can be trusted. All the answer these simple question: *Is Andy Gibbons really innocent? Is the price of his freedom worth paying?* **Don't miss this** **crime suspense-thriller about a corrupt organization with a sinister agenda that exploits every weakness and every dark corner of the fallible justice system.**

Get Unguilty Now!

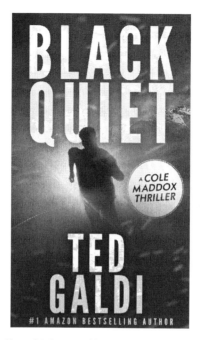

They thought they could run the town... Until they attacked the brother of an ex-Special Forces commando. Cole Maddox just moved back to his hometown in Montana after leaving the Army's most elite unit because his superiors lied to him. But his town has changed. A ruthless gang of bikers has flooded it with fentanyl, and when Cole's brother defies them, they put him in a coma. Big mistake. Cole unleashes his arsenal of Special Forces skills to take them down. However, he soon learns the gang is only the bottom layer of a criminal network much larger and deadlier than he imagined. **Can Cole get justice for his brother while keeping himself and those closest to him alive? Find out in this fast-paced, adrenaline-surging thrill ride from Ted Galdi.**

Get Black Quiet now!

For all our Thrillers, visit our website.